THE RED CABBAGE CAFÉ

THE RED CABBAGE CAFÉ

JONATHAN TREITEL

PANTHEON BOOKS • • NEW YORK • •

TO CAROLINE

Copyright © 1990 by Jonathan Treitel

All rights reserved under International and Pan-American Copyright Conventions. Published in the United States by Pantheon Books, a division of Random House, Inc., New York, and simultaneously in Canada by Random House of Canada Limited, Toronto. Originally published in Great Britain by Bloomsbury Publishing Ltd., London, in 1990.

Library of Congress Cataloging-in-Publication Data

Treitel, Jonathan.
The Red cabbage café / Jonathan Treitel.
p.   cm.
ISBN 0-394-58766-9
I. Title.
PR6070.R3634R4   1991   90-52526
823'.914—dc20

Book Design by Anne Scatto
Manufactured in the United States of America
First American Edition

If you had been passing through Moscow in 1922, you might have dropped in at the Red Cabbage Café. There, posing under a pugnacious banner, might have been Sophia, avant-garde artist and waxwork maker to the Romanovs and the Revolution. Charging through the doorway might have come the self-destructive poet Gritz, who'd have thrust on you his noisy verses and his vodka. And over there, in a dark corner, you probably wouldn't have noticed Humphrey Veil, scratching his head and wondering what on earth was going on.

Humphrey has worked in Moscow since 1919. An Anglo-American-German-Jewish Marxist engineer, he wants to do his bit for the workers of the world. He is one of the designers of the city's underground railway. Somehow he has stumbled into an amorous triangular relationship with Sophia and Gritz.

Lenin is stumbling too. He has put up with food riots in Petrograd, a counter revolution in the Crimea, not to mention his curious intimate problem. One day quite soon, Humphrey will be summoned with Sophia into the Kremlin, and there our passionate, wimpish hero will strut in his first great role on the stage of history. How Comrade Stalin, red and other cabbages, plenty of wax, and *doppelgängers* come into it may well disarm the unsuspecting reader. What is certain is that Jonathan Treitel's tragi-comic Soviet epic marks an indisputably triumphant literary début.

THE HOUSE OF ICONS

History repeats itself, the first time as tragedy and the second time as farce.
    – Karl Marx

1

As they say in Russia, 'An icon is a window into eternity.' (It sounds better in the original.)

I'm not quite sure what this means. Something along the lines of 'Art shows the world as it should be . . . ' Anyway the Russians have always been chasers after perfection. When I came to Moscow from New York in December 1919, I was struck by the beauty of – not what had been done, but what was dreamt.

The Moscow Transport Workers' Soviet found me an apartment in a seventeenth-century building which used to be the residence of a sugar-millionaire antique collector. The building was very central (just leave St Basil's by the exit near the iconostasis, turn left at the first crossing, left, and left again). I lived in a round apartment under a turret. When I looked through the oriel window of my bedroom, I could almost see down into Red Square, were it not for an oblong sugar warehouse – the shape of a sugar cube – blocking the view.

The walls of my apartment were covered, in a close tessellation from ceiling to floor, with icons. Nowhere else to store them, I suppose. My concierge – Nadia Gavrilovna Stepalina, a middle-aged ex-ballerina with rabbit teeth – assured me the building would eventually become a museum, once the State could afford it. I tried to avoid looking at the icons too closely. I kept reminding myself that these were only images, and the gilt haloes over their skulls signified no more than a kind of painterly hoopla. But I couldn't dodge the collective stare of their oval Byzantine eyes. They brandished their crosses at me. They were stiff with fanaticism. I felt I was living in the midst of a crowd of religious maniacs.

I found myself posing in iconic postures, especially in the mornings when I woke with a start and stumbled giddily around the apartment. I flattened my lips and gazed straight ahead through the window. I yawned with my arms spread horizontally, crucifix-wise.

3

There was little furniture in the apartment. My greatcoat used to be draped over St Cyril, and my fur hat would be on the Madonna. A 'Jesus Throwing the Moneychangers Out of the Temple' had a projecting ledge at the top, so I rested there my brush and comb, my toothbrush, my tooth mug and shallow tin of toothpowder.

I dressed rapidly because the apartment was chill. The only heat was a round charcoal stove in the middle of the main room, of the type called a *burzhuika* (literally a 'bourgeois woman'). My concierge (who came from a bourgeois background herself) would knock coyly on the door, so quietly I couldn't hear the rap; then burst in shouting, 'Why don't you listen, Comrade Fraya?' (*Fraya* was her home-made diminutive of 'Humphrey'.)

I'd take her bucket of warm water, and give her a small tip. 'Many thanks, Comrade Nadia Gavrilovna.'

She'd smile crookedly, and depart.

A hurried wash and shave. I'd slip into the high boots, the greatcoat and hat. A final check on my multiple reflections in the shiny silver and gold surfaces of icon-casings – yes, I looked convincingly Russian.

Then off to work.

There were two Moscows in those days: the real and the ideal. The real city was a decrepit place, broken down by years of war and revolution. As I walked down Heroism Boulevard (its official name; everybody called it Salt Cabbage Alley) on the way to work, I had to climb over a pile of rubble. This was the remnant of a barricade built three years ago by some group or another; nobody had yet got round to removing it. (The traditional method of barricade-making in winter is to use water as cement. It freezes solid. In summer the barricade collapses. Freezes again. Melts again. After a few years, what is left is a shallow irregular hillock.) Then I caught a bus (because the tramlines had been recast into cannons or something) which usually had a bullet hole or two in the side, through which the wind whistled.

The ideal Moscow was the capital of International Socialism. Red flags protruded from snow-coated buildings, startling as a tongue stuck out from a pale face. Banners were strung from church and synagogue domes, declaring: RELIGION IS OPIUM. The gas lamp-posts were scrawled in crimson paint with a quote from Lenin: COMMUNISM = RULE BY THE SOVIETS + ELECTRIFICATION. As I looked through the bus window, I'd often see some ragged group of workers or soldiers trotting along, carrying placards with portraits of Marx, Lenin and

4

Trotsky, en route to yell a slogan here or lay a wreath there. Everybody in the bus would wave to them and clap (which also kept our hands warm).

I said 'everybody' – but there were always a few rebellious souls. When the bus turned a sharp corner, an old woman hanging on to a window-pole would cross herself (but – if somebody was looking – pretend to be idly twisting a loose thread in her shawl knot). A fat young man occupying two seats would wink, go *psst* like a deflating balloon, and offer black market sausages.

I left the bus just on the far side of the Moskva river. Then I had to walk along the bank to the headquarters of the Moscow Metropolitan Transport Soviet. In the depth of winter the ice along that path was a blackish-green and sharp as broken bottles.

I leaned on the parapet and looked into the frozen river. I took a good breath of the chill fresh air. Then I crossed the road, entered a red-brick building, and began climbing the five flights of stairs towards my office.

There were originally seven of us engineers in the Planning Section – three native Russians, a Latvian, a Scot and myself: an Anglo-German-American. Our leader was a hairy, bearish Jew whom everybody called Lev (though his real name was something Yiddish). Because he worked us so hard, behind his back he was nicknamed 'The Taskmaster' – but this was intended affectionately (at least by me). We were each assigned a section of tunnel and a station to design, but he insisted we do this with great thoroughness. 'It's no good finding out the tunnels don't connect *after* the metro's finished!' he used to exclaim. He'd sweep his fists past each other to illustrate the non-connecting tunnels. The fists would usually finish up slamming into a wall or table. 'Sorry wall. Sorry table,' he'd murmur. Then he'd kiss the cement and wood.

The Latvian was arrested for political reasons. One of the Russians was conscripted by mistake (despite his official exemption). Another Russian simply disappeared. That left just four of us to plan the entire underground railway network for Moscow. Apart from Lev and myself, there was Yuri (a small young man with a dancer's build) and Jock.

'Jock' was what the Scot liked to be called. He had the misfortune officially to be named John Brown. About the only words of English Lev knew were the chorus of 'John Brown's body'. So whenever Jock entered the room, or said or did anything, Lev would, while slapping his own thigh (or anybody else's within reach) in tempo, sing out ' . . . hiz zoul koez mushtchin onyonyony!'

5

By way of revenge, Jock could mimic Lev's jocular patriotism to a tee. 'Are not humble vegetables more worthy than nancy-boy flowers, hnn?' Jock growled, then added an imitation of Lev's expressive eyebrow twitch. (Lev at the time was in the storeroom, trying to get hold of a slide-rule that actually slid.) Jock took a red cabbage from his shopping bag and tore off a leaf. 'Hnn? Hnn? Yes, yes, this cabbage is as red as the Revolution!' He folded the leaf and put it in his buttonhole.

At this point, Lev returned. We all debated the choice of track gauges. Throughout the discussion, Jock nibbled at his leaf, until it was reduced to a stump.

Afterwards, Lev took me aside. 'Did you notice something funny about Jock?'

'No.'

'His . . . flower . . . buttonhole . . . '

'No. I didn't notice anything.'

Lev, puzzled, hummed the chorus of 'John Brown's Body'.

Jock could also imitate Yuri. Jock would cross his feet in an awkward balletic posture, open his eyes wide like a child, and say in a high voice with an aristocratic r, 'I wonder . . . oh no, no!'

In return Yuri – with his face arranged characteristically, his cheek angled on an extended finger – would peer at Jock's hairline. Jock had curly ginger hair which was falling out rapidly. 'Hmm,' Yuri would go, 'provided he grows a little beard, in five years' time he'll look just like Lenin.'

As for Jock's mimicry of me, I have to say I didn't think it very accurate or funny. Jock would stand very straight with his arms at his side, and make himself look tall. He would blink a lot. He would speak Russian with a funny accent (the English long *i* and the German *r*). He would tell a ridiculously muddled anecdote about Karl Marx and fish soup.

Jock and I used to quarrel (although we both admired each other's dedication to the cause – at least on my part). The thing is, nobody can accuse me of lacking a sense of humour. I appreciate wit. I am all ears for a comic anecdote. I can even belly-laugh at a juicy pun. But I cannot see the point of so called 'sarcasm' and 'irony'. Jock – who had been a dedicated Communist union organiser among the Scottish railway workers – would make the most cynical, *negative* comments about the Revolution. It was worse than I have heard from any capitalist.

'You know it won't happen,' he used to murmur, out of the blue.

'What won't?' I'd ask, puzzled.

'The Moscow metro, of course. It's all just a propaganda ploy.'

'That's nonsense! Lenin himself – '

'Be serious, Humphrey. The Reds are on the losing side. The armies of Britain, France, America, are all – '

'But the inevitable process of history – '

'Look around you, Humphrey! Look at Moscow! People are starving on the streets.'

'The food is quite – '

'Oh, *we* eat well. We get special rations in our canteen. But the common worker or peasant . . . '

Jock would then start swearing in quick colloquial Russian. I'd ask him to translate this into English. He'd continue in his Glaswegian dialect – of which I couldn't understand a blind word. He'd switch into normal English:

'Och, I can speak your posh Sassenach, if I have to, Humphrey. I can put on the smarmy voice. You're so soft in the south. You think life is easy. Life is hard in a revolution. Millions of Russians are dying. Don't fool yourself, man!'

For a moment, I'd be shocked. I'd think of the Muscovites I'd encountered on the buses and in the streets: the cripples, the beggars, the unemployed . . . and I'd wonder how much the Revolution had so far helped *them*. Then I'd realise Jock was teasing me, and I'd guffaw as loudly as I could.

But it wasn't all fun and games. Within that office, beneath its low sloped roof, under the dangling bare light bulbs flickering as the power supply fluctuated, working on the blackboard and the drawing boards, we plotted the future course of the metro. I felt as if I belonged to a cell of revolutionaries conspiring for a better world – like Lenin in Zürich. (I told this to Lev and Yuri, who agreed; Jock thought the comparison hilarious.)

We didn't finish work until late at night. Anyway I knew of nothing else to do in the evenings. Lev would go home to his wife and Yuri to his boyfriend. Jock used to mooch in semi-legal bars. But I preferred to walk slowly and solitarily through Moscow, en route to my home among the icons.

The streets would be quite empty by ten or eleven. Rats and stray dogs would scamper. An occasional soldier or policeman might check my papers. Long clear vistas – apart from the odd staggering drunkard.

I would return home by an indirect route – along the bulldozed path by the solid walls of the Kremlin, then left, then right, and circle round the Kremlin through small streets. As I walked, I imagined the metro tunnels that would one day lie beneath my route. I passed the ruined site on Coachmaker's Row – just snow and a bombed smithy – where a major interchange station would inevitably stand.

At the crossroads where Salt Cabbage Alley meets Milk Lane, beside my apartment building, a small bonfire was blazing throughout January – sometimes just reduced to a charcoal brazier. A dozen or so men and women – soldiers, shift workers, husbands coming back from a night out – would be gathered around it. I'd greet them. I'd lean over the low flame and melt the icicles off my eyebrows. The dripping water would hiss on the coals or slow-burning wood. The smell of steam and wet fur would fill my nostrils, combining with the indescribable odour of Moscow itself. I loved everybody – not as individuals – I was in love with Mother Russia.

Then I'd go into the apartment building. The concierge would always be awake. She'd shout to me as I climbed the stairs past her rooms, 'Comrade Fraya! All's well?'

'Splendid, Comrade Nadia Gavrilovna!'

And I would enter my apartment.

I'd take my boots off, levering the heels on the rim of the cold *burzhuika*. I'd hang my overcoat over St Cyril and rest my fur hat on the Madonna.

I'd peer through the frosted glass of the oriel window at the bonfire below – and other more distant flames across the city – and rub my hands together as if warming them over the far glow. How wonderful, I'd think: fire for a Revolution!

The hoarfrost pattern on the window would be superimposed on my view of the bonfire. It would seem that some white figure was couched on the flames.

Then I'd turn the gas light off. I'd climb into bed. I'd suck a sugar lump (set aside from my ration). The last thing I'd see before falling asleep was the array of icons, lit by the moonlight diffused through the frosted pane. Now the icons would look like a crowd of typical Russians. I'd recognise the faces. St Martha . . . why, that's the old woman on the bus who crossed herself. St Basil . . . he's the black market dealer. My mouth would fill with sugary saliva, which had not yet turned acid . . . Nadia is the Holy Ghost. Jock is John the Baptist. Yuri is Mary Magdalene. Lev is the bear accompanying the prophet Elisha . . .

Then the final iota of sugar would dissolve. I would leave the real Moscow entirely, and enter the ideal Moscow – the city as it should be.

2

On 29 February 1920 I had the day off work. (The nightwatchman at the Metropolitan Transport Soviet had been arrested for black marketeering, and nobody could find the spare keys to unlock the building.)

So, having nothing better to do, I dressed up in my warmest clothes. (It was my custom to wind copies of *Pravda* round my legs, between my long johns and my trousers, for extra cosiness.) My belt was broken, so I held my trousers in place with a safety pin at the front. I muffled myself in my furs. Then I strolled through Moscow – along and across the river, past the Church of the Resurrection and the Church of the Oppressed, and back up to the Kremlin and St Basil's.

It was queer to see the city during a normal working day. For one thing, it was almost exclusively female. Apart from some policemen, soldiers and road builders, Moscow seemed populated entirely by bulky women heaving net shopping bags. They tramped through the snow. They formed long grumbly queues outside shops and stalls, and swung their bags like a row of pendulum clocks. Out of idle curiosity, I gazed at what I could see of the women's skin: reddish patches of exposed cheek and nose – and wondered what the rest of their bodies looked like.

In Red Square (just about where Lenin's Mausoleum now stands) was a square canvas tent. The tent flap was screened with a drape of blackout material. Pinned on to that was a sheet of corrugated cardboard, scrawled with:

HOW ARE THE MIGHTY FALLEN!!!

SEE THE SO-CALLED

LITTLE FATHER

DEGRADED!!!

SEE THE SO-CALLED
LITTLE MOTHER
IN ABJECT DEJECTION!!!
SEE!!!

It was beginning to snow again. To get under cover, as much as out of curiosity, I paid my two thousand roubles (worth about ten cents, you understand; this was during the inflation) and entered the tent.

At first – coming out of the bright snowscape – the interior of the booth seemed dim as an aquarium. A few other inquisitive people – housewives, mainly, with shopping under their arms – floated through the semi-gloom. A little brown light filtered through the canvas; and there were candles here and there, dripping tallow on to saucers.

Then, as I penetrated deeper into the tent, I noticed other people dressed in rich materials and bulky jewellery. These grandees were posing on low pedestals, against the far wall. There was a man with a neat beard and a crown, standing with arms akimbo. His arm was linked with a younger fellow in plus-fours, who much resembled him. Three ladies – one aged and two young – in satin dresses (mauve, royal blue, primrose) and very white skin were lifting their noses haughtily. A girl in cream silks was gripping a tennis racket as if her life depended on it.

I recognised this grouping as the former imperial family: the Romanovs. *There* was the Tsar and the Tsarina. *There* was the brash heir to the throne. *There* three of the Grand Duchesses. I had often idly wondered what had been their fate (there was a rumour that they had been executed, but this had never been confirmed in *Pravda*). Now I knew. It seemed a wonderful comedown: that the former rulers should be on display to all and sundry for a few copper coins.

The Romanovs were partially screened from my view by the mêlée of oglers. I happened to have *The Communist Manifesto* in my coat pocket. I took it out and waved it, over the heads of the crowd, at the royal family. 'Yoo hoo!' I called – in what I intended as a tasteful taunt. Then I hastily put the *Manifesto* back in my pocket. I didn't want anybody to think I was making a 'pass' at one of the Grand Duchesses.

I approached the Romanovs. I could see them more clearly now, from the side. They were cordoned off by a hemp rope. A line of women was pressing against the rope, leaning close to the royal family, inspecting details.

10

Near my elbow, was a collection box tied on to a tent pole. (It had originally been a tin of soap powder or something, with a slit cut in the lid.) A paper wound round it was inscribed: *Five hundred roubles per prick*.

Now that I looked more closely, I noticed the gawking women had pointed items in their hands: sewing pins, needles, hat pins. They'd drop a coin in the tin; then lean forward and stick a pointed item in the face or hands or clothes of their choice Romanov.

I put my coin in the tin – and the penny dropped (metaphorically as well as literally, if you see what I mean). I realised the imperial family were in fact dummies. Very convincing ones – at least in the dim light. The Tsar's lips were curled in an authentic snarl. The Tsarina's nostrils flared proudly. Grand Duchess Anastasia's buff tennis dress was unbuttoned at the neck; if you peered down it, you could just see the bulge of her left nipple beneath a single layer of silk, and even a faint rosiness. All their wazen complexions were rather pockmarked, having been gouged by numerous sharp objects already.

I scanned the dummies, trying to decide which one I would impale. I had half a mind to stab the Tsar through the heart. There again, there was something to be said for piercing the fair breast of young Anastasia (though I could not convince myself my motive was purely political). I sidled to and fro, eyeing one dummy then another, enjoying the suspense before making up my mind.

Then I saw another figure, posed in the shadow behind the Tsar. It was a female – presumably one of his sisters or sisters-in-law. I moved close to her. She was the most regal lady I had ever seen. Although she was of average height, she gave the impression of a mighty stature. Her bosom projected horizontally. Her skin was lily-white, with a beauty mark under her chin. Her eyes were emerald. She was wearing a purple satin dress, a string of pearls, and, over her right nipple, a ruby brooch which (I bowed to examine it with care) oddly was in the shape of a hammer and sickle. She was my choice for pricking.

At this point, it occurred to me that I didn't have a pin or needle on me. I considered borrowing one off somebody in the crowd – but I felt a queer reluctance to share anybody else's. Then I remembered I had fastened my trousers that morning with a safety pin.

Yanking my trousers up with my left hand, I opened and took out the safety pin with my right. I bent the pin between my fingers so the point projected. I held it between index finger and thumb. The pin moved closer and closer to the regal dummy. Where would I perforate her? Her

11

lips? Her nose? Her eyeball? The tip of the pin touched her delicately rouged cheek.

The woman screamed and screamed. A ruby of blood was forming on her cheek. My arms flew up in winding gestures of apology. She glared at me and kept screeching till my eardrums thrummed. I could think of no excuse. I was transfixed. My trousers fell down. The newspapers unwrapped themselves from around my patched long johns, and fluttered away. Articles on the battles in the Crimea and meat rationing and poetry recitals flapped, crumpled and disappeared among the crowd of housewives and Romanovs. The woman stopped screaming and burst into laughter. Her bosom heaved. She chortled at a high pitch with her lips wide apart like a prima donna. Great gouts of laughter were shaking from her throat. Her noise was scarcely distinguishable from a wail of pain. She leaned forward, and hugged me, and patted my cheek.

She was my wife to be: Sophia.

3

Sophia Arkadievna Bellechasse is the greatest creator of imitation humans in the world.

She comes from the famous Bellechasse dynasty of wax artists. Her great-great-grandfather, Pierre-Marie Bellechasse, had been the art tutor to Marie Antoinette at Versailles. It was the custom there for the King to carry out his daily activities almost entirely in public. His supping and going to bed – *Le Dîner* and *Le Coucher* – were ceremonies to be attended by devout courtiers. The King tired of this formality. Pierre-Marie proposed that His Majesty be substituted for on such occasions by a wax dummy. The artist's mock-King was so authentic seeming that Marie Antoinette herself could not tell it apart from her real husband, except on the rare occasions she drew close enough to note its lack of smell. Even the palace flies, which (so it was said) were in the habit of circling the King's head in a kind of black halo and emitting a pleasing hum, performed the same service for the dummy.

Soon Pierre-Marie was called upon to mimic Marie Antoinette. He produced – not a mere imitation of the Queen's surface – a re-creation of Her Majesty as she should have appeared. The real lady may have been a trifle dumpy and thick armed; the ideal dummy was svelte and slender wristed.

Before long all the courtiers were demanding copies of themselves. Pierre-Marie hired a team of forty assistants who built wire armatures and arranged the clothing, the wigs and the glass eyeballs. Pierre-Marie personally supervised the construction of the skulls. Each courtier's face was smeared with a fine plaster; two straws were inserted up the nostrils to enable minimal inhalation. After only half an hour, an assistant tapped just above the cheekbones with a small chisel; the plaster mask slid off. Flesh-tinted hot wax was poured into the masks, and left to cool; so a model of the face was produced. Assistants fixed the eyelashes, eyebrows, eyeballs and any facial hair or beauty marks. Finally Pierre-Marie stroked the still warm faces, and, by a gentle impress of his finger, applied that *je ne sais quoi* that made them seem perfectly alive – the dilation of a nostril or the sag of an eyelid.

The introduction of dummies made court life far more restful. *Le Coucher* was reduced to a tableau: a dummy lay in bed; other dummies observed. Grand balls took place till late in the night: orchestras played, servants moved the dummies around in graceful *pas de deux*; meanwhile the courtiers lay snoring in their beds. Eventually most of the courtiers went away to Paris or their country estates, leaving Versailles populated almost entirely by dummies and underlings.

The soft-hearted monarch found dummies convenient in his system of justice too. Naturally one had to carry out the law with the utmost severity, and execute malefactors as an example to others. But what was strung from the gallows was seldom a creature of flesh and blood. Likewise the Bastille was occupied by a half a dozen genuine prisoners selected for their noisiness; the other cells contained mere imitations.

When the Revolution came, the dummies saved the lives of many aristocrats. Often the mob would invade a château, rampage up the broad marble staircase and through a tapestried hall, finally attaining the balcony where a Count was posed . . . only to discover that the genuine Count was absent, having escaped through the kitchen window disguised as a washerwoman two hours earlier.

After the Bastille was stormed, the dummies there were tied together like firewood, and carted away on a tumbril to be auctioned at the Place de la Concorde. An entrepreneur bought the job lot. He cut off the wax heads using the public guillotine located in the Place. The clothes were sold to second-hand dealers, the metal armatures were salvaged to be re-forged for munitions, and the heads were melted down and cast into candles.

In 1792 Pierre-Marie was arrested by the Committee for Public Safety. This was despite his protestations of loyalty to the Revolution. (He had cut his hair short, wore trousers instead of breeches, and always carried a copy of *Candide* in his breast pocket, just in case.)

Following a year in jail, he was arraigned in January 1793 – a week after the execution of the King.

Danton – that bull-headed, big-shouldered man (whom I always visualise as rather like somebody I'll tell you about later called Gritz) was prosecuting.

'Bring on Exhibit Number One!' he commanded.

A dummy of Louis XVI was carried into court. It was propped up beside the accused.

14

Danton bellowed, 'Look at the face of privilege and tyranny! Look at the prisoner Bellechasse!'

Jean-Marie smiled politely.

'Bellechasse! Did you or did you not construct this dummy?'

'Certainly, sir.'

'Does it or does it not glorify the personage of the so-called monarch?'

'If I may, sir, I would like to point out – '

'Judges! Jurymen! Examine this dummy closely! See its noble brow. See its strong chin. See its far-sighted gaze. It is the prisoner Bellechasse who portrayed the King thus!'

The judges and jurymen examined the dummy; indeed they all noted its noble brow, strong chin, and far-sighted gaze.

Pierre-Marie replied gently. 'If I might quote Voltaire . . . '

The court waited, anticipating some ironic claptrap about 'this best of all possible worlds'.

'Voltaire wrote, "The secret of Art is to correct Nature." My learned Judges and Gentlemen of the Jury, might I turn your attention once more to this dummy of my manufacture, this simulacrum of the so-called King – or, as I prefer to call him, Citizen Capet. It has been suggested to you by the honourable advocate, Citizen Danton, that this model is an homage to Capet. I am sure you will all, on closer perusal of the dummy, agree that it is in fact an attack on the monarch, a deliberately absurd and derisive caricature of his person. Observe the frowning low brow. Note the dangling jowls of the double chin. Glance into the watery eyes . . . I rest my case.'

And everybody in court looked at the dummy. And they all saw a low brow, dangling jowls and watery eyes.

So Pierre-Marie was acquitted.

He wasted no time in 'cultivating his garden'. That very evening he set out for the Swiss border. Within two weeks he, his son Pierre and his surviving dummies arrived in London.

Posing as an ardent Royalist, he set up an exhibition in King's Cross (located, in fact, where today lies the juncture of the 'Tube' and the mainline railway terminus). He shared premises with an exhibition of dancing poodles and a Punch and Judy show. He charged half-a-crown entrance fee, or sixpence for the working classes.

The *Bellechasse Simulacrum Exposition* was all the rage for about six months. Then it fell out of fashion; he made little money for the rest of his life.

A fire in 1810 destroyed most of the dummies and all of Pierre-Marie.

15

Pierre Bellechasse, his son and heir, promptly returned to Paris. By then Napoleon was in power, and there was much nostalgia for the old royalty. Pierre made his fortune exhibiting Louis XVI, Marie Antoinette, Danton, Robespierre and a two-headed calf born near Dijon.

A self-portrait of Pierre survives – a charcoal sketch. (It's one of Sophia's most treasured possessions: she keeps it concealed between the frame and the glass of her mirror.) He is a dapper man dressed in the mode of the *jeunesse dorée*: a tight-buttoned tailcoat, and boots with an upcurved narrow tip.

He was ambitious. By some stratagem (it was rumoured he was 'friendly' with Josephine), he managed to persuade the Emperor himself to pose for a portrait in wax. Napoleon was delighted with the end product, not least because Pierre had added ten centimetres to the imperial leg length.

The upshot was that Napoleon ordered Pierre to accompany him on his military campaigns, to provide moral uplift to the troops. Pierre could hardly refuse this arduous assignment. (Perhaps the Emperor had found out about his relationship with Josephine?)

That is how come Pierre, along with his waxworks, found himself in Moscow in 1812. He entered the deserted, burning city. French troops were looting what little there was to loot. It began to snow.

When the French retreated later that year, Pierre, weakened by typhus, stayed behind in Moscow.

We understand the pattern of history (Marx has revealed that), but we know so little of the details. Nothing is recorded of Pierre's life in war-torn Moscow (though often, in Moscow during the Civil War, I tried to imagine it).

He does not appear again to history until 1821, when he was owner and manager of the Imperial Waxworks Museum on the Nevsky Prospekt in St Petersburg, by Appointment to the Tsar.

He was succeeded in this post by his son, Robert.

Who was succeeded by his son, Arkady.

So far – in the Bellechasse family history – women have featured little. At this point in history (circa 1890), the Bellechasse family ran out of male heirs. Arkady's wife, Serafina, gave birth to Sophia. Then she retired to her chaise-longue and refused further marital relations with her husband.

So Arkady, an eager young chap in a striped blazer, put his energies into training Sophia to take over the family firm. She has often described to me how he taught her the correct technique for gluing eyebrows in place, or how to attach an earring without distorting the waxen lobe. He patted her head a great deal and offered lots of little smiles. When his monocle would pop startlingly from his eye socket, he'd make an 'oh, oh' noise.

Both Sophia's parents 'perished in the Russo-Japanese War of 1905'. That's what she told me at first. It turned out they died in a railway accident near Voronezh in 1908. Apparently, the track was poorly maintained – which could, I suppose, indirectly be blamed on the shortage of manpower due to the war.

'History repeats itself,' as Marx said. Sophia was running the St Petersburg waxworks when, out of the blue in August 1914, a summons arrived to attend the imperial court. There she was informed that she was henceforth the art tutor of Princess Anastasia.

She travelled with the Court, shuttling between the Summer and the Winter Palaces. She had to place the family business under the control of a manager – who promptly absconded with most of the assets. The waxworks went bankrupt.

I used to ask Sophia what it was like at the Court, at the very centre of the web of that corrupt regime.

'Oh, it was awfully . . . to be quite honest, Humph . . . *boring.*'

'What about the Tsar . . . and Rasputin?'

'Rasputin, yugh! Always mumbling away in his dreadful accent. Smelled of damp, too . . . The Tsar and the Tsarina: he called her Sunny and she called him Bunny.'

'What? In English?'

'Of course. Sunny (that's the Tsarina) was brought up at the court of Queen Victoria. You never heard such dated English! I actually heard Bunny call for "a dish of tea"!'

(In fact Sophia herself used to pronounce 'habit', 'humble' and 'humour' in the old-fashioned h-less manner. And when she was in her melancholy mood, she would claim to be 'hipped'.)

I'd ask Sophia for more details.

'As the Great War became more horrible, was the Court pessimistic?'

'Oh no, Humph! No, no. Bunny used to love dressing up in his fancy dress with all the tinkly medals. Him and the dear young Tsarevich, too. I had to keep changing the uniforms on their dummies . . . But no pessimism, no . . . The worse the war became, the more frivolous everybody was. We played Charades, Consequences, Animal Noises, too. Awfully jolly. We drew our animals out of a top hat. I was a cat – I

17

made the dearest little miaow. Bunny was a rabbit, of course. The
Tsarina was going oink-oink. So was Rasputin, so those two liaised. My
fellow cat was the Tsarevitch, Alexis. He went miaow, too. I'm sure he
cheated. Then he kissed me.'

'Did you kiss him back?'

'We all knew the regime was doomed.'

'When did you leave the Court?'

'Ah, Humph! Now there's a question!'

Sophia would tickle me under my armpits or chin, or kiss my nose.
She'd tell me a different story each time I asked her how she came to
join the Bolsheviks.

I'll tell you her account that struck me as . . . well, about as convincing
as any other.

'Actually Humph . . . I became a Communist through a misunder-
standing. It was in November, a few weeks after the second Revolution,
and we were in Siberia. Horribly snowy, it was. I got chilblains on my
toes . . . The imperial family, all sitting round having dinner. And I was
near the bottom of the table, of course, trying to wriggle my shoes off to
ease the pressure on my toes. So . . . well it turned out afterwards that
the Tsarina had asked me . . . I didn't hear at the time . . . "Are *you* at
least still loyal to us, Miss Bellechasse? Or will you too follow the path
of expediency and ally yourself with the Communist atheists?" And I
said – now, the wine waiter was coming round at the time, and we were
having salmon – "I prefer the red, thank you." So it was settled. My
things were packed. I left for Moscow the next day.'

Of course, I can't vouch for the truth of this history of the Bellechasse
family, I've pieced it together from anecdotes Sophia has told me over
the years. And though Sophia never lies (well, hardly ever), it's not
beyond her to embroider the truth.

I feel I have a duty to Sophia to relate her family background. If what
she has told me is true: it throws light on her character. If it's untrue: it
throws light on her character. Much that I'll write about her in later
chapters might seem uncomplimentary. You may come to think of her
as 'selfish', or at least 'highly strung'. But I want you to understand she
bears the weight of a great deal of history.

4

After I had impaled her cheek, Sophia invited me back to her place. (Rather forward of her – had I thought twice about it; but of course I didn't think twice.)

We waited at the bus stop under the St Nicholas tower of the Kremlin, and caught a bus going north.

Without consciously working it out, I'd vaguely supposed Sophia resided in a splendid palace. Or, there again, she might voluntarily be living the life of the poorest worker, sharing one basement room with a family of street sweepers and abattoir assistants.

So I was surprised when she guided me off the bus and into a rather pleasant bourgeois district (not so different from my own former residences in Highgate or the Bronx). Wintry birch trees lined the pavements. There were blocks of flats interspersed with newish detached houses, all in an antique style of turrets and overhanging eaves (the Russian equivalent of Victorian Gothic).

Sophia lived on the ground floor of a house; the storeys above were inhabited by a family of insane aristocratic deaf-mutes, she told me at first – later admitting that in fact the upper floors had been looted in the Revolution and were unoccupiable. Sophia had her own separate entrance – quite a luxury for Moscow.

Her place wasn't large, but it was neat and cosy. Persian rugs on the floor. Elongated rectangular furniture with brass fittings. A circular mirror. A fireplace where a log burned tidily behind a fire screen. I crouched there, warming my face, pleasurably wrinkling my nose as it once more became flexible.

Lots of paintings everywhere. Country scenes by Russian imitators of the Barbizon school hung in the bathroom and kitchen. The living room was decorated with tall frameless canvases painted with triangles and circles: semi-abstract Constructivist works that I could make nothing of. Sophia would point casually at the art works: 'Oh, that's by Katya. That's by what's his name. That naughty one's by Tolya, the little dear.'

19

As soon as we arrived in the house, her fingers scampered through a shallow drawer under a display cabinet, and she produced a strip of black velvet, sewing scissors and a bottle of glue.

'Be a sweetie, Humph. Patch up my wound.'

'What, on your cheek, Comrade Bellechasse?'

'Call me Sophia, dear. Simply *everybody* does.'

So I gummed a square of black cloth over the droplet of dried blood. I put it on at an angle; so it looked like a diamond-shaped beauty patch, and gave her (I decided) a rakish eighteenth-century appearance – like one of her French forebears.

Sophia always thought of herself as very Gallic (although, according to my calculation, she had only one thirty-second part French blood). At moments of emotion, she used to twist the ruby ring on the middle finger of her right hand and murmur, 'Mon dieu', or 'Merde'. She would sometimes speak Russian in an exaggeratedly French accent: nasal and dropping *h*'s.

She had me sit on the upright purple sofa. 'You look so tired, 'Umph, *mon petit*. You must have a drink, a little French drink, called *kir*.'

What she called kir turned out to be some kind of wild berries preserved in vodka: fruity, sweet and potent.

She sat beside me and clinked glasses. The bottle was on a low table in front of us. She kept refilling our glasses, with cries of, 'No, no, I insist.'

I was shy at first, but I became steadily more drunk and talkative. I began to realise just how lonely I had been, working in the shadowless office and sleeping in the dim icon-walled apartment, how much I pined for charming female company.

'I want you to tell me *all* about yourself,' Sophia said, tapping me on the wrist.

And I told her all about myself. I told her about my upbringing in London. I'd lived in a tall thin house with Papa (my mother had died giving birth to me), a miserable old man with ill-fitting false teeth and socialist principles. As a youngster, he'd worked with Karl Marx on the *Rheinische Zeitung*, and had fled Germany during the 1848 troubles. Papa had impressed on me umpteen anecdotes about Marx: his politics, his dermatitis, his fondness for fish soup . . . And I also told Sophia about my youth in New York, staying with my uncle's family. (This was during the Great War; I'd had to leave Britain to avoid internment as an Enemy Alien.) I'd been an apprentice engineer on the subway system there. I described, with appropriate circumlocutions, my first kiss, flirtation and other erotic experiences. Sophia listened with lips slightly parted. Then in 1917 I'd been interned as a pacifist Communist, and had come to Russia as soon as I could. I emphasised my commitment to Communism. I told her about my love of engineering and the plans for the Moscow metro.

I did noisy, sozzled imitations of my colleagues at work.

'Oy, oy . . . ow!' I said, mimicking Lev banging his fist on the wall.

I stood on one leg on the Persian rug and pirouetted. 'You can*not* balance a thousand kilogram load on a teensy weensy strut-ling-ette-ikin,' I quoted Yuri. (This doesn't translate well since in English – unlike Russian – one can't form naturally a triple diminutive for 'strut'.)

Sophia – who was getting tipsy herself – clapped the heels of her hands together and screeched with laughter.

I teetered over during the pirouette and fell back on to the sofa – almost but not quite landing on her lap.

I even parodied Jock: his savage cynicism, his conviction that millions of Russians were worse off now than under the old regime. I spoke Russian with a Scottish accent, trilling the *r* with the back of the tongue raised (though in fact Jock spoke Russian perfectly). I exaggerated his complaints for the sake of a comic effect. 'The R-r-revolution is doomed! R-r-russians are starving!'

Somehow, this wasn't so funny.

Then Sophia got up, rather wobbly on her feet. She turned the handle of a door in a painting – which turned out also to be the real handle of a real door.

She guided me through into another world.

A cold place with a high ceiling. Mounds of wax on the floor, mainly flesh-coloured, but also reds, blue, yellows, a little green. We moved forward together, slithering occasionally and gasping, then regaining our balance. We passed iron frames fitted with dangling hooks. Wooden work benches. Wire armatures twisted into the approximate shape of a skull or a torso. Long strips of canvas, some of them wound round the armatures. A table loaded with wigs, like the scalp collection of a Red Indian chief. Sophia swung her arm in a broad inclusive gesture. 'This is where I copy people,' she said.

At the time I couldn't make sense of the huge contrast: the neat bourgeois comfort of her home – the messy hotchpotch of her studio. She even used different voices in the two places: a high, airy, fluctuating voice for domestic use, and a straightforward monotone when talking about her art. As I came to understand her better, over many months, I

realised that this split personality was essential to her. She wouldn't have
been able to maintain the charming frivolity of her social life if she hadn't
been able to retreat into the steady get-on-with-it of her dummy making
– and vice versa.

I was shivering. Pink icicles clustered around the rim of a pot of red
paint. There was a croaking sound like a crow's call from somewhere
above – a rafter bending under the weight of snow, I expect.

'I want to go back,' I said.

She nodded. She gripped my arm.

'I just wanted you to see this side of me.'

So we returned to her warm house.

We walked back into the living room, and through its far door.
The bedroom was square and low; it smelled of lavender. All the
fittings apart from the bed were pressed against the walls. A round
mirror within a simple carved pine frame faced me as I entered,
reflecting my collar. A shallow pine dressing table stood beneath it.
When I turned, I saw a long painting hung on the door, signed
Maximilian Gritzshtayn: at first glance it appeared to be a view of
red skyscrapers but it was in fact an ingeniously calligraphed selection
of quotations from Marx and Lenin.

The bed, a solid square item draped with a purple satin coverlet,
floated in the middle of the room. A polar-bear rug lay on the
floor in front of it. We walked forwards, side by side, stepping over the
snow-white fur.

I know that bed so well, every inch of it, every small lump and twanging
spring – for we made love there I don't know how many times . . . I
remember, in the cold nights, we used to lift the polar-bear rug from
the floor and pull it over us. In the small hours I'd often wake and find
that most of the bear skin had found its way to Sophia's side of the bed,
so I'd have to slip my hand in the jaw, grip its teeth and drag the whole
bear across.

But, no. On that occasion, on my first visit to her house, we didn't
make love. We didn't even sit on the bed – although Sophia patted the
pillow suggestively.

I yawned and said I must be returning because I had a hard day at
work tomorrow.

She said, 'Must you?'

I yawned again.

Then I put on my greatcoat and hat. She let me out on to the street.
On the doorstep, before we parted, she extended her hand. I turned

it over and kissed her on the palm, between the life line and the love line. (This is an American romantic trick I'd acquired in New York.)

I leaned forward and kissed the black diamond-shaped patch on her cheek. A little blood had seeped through. It tasted like rust.

5

Iron girders. Iron tubing. Tension. Compression. Grand visions of subterranean tunnels and tracks constructed in stainless steel and flecked with red where flags waved occupied my head during the spring of 1920 as the planning stage for the metro neared completion. The Planning Section had set a July deadline. The plans would be submitted to the Metropolitan Transport Workers' Soviet. They'd rubber-stamp it. Then it would ascend the pyramid of power, having to be approved on each level, right up to the Central Committee and the Politbureau. We kept a bottle of warm French champagne (acquired by Lev through some black market swap) in the office (behind volume VII of an outdated edition of Khlebanov and Shlovski, *Elements of Engineering Thermodynamics*), to be opened on the day when our proposal would finally be accepted.

Meanwhile Sophia and I were en route to becoming lovers. It was a slow journey. We met whenever we could spare the time, which was about twice a week, at museums or parks, her place or mine.

I can't describe for you the gradual increase in the intimacy of our kissing and fondling (I was permitted to touch her ... here ... here ... and finally here ...) because this is private, and because anyway now, as I write these words, nineteen years later, I've forgotten too much. (Or so I think. Perhaps if I shut my eyes and let my fingers grope in thin air, and remember ... I will find some way to retrieve that love after all.)

The world which Sophia inhabited, and which I was permitted to enter on occasion, hardly seemed the same at all as the quotidian one where a Civil War was taking place between Whites and Reds and the Moscow metro was being designed. If the two worlds meshed at all, it was only in the way a symphony or an opera works (I'm not very musical, so please excuse my ignorance): from time to time you have a jolly

24

rousing melody, with boring transitional sections in between to glue the nice bits together.

Meanwhile we four engineers were getting on each other's nerves.

Yuri was becoming skinnier and skinnier. I used to sit beside him at the canteen, and urge, 'Have another potato,' but he wouldn't.

In the office, he'd carry out complicated calculations, in his head or scrawled on little bits of paper, proving that:

'According to my extrapolation, by 1992 everybody in Russia will be as rich as the Queen of England.'

'Queen?!' I'd say. 'They have a King there now.'

Jock, 'You can't trust statistics.'

Lev, 'Get on with your work, Yurochka.'

Yuri, insulted, would stick out his lower lip. He'd arrange himself in some bizarre posture – one leg projecting horizontally on to a chair and the other raised vertically, say – and flip through a table of anti-logarithms.

As for Lev, his jokes became sillier yet. He made complicated puns (most of which of course I can't translate). For example, he argued, 'God is Love. Love is blind. A meths drinker is blind. So God drinks meths. QED.'

I think I annoyed my colleagues by my relentless optimism. I'd whistle catchy Bolshevik hymns and vaudeville songs. I'd declare that the metro planning process was far ahead of schedule. I'd tell everybody about Sophia, all her charms and foibles.

'We really don't care about that woman,' Yuri would interrupt me.

'For Marx's sake!' Jock would swear.

Lev would bawl, 'Shut up! She's not your first-born baby!'

But the most irritable and irritating member of our team was certainly Jock. He'd acquired scabies – a skin infection which meant he was always scratching his inflamed cheeks and tugging at his eyelids. What's more, he was upset about politics.

'Bolshevism was defeated two years ago,' he declared to me in March, during the ten-minute afternoon tea break, as we strolled along the banks of the Moskva river.

'What *are* you talking about, Jock?'

'Bolshevism means rule by the workers, yes?'

'Yes.'

'The workers organise themselves in soviets and the soviets run the industries?'

25

'But the soviets *do* run Russian industries!'

'This precious metro of ours,' he said, apparently changing the subject, '*if* and when it's built, who do you think will control it?'

'The dictatorship of the proletariat, I suppose.'

'I mean who's going to drive the trains, direct the signals?'

'Surely experienced rail workers.'

'And do you know who's in charge of the railways? I'll tell you who's in charge of the railways. The Ministry of War! Under Trotsky. That's who!'

'There *is* a war on . . . '

Jock scratched furiously at his cheek till a dew of blood formed.

'Humphrey. Have you talked to *any* real workers in Moscow?'

'Well, to be honest, their accents . . . And the proletarian class consciousness isn't all it might be – '

'Until March 1918 the Railway Union ran the rail system. Separate soviets – groups organised by Communist workers – controlled each section. Then the Party demanded the soviets should merely parrot the orders of the Politbureau. Fine "socialism" that is! The workers refused. They went on strike. Trotsky sent in the strike breakers, the scabs, the – '

'I beg your pardon?'

'The so-called Labour so-called Army! A rabble of scabs armed with machine-guns . . . I've been buying workers drinks in a hundred and one railwaymen's bars. I've been listening. I *know*!'

I breathed in the clean spring air.

'Ahh! Fine weather,' I said. 'Look, most of the snow has melted from the roads.'

I glanced at twin heaps of melting snow on adjacent turrets on the Kremlin wall . . . and thought of Sophia's bosom.

Perhaps I should have been listening with greater attention to Jock, who was quoting from memory the entire relevant decree of the Council of People's Commissars, as published in *Izvestia* No. 57.

I jerked myself back to political consciousness. 'Ah, yes. *But . . .*'

'You know what you are, Humphrey? You're the greatest but-nik in Moscow!'

'*But* it's expressed better than I could in the immortal words of Lenin . . . '

I took my diary from the inside pocket of my jacket, and fumbled through it till I found the page where I'd written extracts from Lenin's speeches (copied from *Pravda*). It was a thin, expensive diary, with a red

26

leather cover, gold-tooled with: *Journal for 1915.* (The day of the week for a given date was the same in 1915 as in 1920.) I'd bought the diary on the black market in exchange for one hundred grams of lard.

I still possess that diary now. (Indeed I have all my diaries; their red, black and blue oblongs are stacked on the desk in front of me; strange that they of all my belongings should cling to me.)

I quoted:

If we are not anarchists, we must admit that the State, *that is coercion*, is necessary for the transition from capitalism to socialism. The form of coercion is determined by the . . . [etcetera] There is, therefore, absolutely *no* contradiction in principle between Soviet – that is, socialist – democracy and the exercise of dictatorial power by individuals.

'You see?' I said. 'It's all quite straightforward!'

'But the railway workers – '

'Just one moment, Jock. I believe I have another . . . '

I flipped forward a page in my diary, and quoted Lenin on the subject of railways:

but be that as it may, *unquestioning subordination* to a single will is absolutely necessary for the success of processes organised on the pattern of large-scale machine industry. On the railways it is twice or three times as necessary.

'Twice or *three* times,' I repeated.

Jock scowled and wouldn't listen to my quotations. He tugged his curly locks; a few hairs floated away on the wind. He scratched his cheek. He spat over the balustrade in the direction of the Kremlin; his saliva fell in the river.

It was time to return to work. We walked back, he striding in front and I trailing behind.

I was tittering. I had noticed in my diary another quote from Lenin on the question of central control: 'Given ideal class consciousness and discipline . . . this subordination would be something like the mild leadership of a conductor of an orchestra.' This evoked an irresistibly droll image: Lenin waving a baton and the Red Army playing their rifles like flutes, or plucking a chain of machine-gun ammunition like a harp . . . But, in his present mood, it seemed best not to tell Jock jokes.

27

We climbed the stairs to the office.

We entered. Yuri was bending over a large sketch plan of the proposed tunnel under the Moskva river, twitching his fingers at details, and Lev was examining the diagram over Yuri's shoulder, nodding and making *um-hum* noises.

'I need a drink,' Jock said in English.

He stretched up, and pulled volume VII of *Elements of Engineering Thermodynamics* from the shelf. It fell face down on the floor. He reached for the champagne bottle that was concealed behind there, clutched its base and waved it like a club.

'My father always told me', I said, nervously, 'that you should hold a bottle by the waist and a woman by the neck – or is it the other way round?'

Yuri giggled alarmingly.

Lev said in a deep voice, in the tone cab drivers use to calm horses, 'Steady, Jock. Steady.'

Jock said in English, 'What're you saying it for? They'll never build the bloody metro!'

I recall Jock at that moment: his entire head ruddy with passion and skin disease . . . and I can't help wondering: if in the spring of 1920 I'd listened more to him, and cheered him up, if only I hadn't been in such a Sophia-obsessed frame of mind, perhaps I could have saved him from his sad fate.

I heard a mighty crash – like the bang of the mightiest instrument in the percussion section.

I looked up. The silvery top of the champagne bottle had struck the shelf. Its neck was cracked. Greenish glass splinters were sliding over the desk top.

Yuri was furious, screaming silently. Lev was shaking his head.

It seemed as if, for an instant, the drink was holding back inside the bottle – then suddenly it all gushed; a glittering foam spurted in a long arc, up to the shelf, down on to the desk, and flowed across the sketch plan of the under-river tunnel.

6

Sophia and I were attending a performance of Tchaikovsky's '1812' Overture by the Railway Workers' Symphony Orchestra at the House of Trade Unions (that's the building with the famous columns everybody still called the House of Nobles) on the evening of 15 April 1920.

(I'm rifling through my diary to check the date. I note this was just a fortnight after we had made love properly for the first time: there are three red stars on that page.)

The orchestra was simply dreadful. Well, most of the younger rail workers had been conscripted into the army or arrested, so the musicians were aged or cripples mainly. The instruments were shoddy.

Nevertheless, the audience clapped and bravoed loudly and often during the performance. This was partly patriotism (the '1812' Overture celebrates the failure of Napoleon's invasion of Russia) and partly because it had become the custom to cheer furiously at *all* public meetings.

At the highpoint of the Overture it is usual for a cannon to be fired. Since every available firearm had been requisitioned for the Civil War, this was not possible. Instead all the members of the orchestra snapped their fingers in unison.

During the interval I spoke to Sophia. We were standing in the shadow of a tall fluted column by the entrance. 'Of course I don't claim to be a musical authority, but it does seem to me the performance was lacking in – '

'They're atrocious!'

'Well, yes.'

So we slipped round the column and out of the Hall.

There was a cold spell in Moscow that April, and it was after dark too. Sophia was only wearing a thin mauve silk dress under her fox fur coat. As we strolled towards Red Square, she shivered.

With both hands I massaged her cheeks till they turned rosy. Her little mouth and nose wobbled.

29

'This is enjoyable,' I said.

'Um yum,' she replied through compressed shaking lips, 'but we can't spend the entire evening doing it.'

It would have been anti-climactic to go straight back to her place or mine.

'Why don't we go to . . . ' I said, and realised I couldn't think of anywhere interesting.'

'Come to the Red Cabbage,' said Sophia.

So we went to the Red Cabbage Café.

The Red Cabbage Café was located in one of the narrow alleys behind the Church of the Assumption. During the day that area was a semi-legal market: people would barter a home-grown cauliflower for a chamber pot, or a Levitan oil painting for a leg of lamb. We wound our way through the streets, stepping over rubbish, and handing a small coin to each of two shawled women who were prospecting for food among the mess of papers, carrot tops, rotten beetroot. The moon was full.

The streets were fairly deserted; there was no convivial noise.

'Are you sure this café exists?' I asked.

'Come on.'

We turned another corner. Sophia pushed open a rickety unmarked door; we walked down a long brown corridor. We still couldn't hear or see the café.

Sophia rapped on a whitewashed oak door.

A voice shouted through it, 'What's the password?'

'Two and two makes five!' Sophia yelled back.

The door swung open, and we passed through.

I'd always avoided meeting Sophia's artistic friends before. I mean, I'm not at all an 'arty' person, and I'd imagined artists as . . . as . . . well, I don't really know how I'd imagined them.

The first thing that struck me was the darkness. I didn't know if there was a power cut (there often was in 1920), or if the building wasn't wired for electricity, or if the gloom was favoured on aesthetic grounds. Anyway all I could see at first were little puddles of yellow light around oil lamps.

The second thing was the smell. A combination of damp furs and alcohol and dandelion coffee and stale tobacco and turpentine and cologne.

Sophia guided me down a couple of steps. We seemed to be in a large semi-basement area – perhaps the ground floor of a house with all the internal walls removed.

'Crouch, Humph!' she called suddenly. I ducked – and just avoided banging my head on a large red cabbage (constructed from plaster of Paris, I think) dangling from the ceiling.

As my eyes adjusted, I saw more details. For no obvious structural reason, a ladder was lying diagonally across the length of the room. It was painted with flowers and vegetables, and slogans such as WORKERS OF THE WORLD UNITE and ¡¡¡FUTURISM!!! and DEATH TO THE RADISHES. We bowed to pass beneath it.

I still found it hard to see more than a few metres in front of me. What windows there were – a few small ones at the back – were daubed with geometric designs, and let almost no moonlight through. I made out some black cuboidal objects on the floor.

And then I saw people. What had looked like flickering reflections of the lamps turned out to be faces, grimacing slightly or puffing at home-rolled cigarettes. Most of the heads were tilted, resting on shoulders or tables: eyes blinked sleepily. Hair was misplaced (it seemed): several men had puffy locks on either side of the chin, or half a moustache, or a triangular bald spot. Women had shaven foreheads, or had wound a plait under the chin like a fake beard.

Sophia stood on tiptoe. 'Wakey, wakey, everybody!'

Voices called out in greeting; they addressed her as (I'm translating approximately) Dearie and Little Grandmother and Queenikins and Waxhead.

Figures in dark clothing sprang up and clustered around her. They clutched her and kissed her cheeks. (I felt somewhat jealous.)

Sophia squeezed my hand. 'This is Comrade Humph,' she said in a big voice, 'and he's an engineer from New York!'

Then I too was welcomed. People smiled and said their names, most of which I didn't catch. They mouthed little phrases – whatever they could say in English. I heard somebody conjugate 'to be'. Somebody else murmured a risqué pun about 'Sophia' and 'sofa'.

Sophia and I sat down on a bench. A skinny blonde waitress put a jar of something liquid and two glasses on a packing case in front of us. She charged us only three cigarettes (this was during the inflation, when cash was seldom used). Sophia took out her silver cigarette case.

'No, Sophia. Let me.' I had some American money in my wallet, and I gave the waitress a genuine dollar bill.

I was startled by the bill's greenness – just as I was handing it over, the electric lights jumped on.

It was like the beginning of a play. Suddenly the café was brightly

31

coloured. People were chatting, giggling, wriggling. Cockatoos and
pineapples were impastoed on the ceiling. The floorboards were painted
with polygons in rainbow colours. Sharp geometrical sculptures, made
of corroded metal and charred wood, were pointing at me.

Human beings – I could now see them as separate individuals with
different expressions and fairly standard bodies – came over and chatted.
They offered or borrowed cigarettes. They patted me all over – but I
took this in good part. I drank the fluid that was in the jar (it tasted like
cabbage water, but it certainly had alcohol in it), and began to feel quite
at home.

To start with there was the waitress, Katya, a dim, hollow-chested
thing with a Baltic accent. Her lips were thin and pale to the point of
non-existence, but she had lipsticked a rose-bud mouth at a slant across
her left cheek, giving her an air of deformity and depravity. She greeted
me with a jolly pleasantry which I couldn't understand.

Next a pair of balding men shambled over. The one in the leather
overalls was Efim; he said he stuffed dead animals by profession (if I
understood the Russian correctly). The quiet one was Vadim; he was,
'well . . . an artist . . . or a musician . . . or a poet . . . I suppose.' He
bought me and Sophia another drink.

And yet another drink was donated by Tolya, a young hairless
man who used to strut with his chin tipped up. He was in the habit of
tapping out his cigarettes on the shoulder of his coat. He was a sculptor,
he said. He volunteered to tell me how poetry works. Apparently it's
all just a formalist construction of sounds; each sound carries a particular emotion, for example the *u* in Humphrey is gloomy. I said, 'Thank
you.'

Alla (alias 'The Nun'), a tall woman with a high forehead, hugged
Sophia. This was dexterous, because Alla kept her hands in a fur muff
throughout.

'I'm a poet. What are you?' she asked me in a low hoarse tone.

'Oh, I'm practically an artist, too,' I said (rather drunk by then). 'Well,
I don't have the artistic temperament, you see. But Sophia's always
saying what sensitive fingers I've got.'

I wiggled my fingers inside Alla's muff and felt her hot sticky palms.

But Sophia slapped my wrists, and I had to detach myself from the
Nun. I ordered another round of drinks to placate everybody.

Tipsy as I was, I could tell this place was 'phony'. Oh, they say
engineers are conservative, but nobody could be more hide-bound by
tradition than artists. What was the point of the dark passage and the

32

password? Why did they meet in a basement instead of above ground like everybody else? Why did so many of them wear black? Why were their hairstyles so absurd? Obviously they were conforming to type. On the other hand, although I'm all in favour of revolution in principle, I have to admit that conservatism (with a small *c*) is relaxing.

I was relieved. I had another drink. I'd met Sophia's friends and they'd turned out to be not too abnormal. Oh, they all had their little eccentricities, but not very much more so than engineers. I'd been afraid there would be some important part of Sophia's life which I wouldn't be able to understand, that at some point I'd lose track of her . . . and that would have been dreadful. I loved her, you see.

And my relief meant I could let the drunkenness I'd been suppressing rip.

As I was bending round to summon the waitress, I noticed a display at the back of the café.

I staggered across to it, weaving between the packing cases and the groups of chuckling arty types.

I smelled turpentine and perfume.

'Art!' I cried, sniffing deep. 'I know what that is! It's Art!'

The back wall of the café – and the adjacent ceiling and floor too – were decorated in the likeness of an aquarium, or perhaps a jungle. Sprays of green horsehair sprouted intermittently. Bodies dressed in work clothes – but cut up and re-assembled into contorted strung-up shapes – were arranged in a tableau. The lighter limb bits twisted and swung on air currents. I stroked the delicately stippled wax of an Adam's apple. I instantly recognised Sophia's handiwork.

Sophia turned out to be standing behind me.

I said to her, 'It's very messy . . . ' I was thinking of the studio at her home, the random splodges of coloured wax everywhere.

A horrifying surmise: did Sophia have complex, morbid, artistic fantasies that I couldn't comprehend? I realised that, although I'd half-known she could be selfish or irritable like anybody else, I'd also supposed she was too divine to have any actual *thoughts* – just vague benevolent notions passing through her head.

'Yes. Isn't it?' she answered.

'Your other . . . your Romanov dummies were neat.'

'But this is my *Art*.'

I touched the concavity of a detached elbow stump. 'Who is this?'

'People . . . Russians.'

'Why . . . why are they broken?'

33

'Futurist art mirrors our society, the fractured state of – '

I jumped as high as I could and landed in a crouch. 'I don't understand! I do not understand!'

I put my arms round her waist and pressed my head into her belly.

'Well, I never!' said a familiar voice in English.

It was an elderly woman in a green woollen dress who was bending down to speak to me. I peered into her cleavage: the breasts were familiar though rather smaller than I'd remembered. It was . . .

I had a hangover. My head ached. The café was blurred and spinning.

I'd known her at the camp in upstate New York where we Communists had been interned after America entered the Great War. She'd taught me Russian. She'd been famous for not wearing a corset, which had greatly impressed me as an adolescent. Her name was Ma Gold.

I stammered, 'Ma . . . Ma . . . '

'Humphrey Veil! Me oh my! So what's new, Humphrey? You got that job on the Moscow subway?'

'Ma . . . '

'Me, I live in Petrograd. They deported me from the States, I guess you know.'

She pressed a leaflet into my hand. 'I'm here as a representative of the Kronstadt Sailors' Soviet, standing for their legitimate rights: free speech, free press, free meetings, the usual ticket. I'm in town to seek support from the Moscow Railway Workers' Soviet. Any of you engineers want to come in with us on this one?'

I wasn't especially surprised at the apparition of Ma Gold. I wouldn't have raised an eyebrow if the Statue of Liberty had wandered into the Red Cabbage Café and hugged me against its bronze bosom.

I chatted to Ma about old times. 'Do you remember', I said, 'how you taught us the Russian *shtch* consonant by rewarding us with spoonfuls of *shtchi* [cabbage soup] and *borshtch* [beetroot soup] only if we could pronounce their names properly? And I – '

'I'll never forget,' said Ma.

The waitress brought the bill for my last drink. She'd apparently made an error in the addition, and we argued about that briefly; it turned out to be my mistake. I reached into my hip pocket – and discovered my wallet was missing. Amongst all those 'friendly' hugs and pats somebody must have pickpocketed it.

This was the last straw – not the loss of the money – but the realisation that I cared about a handful of dollar bills. I burst into tears.

Sophia tousled my hair.

The café rotated faster. Vadim and Efim were performing a crouching dance. Alla was reciting Pushkin. Two old women were waving shawls. Tolya was juggling cutlery. The waitress was singing, 'Oh you owe me for your drink oh!' in a fine soprano . . .

Ma Gold, hovering above me, fissioned.

I had a vision of the past. I recalled Ma offering me a taste from two big bowls. Accidentally I'd spilt some cabbage soup on her, and she'd tipped beetroot soup on me. A green spew had sloshed up and drenched her. A redness had descended . . .

A colossal red cabbage, as big as Russia, opened its leaves and swallowed me up.

7

It took me three days to recover from the hangover. I somehow stumbled into work (Yuri made cutting remarks; Lev was sympathetic; Jock grunted to himself), but spent most of my time in bed.

I slept as much as I could. When I awoke, I stared across the room at an icon of St Basil (who fixed me with a sly wink) and another of St Paul (who was fiercely unforgiving).

My concierge used to come in with cups of tea.

'A man must keep his strength up, Fraya,' she'd say.

'Thank you most kindly, Comrade Nadia Gavrilovna,' I'd reply in my maximally formal manner.

Then she'd sit on the end of the bed, and narrate comic anecdotes about her dead husband. They all concluded with the same sentence: '. . . and then he said he loved me always!' Her eyes glistened.

'Well, that's an interesting tale, Comrade Nadia Gavrilovna.' I sipped the tea. I hadn't the heart to turn her away.

Besides I liked female company. I was rather surprised that Sophia hadn't shown up. Of course I would quite understand if she preferred to avoid my sick-bed; it's not the sort of environment she belongs in. Also my memory of the events at the Red Cabbage was hazy. It was possible, I thought, that I had somehow offended her there: perhaps I had insulted her or shamed her or vomited on her lap.

I asked her about this when she finally did arrive, bringing me a beautiful bunch of daffodils, on the third day.

'No, no, Humph,' she said. 'I was . . . busy.'

She gave the daffodils to the concierge, who put them in my tooth mug (which was in its usual place on top of the Angry Jesus icon). A fine splash of yellow among the gilt frames.

Sophia half-sat on the edge of the *burzhuika*, warming her bottom. I noted that Sophia was a little nervy in the concierge's presence. (Sophia was always at her best, her most regal, in purely male company.)

After the concierge went out, Sophia said, 'She's after you, Humph.'

'Who? *That* woman?'

'Don't say I didn't warn you.'

Sophia shook her head, as an indication she wanted to switch topics. 'Humph, it's practically noon! Out of bed, you lazy man, you.'

I was feeling better already: Sophia's scolding always put life into me.

I said coyly, 'Hangover's not infectious.' I indicated by little gestures that she might care to join me in bed.

Sophia's face hovered over mine. Her hands slid under the top sheet. In one extended yank, she levered the sheet, blanket, coverlet, up, down and on to the floor.

I lay on the bed, shivering in my underwear. I struggled up. Sophia un-hung my trousers from the icon of St Cyril and shook them out. 'Humph!' She slapped my bottom. I stepped into the trousers.

Sophia's bossiness was comforting (I reflected). Children liked to be looked after by a mother who knows what's what. I relished the pleasure of dependence.

I mulled over the political implications of this idea – and meanwhile I was getting dressed and following Sophia out into the busy street.

There, in front of the apartment block, a Model 'T' Ford was parked. Cars were rare then; only foreigners and high-ranking Party *apparatchiks* were able to obtain them.

A youngster in military uniform was holding open the back door.

I was frightened. 'W-where are they taking us?'

'He's only my chauffeur, silly. He's Volodya. Say hello to Volodya, Humph.'

'Hello, Comrade Volodya,' I said.

'That's a good Humph!' Sophia kissed my cheek.

We sat in the back.

The soldier wound the starter, got into the driving seat and drove off.

The city unwound itself past the car windows. We were headed north. We were silent for a while.

'Well, if you *really* want to know, Humph, I borrowed the auto from a friend of mine, a General.'

'A *man* friend?'

'Of course, Humph. There aren't any female Generals . . . a sweetie!'

I chewed my lower lip. The car was bumping over ill-made roads.

'Oh such a sweetie! I modelled his wife's bust for him, and he was ever so grateful.'

'Bust?'

'In wax. Isn't it nice to have oodles of good friends?'

'Oh . . . yes.'

'And a *sympathique* official at the Socialist Artists' Mobilisation Campaign gave me those daffodils. Such pretty blooms.'

'Well . . . '

'Friends are *so* essential in a revolution . . . Russia is full of gallant comrades.'

I had no opportunity to ask any questions about her men friends before the Model 'T' drew up outside her home.

We got out.

A queer idea was troubling me – a blasphemy – I was wondering why Sophia loved me. Oh, I loved her, that went without saying: she was so sublimely lovable . . . But what did she see in me? I realised I had thought of her as some divinity who demanded love and bestowed a matching quantity from her own endless supply. But if she was a mere human, and so had a finite capacity for love . . . why me?

I thought of my father, of his (presumable) love for a sixteen-year-old golden-haired statuesque beauty – my mother. And then I considered his youth in Prussia, his rebellion against his orthodox Jewish family and conversion to Communism. What had it been like for him to lose faith in a loving God?

I shivered – although it was less cold in Sophia's studio than it had been on previous visits. (We'd wandered through the house and into the studio while I'd been thinking about Papa.) Definitely it was now spring. Besides, Sophia had lit a charcoal stove on which a pot of flesh-tinted wax was warming.

Bits of bodies were attached to hooks or lay in piles. I wasn't sure whether these were incomplete realistic dummies, or whether they were artworks in which the fragmentation and brutal re-arrangement were deliberate. I would have asked Sophia – except I didn't want to show off my ignorance on artistic matters.

'I'm going to model you, Humph.' Sophia was speaking in the serious let's-get-down-to-business voice she used when working on her art.

'Me?'

She pointed at a chair – a bumpy old-fashioned one, with an orange towel spread across the seat. I hung my greatcoat over the back of it. I sat down.

'Take your clothes off, Humph.'

I took off my waistcoat. I undid my shirt buttons. She helped me with the collar stud; her fingers were cold, and I wriggled. Then I pulled down my trousers, sliding them over my shoes.

Sophia was stirring the softened wax.

She glanced round. 'And them too, Humph. Take them off.'

'You don't mean . . . model me *without my undies?*' The prospect shocked and thrilled.

My small paunch was poking between my woollen vest and my long johns. I hummed Arab-ish music, 'Ma mum mam mom . . .' and wriggled my middle in a kind of belly dance.

'Don't be ridiculous, Humph . . . I meant take off your shoes.'

Sophia was in her no-nonsense mood. She rolled up her sleeves and kneaded a large ball of grey clay.

She pointed at a hook which bore a clothes hanger draped with a full military uniform.

Dutifully I dressed in the elaborate costume. The boots were long and shiny. The coat was clanky with medals. I recognised the Iron Cross. 'I'm a *German?!*'

She gestured at a shiny item on a low shelf: a *Pickelhauber* spiked helmet. I put it on. It slid down my forehead. I pushed it back. It was heavy and cold. Its rim pressed into my skin.

She nodded at a wire armature. 'Take care not to crease or stain the costume. The uniform will be transferred on to this, afterwards.'

'I'm the model for – ?'

'You're Kaiser Wilhelm, of course . . . Chin up! That's better.'

In a flash of humour, she saluted me and stood to attention. Then she pummelled her clay again.

'But . . . ?'

'Oh, part of a tableau. The exhibition in Red Square. I've been asked for a line up of Russia's enemies: the Tsars, the Mensheviks, the Right Socialists, the Left Socialists; the American, French and British Presidents. The Kaiser, for good measure. You look like the Kaiser, don't you, Humph? What *does* he look like?'

'I'm afraid I really don't – '

'You're tall and fair . . . Teutonic, at any rate.'

I raised my right shoulder and twitched the right fingers. Then I repeated the action but on my left side instead. 'The Kaiser has a withered arm,' I said. 'I can't remember which one, though . . . '

The clay lump was about the size of my skull. Sophia worked rapidly. She drew up a bulge of it between finger and thumb, alternately pressed it thinner and pulled it, till it resembled a nose – *my* nose. Then –

taking the nose as the fixed reference point – her palms spread out, massaging the clay cheeks and eye sockets. (I imagined the firm rub of Sophia's hands on my own face.) She built up the cheekbones. The ridge of the eyebrows. The forehead. Then she returned to the lower face. As she constructed the Kaiser's mouth, she ground her teeth, and frequently inspected my face with her head cocked like a bird. She roughened the texture of the mouth using her knuckles. (I licked my lips. 'Don't!' she said firmly.) Then chin and jaw appeared. The neck tapered.

It didn't exactly look human. The head had an unshaped top and back, for one thing. And it was a dull mauve-grey.

The next stage of the manufacturing process was remarkably simple. Sophia rested the clay face-down in a tray of fine white sand. When she removed it, the impression of the features was left in the sand.

Using a couple of rags to guard her hands, she lifted the pot from the charcoal burner, and poured its contents into the tray. Molten pinkish wax ebbed into the sand mould. She inserted a wire handle in the soft wax.

'We have to wait now', she said, 'until the wax cools.'

She set the sand tray inside a larger tray containing cold water to speed up the cooling.

While we were waiting, Sophia talked and I listened. She told me the history of her family. Of her great-great-grandfather, Pierre-Marie Bellechasse, who had made a dummy of Napoleon. Of his son Pierre, who had come to Russia and worked for the imperial family.

She described the old-fashioned method of dummy making: the face of the subject is smeared in plaster, which is left to dry. (I could feel in imagination the sticky damp plaster clinging. I blinked and twisted my mouth, freeing my face-skin.)

'Just one moment, Humph.' She disappeared into the rear of the studio.

I turned round a moment later, and she was standing behind me, arms akimbo. She seemed to have changed rapidly into different clothes: an elegant and impressive purple silk dress with a ruby hammer and sickle brooch over the left nipple.

'Mmm, nice,' I said. 'Suits you.'

Silence.

'A penny for your thoughts?'

Silence.

'Not sulking, are you? Sophia? . . . Soph? Was it something I said . . .

or did? . . . or didn't? . . . I'm sorry. Whatever it was . . . No, honestly, Sophia, I really do apologise . . . '

I knelt on one knee and kissed her hand. It was wax.

The real Sophia was snorting over my shoulder. 'I plan to put it on guard at the entrance to the Red Square exhibition. So if any visitor has a penchant for pricking ladies, he can take out his aggression on the dummy.'

I blushed. I recognised her reference to our encounter back in December. Embarrassed, I stepped back . . . and banged into the dummy.

The mock-Sophia tilted and fell against the armature destined to represent Kaiser Bill. The pink wax hand with lacquered scarlet finger-nails penetrated the rib cavity of the wire Kaiser. The two tipped. They rolled together on the floor.

Fortunately nothing seemed to be broken.

Sophia threw me a queer look of . . . I'm not sure what, exactly.

She separated and raised the dummies.

She rested a finger on the wax in the mould to check its warmth. She nodded to herself. Gripping the wire handle, she gently eased up the wax head. She showed it to me. It was curiously inhuman – the face of an abortion rather than a corpse. It was all a monochrome pale pink. Eyeless. Hairless. A scatter of white sand stuck to it, but she blew this away.

'It doesn't look a bit like me,' I said.

She pressed its chin against her lips, to gauge its temperature. Satisfied, she lowered it face up on to the orange towel on the chair where I'd been seated.

'Don't go near the Kaiser,' she warned me. 'He's very delicate.'

She slapped her hands together to wipe off the sand.

Quickly she strode through the studio and into her house – I followed. I had to trot with precision to avoid catching the jackboot spurs on the carpet fringes or the furniture.

We entered the bedroom.

'Take me,' she said.

'Take you where?'

'Here . . . here, Wilhelm.'

'I'm not actually called Wilhelm, you know. I'm – '

She dived into the polar-bear-skin rug, and pulled me down on top of her.

'Er, Sophia. Wouldn't it be more comfy on the bed?'

41

She sucked in her breath sharply.

I started undoing those fiddly little buttons at the back of her satin dress . . .

'Tear it all off, Wilhelm!'

So, with care, I ripped the fabric along a seam. (I reckoned this way it would be easier to sew it back as good as new.)

Next, the *Pickelhauber* slumped down across my face. Sophia was shouting rude words. She was urging the Kaiser to do violent things to her. Of course I did my bit and we began to make love, more or less. Her nails were long so I got rather scratched.

She bucked about a lot. I hung on to something to avoid getting thrown off the rug, which turned out (as I saw when the helmet rolled off my head) to be the ears of the polar bear.

It didn't seem altogether right (when one considers what Germany had done to Russia) that she should have a 'pash' on the ex-Kaiser.

Besides, I was just a little jealous. I was sorely tempted to cry some other woman's name – just to tease Sophia – for example, 'Nadia Gavrilovna!' But I didn't.

The rug rode up and the bear head flopped over my face. Again I couldn't see Sophia. She was shrieking with . . . well, I don't really know which emotion.

I was exhausted. My hangover was returning. I could make no sense of these exotic Russian modes of love making. I couldn't hear her any more. I wasn't sure if she was still fondling me, or if it was just the old scratch marks smarting. 'Where are you?' I called softly into the bear jaw. 'Where are you, my Sophia?'

PART II

THE PERHAPS BAG

When I grow up, I shall drink nothing but
shampoo, I mean, champagne.
                    – Maximilian Gritzshtayn

1

The famous poet and artist Gritz marched into the Red Cabbage Café. He posed on the step leading into the main room. He swung his left fist in a cross between a boxing punch and a military salute. 'Comrades and buggers!' he roared. 'Gritz is here!'

He strode into the body of the café, and set about greeting everybody. He biffed the men in the solar plexus and slapped their back. The women he merely kissed.

This was a few days after the creation of the Kaiser dummy. I could still feel the scratches on my back left by Sophia's nails. We had just come from the Red Square exhibition tent where she'd been setting the Kaiser in his place. A photographer from some news agency had insisted on taking pictures of me with my arm around the German ex-Emperor . . . And it was horribly hot: the summer had just struck. The café was stuffy and dusty and smelled of rot . . . *And* I felt guilty because I wasn't at work (I'd promised to go in that evening and check some stress-strain calculations).

I was sitting moodily beside Sophia, drinking nothing but cold tea. Since this resembled whisky in appearance, I was becoming very mildly tipsy and lugubrious.

I could see through the pretentiousness of the Red Cabbage crowd. Great artists and writers they may have been (I don't pretend to be a judge of these matters), but that didn't seem a good excuse for lounging in this oh-so-atmospheric gloomy café. Why didn't they get on and *do* their art?

Gritz was smacking the Nun (Alla, the pale poetess) on her bottom. '*No more* Art for Art's Sake! By order of Lenin and Gritz!'

She – using her hands linked together inside her fur muff – pushed him away.

Gritz marched off to impress himself on somebody else. His hobnailed boots clattered. He walked with a long stride and a twist of his tight-trousered hips: most unpleasant.

Gritz was the ugliest man I'd ever set eyes on. He wore nothing but black – a docker's tunic and army boots. His head was shaven. His skin had a yellow tinge – perhaps jaundiced, and gleamed with sweat. His lower lip drooped like the Habsburg emperors'.

Shielding my mouth with my hand, I whispered to Sophia, 'Who is he?'

'Oh, such an *energetic* man.'

'I'm sure.'

'Gritz.'

'Pardon?'

He was engaged in annoying Katya by twitching his fingers over his mouth in the guise of whiskers and squeaking. She was tittering, 'Oh, no, Gritz! No!'

'That's his name. Well, his *real* name is . . . but nobody ever calls him that,' said Sophia. 'Gritz suits him better, don't you agree?'

'What does he do? Artist? Poet? Sculptor? Musician?'

'Oh, yes!'

'Which one?'

'Them all, I think.'

Now he was asking bashful Vadim whether he had any counter-revolutionary tendencies and whether he could prove it in writing and just how had he avoided execution by the C H E K A so long; Vadim was replying, 'Er, um.'

Sophia ordered another round of tea from Tolya. (The Red Cabbage worked on a co-operative system: every regular customer got to be a waiter once every so often.) Tolya nodded, which sent a little cigarette ash snowing from his shirt on to our table. He soon returned with a jug of cold tea, and was refilling our glasses.

'Thank you, Bald Eagle,' I said – using his nickname with deliberate casualness.

Gritz leaned out and raised the flat of his hand like a traffic policeman. 'Oy, Pigeon!'

Tolya looked across.

'Oy, Albatross. Give Sophia and her young man a bottle of vodka. Gritz's treat.'

'I'd really rather have – ' I said.

Gritz swaggered over. His head closed in on mine. He stared with condescension into my eyes. His lower lip dangled and puckered.

'Sophia,' he said, 'who *is* your ungrateful young man?'

I said, 'Hello, Comrade Gritz. My name is – '

'I did *not* ask *you*!'

Sophia placated Gritz by kissing him on the mouth. I looked the other way for the duration of this activity.

Then Sophia sat down, and Gritz leaned on her, resting a fist on her shoulder.

'Now, Gritz, be a good poet and say hello to my best friend, Humph Veil. Humph is an American.'

'No, he's not. He speaks with a German accent.'

'Ah, well, funny you should remark on that . . . '

'Are you a Germany spy or an American spy? Which?'

'A British engineer, actually.'

'What the hell does Sophia see in you? Do you have any hidden talents? Some special knack?'

'I . . . really . . . '

'Take my advice, Veil. Take the advice of one who knows. Sophia's too old. She's worn out.'

Sophia bit Gritz's wrist.

He emitted two sharp laughs. He extracted his hand and examined the red toothmarks. He seemed pleased.

'But she does have fire in her belly, our Sophia.' (I hated that 'our'.)

The jar of vodka arrived. Gritz paid Tolya in cigarettes.

Gritz pulled a packing case over, and sat down between Sophia and me. He took a long swig of the vodka.

He scanned the café. He remarked conspiratorially, 'Gritz sees a lot of radishes here.'

'I only see a red cabbage,' I said, pointing at the plaster vegetable by the entrance.

He ignored my remark. 'A radish is red on the outside and white on the inside. Russia is full of traitors.'

'Ah, I wonder if you're familiar with Lenin's comments on the counter-revolutionary element within the rural bourgeoisie, as printed in the latest edition of *Izvestia* . . . ' I said, eager to steer the conversation into a political channel.

'Gritz worships Lenin! If Lenin did not exist it would be necessary to invent him.' Gritz took another swig of vodka, then pressed his hands together as if praying. He chanted, 'Lenin is the voice of the future. The voice of Russia. The voice of Revolution. Lenin is prepared to sacrifice anything and anybody to crack open the rotten Fabergé egg of Russia and make an omelette of it.'

'What interesting poetic imagery,' I said politely.

Sophia was looking bored. She was never much interested in politics – to be frank.

I recalled an argument I'd been having with Jock over many weeks, as to whether Lenin was justified in establishing a personal dictatorship.

'What do you think, Gritz? Is it true what Lenin says, that the truest form of socialist democracy at the present time is autocracy?'

'If Lenin asked me to unscrew my wooden leg so he could hurl it at the Whites, I would unscrew it willingly! If Lenin asked me to remove my dentures so he could carve them into ivory chess pieces, I would spit them out willingly! If Lenin asked me to uproot my hair so as to knit it into a skullcap to stuff down the flushable plumbing of the bourgeoisie so their sewage outlet overflowed and drowned them in shit, I would scalp myself willingly!'

I said, 'Oh.'

I found his remarks rather reassuring. I'd had to put up with Jock's negativism, his insistence that millions of Russians had perished in the Revolution, or were starving or being shot. Gritz's certitude was comforting.

In this respect he reminded me of Ma Gold. Politically, of course, they were poles apart (she was an anarchist at bottom; at that date presumably in Petrograd, stirring up the Kronstadt sailors) but both were decisive and determined. As a muddled person myself, I appreciate that quality in others.

I began to see how Sophia might actually like the man. She and he were laughing together as they swapped anecdotes about philistine officials of the Artists' Union (one who objected that a portrait 'wasn't very like'; another who thought it 'modern' not to care which way up a picture was hung).

Of course I trusted Sophia. Utterly. I didn't ask her what she got up to with other men. I knew our love was stronger than any . . . distractions. But I was afraid that if she became fond of some thing or person I didn't like, I might become detached from part of her. (For instance she once expressed a taste for gooseberry jam – which I can't stand – and a shudder ran through me.)

'Sophia,' I said, 'tell me why you like me.'

She turned round. Her right hand was scarcely a centimetre from Gritz's at the closest point.

'What? *Here*, Humph?'

'Here. Now.'

'Oh, Humph, you're *such* a sweetie.'

'More. Tell me more.'

She shrugged. 'You're handsome. You're tall and fair, like a Crusader knight . . . '

'More.'

'You're comforting. You're not complicated. You say such nice things to me.'

'More!'

'You don't ask me too many questions. You're an exotic foreigner. You have a dimple on your chin. You kiss me in funny places.'

'More!'

She leaned forward and hugged me. I closed my eyes and snuffled up her perfume and sweat. We kissed.

We were disturbed by Gritz's voice calling, 'Oy, Sophia, say why you love *Gritz*!'

I opened my eyes. He was tapping her between the shoulder blades.

Still hugging me, she turned and said scornfully, 'Oh, Gritz, you *know* I hate you.'

He grinned.

Just then a figure appeared in the doorway, beneath the red cabbage model. Someone with a crimson face and curly ginger hair. I recognised Jock instantly. What on earth was he doing here? I freed a hand from Sophia's grasp and waved to him, but he didn't see me at first.

Jock glanced from side to side. He strolled through the café. He drew many inquisitive glances because of his manner and because he was dressed in an unpretentious white shirt and grey trousers, unlike the regular Red Cabbage crowd.

He spotted me. He came over.

'Ah, hello, Jock,' I said. 'May I introduce my good friend whom you have heard so much about, Sophia, and – '

'What the devil are you doing here?' He was speaking English.

I replied in English, 'I might ask the same of you.'

'Looking for you, of course, you idiot! Taken me two hours to trace you from that infantile waxworks to – '

He was panting. His hair was dusty and plastered with sweat.

I asked, 'Would you care for a drink?'

'Get up! We have to go to the office!'

'An . . . emergency?'

'The deadline for the plans is . . . You promised to work on the

49

stress-strain ... Yuri's hysterical and Lev's daughter's got typhus. I can't do it all on my own. Get moving!'

'Just a quick one?'

I dragged over another packing case for him to sit on, and grabbed a glass of cold tea and a plate of bread softened with sunflower oil (butter was unobtainable that year) from the waiter.

Jock moaned, 'Och, I'll stay one minute.' He sat on the edge of the packing case, as if always on the point of rising. He drank in quick gulps.

So there we were, the four of us, seated round the table like bridge players. We passed bread and tea. It was one of those strange combinations of people from different arenas of one's life that occur often in dreams and memories, but seldom in reality. Jock and I were speaking in English about engineering. Gritz and Sophia were gossiping maliciously in Russian about fellow artists: who's-sleeping-with-whom talk.

I felt awkward; it took me a while to work out just why. You see, anybody casually glancing at us would naturally see us as two pairs: the arty Russians versus the conventional British. And what I realised was, in a way, that division was correct. I did indeed have more in common with Jock than I did with Sophia. But Jock wasn't the one I was in love with ... I began to wonder whether it was possible to love somebody whom I didn't particularly like.

The Eagle strolled past, carrying a tray of drinks. He was whistling a popular tune of the period, whose lyrics ran: 'May a young man sigh beneath the moon? Yes! even a Young Communist may!'

My eyes moistened with mock-drunken self-pity.

Gritz interjected to Jock, 'Ah, you are English too?' To my surprise, Gritz was speaking passable English.

'Scottish.'

'Same thing. Another English spy?'

Jock glanced at me. 'This fellow's off his rocker!'

'Ah, no, my ruddy friend, it is you whose rocker is off.'

I explained to Sophia (I had introduced Jock earlier, but she hadn't been attending), 'This is John Brown, a fellow engineer. He wants me to go – '

Gritz set down his glass of vodka, and interrupted again. 'Has not Lenin described foreign experts as "mercenaries"? Has he not called the moneys paid to them "tribute"?'

Jock's cheeks bulged with fury. He rose from his seat. He shouted in Russian, 'You know what Lenin can do with himself!'

Jock paused for an instant. (One did not insult Lenin in public in

50

Moscow in 1920. It was assumed there were police spies in every gathering.) Sophia got up and stood alongside him.

Jock roared, 'Lenin can – '

Sophia stamped as hard as she could on Jock's left foot.

He squealed and hopped.

Sophia smiled with her eyes, revealing a twinge of joy at her necessary, minimally brutal act. That smile frightened me.

I linked my arm through Jock's.

'Come along, Jock. We really must return to work.'

As we walked through the door, I glanced back. Sophia was waving at me (I noted with pleasure). Gritz grinned.

2

Now let me tell you the fates of Jock and Yuri. I will try to be factual and dispassionate. I apologise in advance if my account should sound cold: it all happened decades ago, I was elsewhere, neither was a close friend, really; one can't – and perhaps one shouldn't – care about the suffering of every individual.

I was discussing this very topic (in general philosophical terms) with Jock himself in July 1920. I was quoting Lenin's dictum that in a war one should shoot first and ask questions later. 'No doubt some of the fellows executed as counter-revolutionaries are in fact quite innocent, but in a war situation, you can't be too careful. You have to look at the overall situation. That's Lenin's genius.' Or so I said.

Jock replied: 'If one innocent person is punished deliberately, socialism collapses. It's a slippery slope! First you say it's fine to shoot *him*, then *him*, then *him* . . . and soon you're mowing them down with machine-guns!'

'Ah, well,' I said, 'ah, well.'

'Yes?'

'Yes, *but* . . . '

The context of our discussion was that Yuri's boyfriend had just been arrested. Yuri was hysterical. In the office, he did little except tear sheets of paper to minute shreds and weep. I sympathised with him – well, we all did. I brought him glasses of tea and patted his back.

Yuri asked us engineers – me, Lev and Jock – to write letters to the Central Committee petitioning against imprisonment of his boyfriend. Jock agreed. Lev hemmed and hawed, saying he had to consider the consequences for his family. I – on Sophia's advice – pointed out that a letter of support from a foreigner wouldn't do the poor fellow any good and might in fact harm him. Besides (I didn't of course say this to Yuri), how could I be sure the man was innocent? I didn't know him personally. He might really be a dangerous Social Revolutionary or White saboteur or hoarder.

Jock emitted a half-laugh. 'You know the true reason he's been arrested. Surely. Some puritan CHEKA man was disgusted by –'

'You don't *know* that!'

'No . . . '

'If it's difficult for me or you to make these ethical decisions,' I told Jock, 'just think how much harder it must be for Lenin. It really shows his genius. He has the fate of millions of people on his conscience.'

'Yes,' said Jock. 'He certainly does.'

We used to sit in the office, Jock and I, in the long hot afternoons, our sweat dripping from our brows on to the engineering diagrams, locked in argument. Lev would be in the back of the office, not saying much. Yuri was usually out by the river, or hiding in the toilet weeping.

There was no urgency so far as the metro was concerned, at least. We'd submitted our plans in mid-July, right on schedule. The Metropolitan Transport Soviet was 'sitting' on the plans, neither approving them nor rejecting them, awaiting word from higher up. According to Jock, the metro was doomed; where would the funding come from in the midst of a civil war? But Lev said that a prestige project was just what was needed in troubled times, and the Central Committee would surely appreciate this. Anyway, we were working slowly, getting on with the job, designing fire-escape stairways for the tunnels and estimating passenger flow.

'Wouldn't it be terrible', I remarked to Jock, 'if they never built the metro?'

'There are more terrible things than that.'

'Yes, but I would feel such a parasite on the Revolution.'

Jack grunted.

'What do you think, Lev?' I asked.

Lev was seated on a high stool at the back, idly flipping through a thermodynamics reference book.

'Me? I'm thinking about my family.'

'Your family?'

'My wife. My three girls. The middle one's completely recovered from her typhus. But the eldest's got a nasty cough.'

'That's wonderful news!' I said. I turned to Jock. 'Don't you think it's wonderful?'

Jock took a sheet of paper from his inside pocket. He unfolded it. It was crudely printed. I read:

**THE WORKERS OF PETROGRAD AND THE SAILORS OF
KRONSTADT DEMAND:
ALL POWER TO THE SOVIETS!
FREE ELECTIONS BY SECRET BALLOT
ALL WORKERS' AND PEASANTS' PARTIES TO BE
LEGALISED
FREEDOM OF SPEECH
FREEDOM FOR ALL THE SOCIALIST PRESS
LIBERATION OF ALL SOCIALIST PRISONERS
EQUAL RATIONS FOR ALL
WITHDRAWAL OF ARMED GUARDS FROM THE FACTORIES
WORKERS OF THE WORLD UNITE!
YOU HAVE NOTHING TO LOSE BUT YOUR CHAINS!**

'Well I never!' I said. 'When your grandchildren ask you about the
October Revolution, you can show them this.'

Jock almost smiled. He showed me the paper again. His thumb was
pointing to the date at the bottom: 13 July 1920.

'But . . . there must be some mistake! The risings in Petrograd . . .
the Kronstadt revolt . . . it all happened in 1917!'

'It's happening again,' Jock said.

Lev said, 'I've seen two revolutions already, and that's enough.'

'Of course,' I said, '*but* . . . '

Now I come to think about it, I'd already heard about the troubles in
Petrograd.

I'd been killing time at the Red Cabbage, sipping a queer murky drink
called *kvas* (made of fermented rye, apparently; the Russians prefer it with
horseradish and honey; it tastes so foul you think it's either good for you
or very alcoholic, but it's neither) while Sophia had been chatting with Alla.

Both of them had been eulogising the place they called by the Greek
name of 'Petropolis'.

'Ah, Petropolis,' Alla had said, 'city of sunlight skimming over water,
of glorious ancient buildings, of clear days and bright nights . . . '

'Ah, Petropolis,' Sophia had continued in the same vein, 'city of my
youth and vanished grandeur . . . '

Naturally, I'd maintained the Hellenic theme by quoting Homer: the
only bits I know: 'Ah, wine-dark sea and rosy-fingered dawn . . . '

They'd both looked at me oddly. Then Alla had smiled, and explained,

'Petropolis is the name we citizens of Petrograd give to our beloved city. Petropolis is the Athens of Russia: its ancient cultural heart; just as Moscow is the Rome: the pivot of imperial might. The prophecy of the Delphic Oracle has come to pass.'

'I beg your pardon?'

'There is ferment and anguish yet again in Petropolis. I have visited the city often these last weeks. Death on the streets. The mother cries for her son. The son for his mother.'

'I see,' I'd said cautiously, sipping the *kvas*. 'I see?'

In August Yuri's boyfriend was released. He was (according to Yuri) half-dead of dysentery and starvation. He was arrested again in September, and died in prison some time before the end of 1920.

I didn't know what to say to Yuri when he came back to the office. His eyes were red. He spoke in a hoarse stammer.

I pressed his hand. I muttered, 'Have faith in the . . . er . . . Revolution.'

He staggered; the business of standing seemed not worth his bother; his legs twisted round each other in a kind of pirouette and gave way; he crumpled to the floor. It took all three of us to haul him up again.

A week later, in December during a bad snowstorm, Yuri didn't show up for work. We thought it was the weather . . . Then Lev got in touch with the authorities, and it turned out Yuri had been arrested for counter-revolutionary activities.

That was the last I saw or heard of him. Where is he today? Perhaps he's living in internal exile in Siberia, happily married to a local peasant woman and bringing up five strapping children. It's possible.

I didn't mourn Yuri much. Well, Yuri was an acquaintance, not a friend. I'd never been invited to his home or met his boyfriend. I had no real belief in his existence outside the office. In an abstract ethical calculus, that shouldn't matter (I know); in reality it does. Besides, I'd been vaguely expecting his arrest for months, and, after he disappeared, I wasn't sure what had happened to him for more months. It's not possible to keep a worry (or a love, for that matter) on the boil for so long . . .

Anyway, I had troubles of my own (trivial ones compared to Yuri's, to be sure: I'll tell you about them later).

By comparison, when Jock died (I'll tell you all about that in a moment) I was far more upset. You see, Jock was like me: a foreigner who'd chosen to come to Moscow to help the Revolution. His decisions – which led to his death – were the sort I might very well have made myself. But Yuri was a native Russian. His patriotism was instinctive. And of course our sexual tastes differed too . . . sympathy means: imagining you're in somebody else's shoes. I could never have stood in Yuri's.

About Jock . . .

On Christmas Day (25 December, I mean; the Russian Christmas is a fortnight later) I brought a bag of mince pies into the office. (I'd got my concierge to bake them in exchange for my last dollar bill.) I'd thought Jock would appreciate a pie or two. But he wasn't in; so Lev and I shared them.

Two weeks later, we got a note – delivered by a swarthy man with a Caucasian accent; his face was swathed in a grey cloth spattered with snowflakes – stating:

I am in Petrograd, as part of a fraternal delegation from the workers of Moscow to the Kronstadt sailors. Long live the Revolution!
Jock.

'Do you remember', I asked Lev, 'the six of us in this office a year ago? Then there were five. Four. Three. Two . . . '
Lev hummed 'John Brown's Body'.

The winter of 1920–1 was bitterly cold. I'd been in Moscow getting on for two years, and felt trapped there. I didn't belong. The days were short. The rations were reduced – even our office canteen had to cut down the portions. Inflation was vast. They introduced million rouble notes (nicknamed 'lemons', for some reason) but you couldn't buy much with them. There was more rioting in Petrograd (so I heard and read) and uncertain battles in the Crimea. Moscow was calm but unhappy.

Indeed I've undergone far worse things in the years since; but personalised suffering at least gives one something to think about and a justifiable feeling of self-importance. Back then I had time on my hands – the Transport Soviet was delaying funding for the metro yet again – so I was bored and guilty.

Of course I had Sophia . . . but she was not much use in time of trouble.

I would sometimes, in my misery, be deliberately rude to her:

'I'm terribly afraid', I'd say, 'of losing my faith and trust in the one person I really love . . . '

She'd hug me and kiss my forehead.

' . . . of doubting the wisdom of Lenin.'

56

She'd push me away.

In February *Pravda* reported a White plot in Petrograd to overthrow the government. According to the paper, they were seeking to re-install the monarchy – which didn't sound very plausible.

I tried to find out what was actually happening through the gossip network at the Red Cabbage. Tolya had just returned from Petrograd; he said the railway workers were on strike, so he'd been marooned there for ten days. Alla had heard from her relatives there: the Kronstadt sailors, bastions of the October Revolution, had mutinied. The soldiers sent against them had refused to fire on them.

Petrograd was cut off. I got no more information for a few weeks. Then the authorities were in control. It is safe to presume that all – or almost all – the rebels were killed, Jock included.

Alla raised her muff above her head. 'Woe, Petropolis is fallen . . . '

Jock. Yes, Jock. I know I should be writing some elegy for him. I should be saying what a fine young fellow he was, how I'd always admired his courage, how he's an inspiration to me even now, how I wept buckets when I heard of his disappearance . . . but he wasn't and I hadn't and he isn't and I didn't. He was a fool.

'Jock. Why did you go and die for some foreign cause?'

'Why did you come to Russia, Humphrey?'

'Answer my question, Jock.'

'Humphrey, you came here for the same reason I did: to help the World Revolution. *That's* why I was prepared to die.'

'Yes . . . '

As I sit here, at the desk, leafing through my stack of old diaries and transcribing scraps of description and conversation into this autobiography (never elaborating them – well, hardly ever), I often argue with the spirit of Jock. I always have the last word.

'I wish I'd seen you die, Jock.'

'Bloodthirsty, eh, Humphrey?'

'All I have is some yellowing newspaper cuttings from *Pravda* on the crushing of the counter-revolution at Kronstadt. If only I'd seen . . . I don't know . . . a bullet smash into your head; seen the blood stream out of your inflamed face and ginger hair . . . If only I had some image, some icon, I could visualise and use to bring tears to my eyes . . . '

'It's all the same to me, Humphrey.'

'Yes, *but* . . . '

3

Meanwhile, Sophia was having an affair with Gritz. (I think I've told you that already; if not, I'm sure you've guessed.)

I feel embarrassed writing about this. In part because it's private, of course. Also, Jock and Yuri were busy getting killed; I knew it was selfish of me to care about my petty troubles.

But I did care. 'Sophia,' I used to plead, 'you love *me*, not him.'

'Not *whom*?' she'd reply, all innocence.

'Not . . . ' (I didn't like pronouncing his name), ' . . . *him*.'

'Honestly, Humph,' she'd say, leaning across my back to adjust the polar-bear rug (we were usually in bed together when we had these conversations), 'you have a suspicious nature.'

'But he admits it! He boasts of his conquests to all and sundry in the Red Cabbage! He asks me for tips on you, says he wants to compare notes.'

'You don't *own* me, Humph.'

'Well, of course . . . '

'I'm a free woman.'

'Naturally . . . '

'Perhaps you have another romance on the side, Humph? You're guilty? That's why you're so bad tempered.'

Sophia would lie on her back, luxuriously scratching under her breasts.

'Oh, no, Sophia! I love only you.'

Mollified, she'd permit me to kiss a little pink flea bite.

The trouble was that theoretical and applied ethics weren't meshing. In principle, I believed in 'free love'. So did Sophia and Gritz and all good Party members. It was evident that the monogamous marriage bond had been a capitalist mode of property acquisition, and that, in the new socialist world, sex would be provided 'from each according to his ability, to each according to his need'. (Ma Gold, I remember, gave a lecture on this topic at the internment camp.) But in practice I wanted Sophia for myself. Obviously, then, my desires were wrong-headed; I did my best to overcome them.

'What's he got that I haven't?' I asked.

Sophia just lay there making *mmm* noises.

'I mean . . . is he violent with you, Sophia? Is that what you fancy? A bit more of the bestial? I could be jolly vicious if I put my mind to it. I could be really nasty.'

I punched her breast softly. It wobbled.

'There! Is that what you like, Sophia?'

She seemed quite content.

I slapped her other breast. It toppled the whole way over.

'Brrr, brrr,' I growled.

'Ah, poor Humph. You're cold . . . '

'I'm not cold, thank you, Sophia. Brrr, brrr. I'm a polar bear.'

'Oh, Humph, you're a sweetie. You and your – ' (She used a Russian slang term that means . . . I'm not sure precisely what; it wasn't in my dictionary. Anyway, the word had a diminutive suffix, which indicates affection.)

'Oh, how nice of you to say so. Brrr, brrr.'

I pulled down the rug and sheet to bare her rounded pale belly. I clasped my fists together and patted it. I must have done this rather too forcefully because a current of air galed from her mouth. She sprawled on her back, her lips apart as if in wonder, wheezing like a deflating balloon.

When I think of her white body and her breath, I think of the snow thick on the ground in Moscow in February 1921, and the wind blowing over. The snow was banked against the houses and rickety shops in the district around the Church of the Resurrection near the Red Cabbage Café. A freakish warm spell: rain was drilling into the snow.

I walked along, arm in arm with Sophia. Our heads were bowed against the drizzle. We didn't talk; just looked down at the thin layer of yellow slush beneath our feet.

We were on our way to a rendezvous with Gritz. Sophia had decided it was about time he and I got on speaking terms.

The rain became heavier. I held my black umbrella over her head. To ensure she was fully rain-proofed, I had to let my own left shoulder get damp. This modest self sacrifice made me feel cosy inside.

Despite the weather and the rigours of 'War Communism' (as Lenin called it), quite a few stalls were operating in the open market in front of the church. No money changed hands. Firewood was swapped for bread, or a knife for a ball of string. You could buy a kilo of potatoes for its weight in leather-bound volumes of *War and Peace*. A lady in a scarlet headscarf (who, judging from her taut vowels, was of aristocratic origin) was trying to persuade a stallholder to accept her grand piano in exchange for a sack of turnips. She was having no luck; she was close to tears. 'I've lugged the damn thing all the way here,' she was saying. The piano was angled in a snowdrift, big and black and shiny.

I wanted to bargain for sour cream. The thick white stuff was stored in chipped beautiful Sèvres vases. I had a net shopping bag in my pocket, just in case I saw something to buy (everybody used to carry an *avoska* – literally: a 'perhaps' bag), and I was mentally working out the best way of balancing the vase in it . . . But Sophia dissuaded me, 'It's half rain water, Humph.'

An old man was standing outside a drink shop, holding up two fingers in a V. (In London, I recalled, this was an insult.) Sophia explained it signified he was seeking somebody with whom to split a bottle of vodka. I seriously considered joining him – I could have done with a stiff drink before encountering Gritz – but, at Sophia's urging, I desisted.

A pair of cart-horses, ambling down the street pulling a wagon loaded with heavy artillery, steered round the stalls and vanished into the distance. A boy trotted after, carrying a broad wooden box into which he scooped dropped dung as occasion demanded.

The rain was washing the centre of the street clean, sweeping away the mud and rubbish. It was battering on the umbrella: a comforting random sound, like a fire in the grate.

We turned under the portals of the church. We entered through the grand door.

When you've been in the rain for even a few minutes you forget that the world could ever be non-wet. So it was queer to lower the umbrella, to stand in the echoing nave, to shuffle to and fro, completely dry. The usual smell of stale incense. Revolutionaries and looters had removed most of the religious memorabilia, but the place was still quite crowded enough with sacred knick-knacks for my taste. A score of Jesus icons within view. A baker's dozen of apostles. The usual scatter of saints and miracles. Striding priests in beards and black robes, like something out of a nightmare, appeared and disappeared. Pious old women were praying with indecent energy. I opened and shut my umbrella several times vigorously, to shake off raindrops.

We sat down at the back of a chapel. We still didn't talk.

The smell of wet clothes, the fume of incense, the swaying of swathed hunched bodies, the crammed narrow space – all this reminded me of a carriage in the London Underground Railway, the 'Tube' (as it was nicknamed at the turn of the century; perhaps it still is). I remembered reaching up for the dangling leather straps and hanging on desperately as the train swerved. Tobacco smoke used to eddy there; a whiff of smog, also. And a curl of steam would drift from a corner, where some old woman would always be crouching, sipping from a mug of oxtail soup. Each Tube journey – like all journeys – had seemed while it had lasted to be the natural state of things, as if there would never be a reason to leave that carriage. Wistful faces on the advertisements papered to the ceiling, 'Grenadier gin keeps you on your toes' ... 'Castro cigarillos are debonair' ... 'Bottomley's instant custard: yum yum', had smiled down at us, and glimmered like the icons in this chapel.

How desperately I wanted the Moscow metro to be built. I craved for the subterranean network of tracks, for the whizzing below-ground trains, for the would-be passengers, ascending and descending at busy interchanges. I yearned for it – my very own medium-sized contribution to establishing socialism – as much as I cared for Sophia or for anything in the world. I analysed my own emotions: I was perturbed. Did this mean I was exceptionally selfless – 'saintly', one might say? Or was I plain perverse?

We waited for a while. I took my watch from the fob pocket, and checked the time. It was three o'clock. We got up and walked back into the nave.

It was here and now we had arranged to meet Gritz – neutral ground in the mid-afternoon. To my surprise, he was on time. He was leaning against the altar. Apparently he had grown green breasts.

As we approached, it became evident he was holding a net 'perhaps' bag up below his collar, containing two cabbages. The bosominess was no doubt deliberate. He must have been there a while – since before the rain started – because his shaven skull was dry. He held up his fingers in a V sign.

His breath smelt of alcohol. 'Opium of the people,' he murmured, 'but I prefer vodka.'

He hugged Sophia without lowering his cabbages.

Then, to my surprise, he hugged me too and kissed me on both cheeks. I pushed him off with the handle of my umbrella.

He recited that famous shampoo poem of his:

61

When I grow up, I shall drink nothing but shampoo,
I mean, champagne. I shall be a pre-revolutionary
capitalist of the old merchant class. I shall wear
a long beard and a frock-coat and a diamond necklace
and silk Parisian knickers. Each morning, for breakfast,
I shall crack open a Fabergé egg. When I grow up,
I shall live in my own shoe and eat nothing but
millet with a boiled herring head, and put kopeks by
towards the maintenance of my moustache.
When I grow down, I shall
la di di wa up grow I when.

'But you haven't got a moustache,' I objected. (I never understand why poets lie about simple facts that anybody could check.)

'Comrade Humphrey,' he roared, 'Gritz drilled a neat hole in your head yesterday.'

'Oh yes?'

'Hammered the nail in beneath the rim of your helmet.'

'Oh, you mean the statue of the Kaiser at the waxworks?'

'Hah! Who's a clever boy? Gritz will make it into soup.'

'What? . . . Oh, the vegetables . . . *shtchi* . . . '

I noticed with dismay that Gritz was fondling Sophia's left buttock. I could hardly tell him to cease if she didn't object.

Sophia took my hand and placed it on her right buttock. 'It's only fair.'

I felt the slick cool satin, and her flesh shifting beneath. I couldn't work out quite what I was supposed to do. Besides the cuff of my coat was damp from the rain; I was afraid that I might moisten her dress. And my opposite armpit tickled, but I couldn't very well let go of her rear without seeming impolite.

'Now,' said Sophia. 'Gritz. Humph. I want you both to be very good friends.'

She pulled my and his spare arms (we had to drop our umbrella and cabbages respectively; they clattered and bumped on the floor) round herself, and linked the hands together.

We stood in that symmetrical position for a while. It was like the finale of a ballet. I smelled Gritz's breath and Sophia's lavender scent. Meanwhile a platoon of priests advanced on the altar, chanting.

'Let's get out,' I said.

We detached ourselves, and walked towards the exit, side by side.

Thoughts swirled in my head about the Trinity: Sophia's the Holy Ghost, of course, but who gets to be the Father, me or Gritz?

We arrived under the portico. It was still raining out there. The snow was dissolving. A cracked Sèvres vase was lying in the gutter, its contents of sour cream flowing away among stringy horse dung. A shawled old woman, drunken, crouched beneath the grand piano was jigsawing together the shards of the vase. I thought: woman: what a wonderful creature. Any man in her position would be lapping the sour cream.

The umbrella problem. We only had one between the three of us, but it was broad enough to protect just two heads. Somebody would have to stand out in the wet.

Well, I'd be damned if it was me! For one thing, it was *my* umbrella. (Yes, yes. 'From each according to his . . . blah blah.')

And I couldn't very well force Gritz to volunteer.

We all looked at each other.

Finally Sophia said, 'So be it. I shall be rained upon.'

'Oh, no!' I said. 'That's quite – '

'I insist,' she said. 'It's the only symmetrical way. It would be unfair if I snuggled under the umbrella with just one of you.'

We set out for the bus stop. Gritz and I walked side by side, our heads close, my woollen coat rubbing against his leather jacket. Sophia strode ahead. The rain was pelting on her fur hat, sliding down her cheeks and nose and gushing into the gap around her coat collar.

I'd never felt so proud of Sophia as I did then, watching her marching up the lane, bravely drenching herself for the sake of amity. I could understand why I loved her – and women in general. Women crave peace; men (at that moment, Jock was besieged at Kronstadt, and Yuri was imprisoned God [who doesn't exist] knows where) do not.

We caught the bus to Red Square. Sophia had to attend her waxworks. Gritz was accompanying her; he was going to spend the night with her. (Sophia had worked out a schedule; she explained it on the bus. I got Mondays, Wednesdays and Fridays; my rival got Tuesdays, Thursdays and Saturdays; Sundays she would spend in solitary reflection. I was rather shocked by her matter-of-fact declaration; but, on reflection, respected her decisiveness.) I was on my way home.

By the time we reached Red Square the rain had stopped. A rainbow was glowing against a grey thundercloud, over the snowscape.

As we descended from the bus Gritz staggered. He seemed suddenly to have become more tipsy – the way some people do an hour or so after drinking. He spun his net bag round his head like a sling. The cabbages shot out and rolled towards the Kremlin.

I began saying my goodbyes, having no wish to go with the other two into the waxworks, where my own dummy (disguised as Kaiser Wilhelm) was on view.

Two chubby middle-aged women scrambled for Gritz's vegetables. They each retrieved one, and came towards him, holding the errant cabbages over their heads.

Gritz accepted their offerings and put them in his net bag. The women stood there, obviously expecting a tip or at least a word of thanks.

'Women in common!' Gritz said to me and Sophia in his strongly accented English.

He repeated this in Russian. 'Women in common! Free love!'

The babushkas, between them, grabbed his 'perhaps' bag. They swore at him – some holy curse. They swung the bag and bashed his middle.

Bits of green-yellow leaf broke off and fluttered on to the thin snow.

The old women kept on hitting him with his own cabbages. He continued to yell as he wriggled in a kind of belly dance, 'From each according to his ... ooh! ow! ... to each according to his ... ahh! eeh! ... '

Thunder rumbled.

I bowed to Sophia. 'Farewell. Till your next appointment, on Monday evening.'

I walked off home alone, swinging my umbrella.

I didn't see where the lightning bolt struck.

4

'Look!' I said. 'Those nutty things are its eyes. That twig is its mouth.'
I was standing under the swaying branches of the (sorry: I'm not very
good at botany) tree with the twisty leaves.

The face grimaced horribly.

I'd set aside that Sunday (5 May 1921) to go on an outing with Sophia.
It had all been arranged: we were to take a cab to the northern outskirts
of Moscow, and wander in a wood there, one famous for its berries (this
was the wrong season, but never mind). Sophia had quoted some English
poem about, 'Annihilating all that's made/To a green thought in a green
shade'.

I could just about manage to take the day off. My time was precious,
as I'd emphasised to Sophia. The Metropolitan Transport Soviet had
authorised Lev and me to obtain supply allocations; we were chasing
through bureaucracies and warehouses in search of non-earmarked
cement.

At the last moment, Sophia had sent me a note at work telling me to
take the bus to the rendezvous; she'd arrive on her own.

Well, where was she? I'd stomped about the clearing for three-quarters
of an hour. No Sophia. Had I misremembered the meeting place? Or
the time? Or the date? Or had something terrible happened to delay her?

At last I heard a voice calling through a thicket. 'Sophia! Come here,
my love, or I'll beat you up!'

I recognised the voice. I made my way towards it. Behold Gritz.

'You?!' he said.

'You.'

'But Sophia promised herself to Gritz!'

'*I* was supposed to be cosseted with her alone.'

'Hah! Gritz knows her games!'

'I think . . . she probably did it on purpose – '

'Oh, no doubt – '

'She just wants you and me to be friends!'

Gritz was startled by my conclusion. He scratched his black fur hat.

I elucidated. 'It's a stratagem, don't you see? To bring her two best friends together. She's always so . . . considerate.'

'That's one word for it.'

Gritz strode back through the high thistly grass. I followed him. He reached another clearing where a Renault was parked, looking as out of place as a stag in a garage (only the other way round, if you see what I mean). A chauffeur in beige livery was polishing the windscreen with a red rag.

'Yours?' I asked.

'The driver's borrowed for the day.'

'I meant, is the car yours?'

'Not exactly.'

'Oh.'

I wandered in a spiral around the Renault. It was a fine machine. Gritz (like Lev) had a knack for commandeering things. The warehouses of Moscow in those years were full of confiscated and misdirected property which could be allocated to an ingenious person with the right connections.

'Another face!' I said. 'In the undergrowth. Made out of those brambly things. Look!'

Gritz didn't look.

I was passing the time by spying out faces. (It's what I do in the countryside – just as other people shoot pheasants or net butterflies.) Faces were everywhere: a wizened countenance in the gnarled bark; a baby's face in the dabs of cuckoo spit on the grass; even a fluffy-bearded fellow in the sky.

Gritz wasted no time in making his opinions known: 'Gritz hates trees! Gritz loves skyscrapers! Gritz hates pollen! Gritz loves steel! Gritz is allergic to nature – '

'Oh, that *is* a pity,' I said. 'I'm just the same with garlic. I come out in spots.'

I waded through a herd of pigmy elephants – which turned out to be a queer shrubbery with flapping grey leaves. I pressed on beneath a canopy of tall trees. The light was flickering like the reflections on a canal wall. This woodland (so Sophia had told me) had originally been set out by an aristocrat for hunting purposes: I listened for deer, pheasant, boar, bear . . . A woodpecker rapped. (I recalled that Alla had once told me that proverbially woodpeckers ask *Where? Where?* – which has a banging sound in Russian.)

I advanced into a shaft of sunshine; then darkness. Then a half-gloom: the forest floor was tigered with gold and ebony. I imagined I was with Sophia (I could almost smell her perfume). She and I were utterly alone in the big black forest . . . We were wandering hand in hand like Hansel and Gretel . . . We were lost . . . 'Where are you?' I called.

'Here,' said Gritz. He was stumbling after me. His big boots were catching in tree roots. His hat was slipping down over his forehead. His head was swaying, open-mouthed.

'You all right?' I asked.

He sniffed. 'My nose is stuffed up.'

'Oh.'

He hooked his hand on my elbow.

I have to admit I was rather pleased by Gritz's condition. A blocked nose is an undignified complaint – I mean, it's not as if he were dying of consumption.

A bird warbled. 'Ha!' said Gritz. 'It is talking your language.'

'Pardon?'

'Everybody knows that English is a kind of bird song, all those *ing ing s s* sounds.'

I whistled scraps of tunes to keep my spirits up: 'The Red Flag' and 'John Brown's Body' and 'Daddy Wouldn't Buy Me a Bow-Wow'.

A brook gurgled. I stepped over it, and forward into a small clearing. Gritz, following more or less in my footsteps, plunged his right leg knee-deep into a rabbit hole in the muddy bank.

He hauled himself up. He looked at me with complete contempt. 'Sophia! How could you leave me in the company of this fool?! Sophia! Gritz will chop you into a thousand pieces!'

'Well, *I'm* pretty annoyed at her, too. She *said* she'd – '

'Sophia! Gritz will dissolve you in concentrated sulphuric acid!'

'I honestly do think she might have given me advance warning – '

'Sophia! Gritz will roast you to a turn!'

'She's not altogether reliable . . . '

Gritz was leaning against a birch tree, trying to scrape the mud off his trouser leg and on to the trunk. He was sneezing in Russian. He blew his nose on his bear fur hat. I sat on a rotten stump and watched him.

Meanwhile, I considered the syllogism: 'I love Sophia; Sophia loves Gritz; *ergo*, I love Gritz.' Well, no . . . in fact, I really disliked him (that's what I thought at first). He was so selfish, like a big baby, caring just about his own interests . . . No (I contradicted myself), he was obsessed with his effect on other people – which is a kind of selfless generosity, really . . . But (I changed my mind yet again) how could I understand him in the slightest? He was an artist and shouldn't be judged by the standards of normal people. Besides there was the language gap. True, he usually shouted at me in brusque, short sentences, but couldn't that be because he spoke so-so English and my Russian was painfully ungrammatical and makeshift! Also he seemed always to declare rather than enquire; however, in Russian there are two alternative intonations when asking a question (Sophia had explained this to me), either raising the pitch at the end as in English, or strongly stressing a syllable in the middle; possibly Gritz was using the latter method, and was really more tentative than I'd supposed? In conclusion I decided that Gritz and I probably had more in common than either of us understood consciously. I told him this. He snorted.

I lent him a handkerchief to clean himself up and wipe his nose. 'Keep it,' I said with deliberately casual generosity.

I'd always supposed that Sophia desired both me and Gritz just because we were opposites (so I reflected as I sat on the stump). I was gentle: he was brutal. I was an exotic foreigner: he was a home-grown Russian. Comforting versus disturbing. Gullible versus cynical . . . In fact I'd pictured Gritz as a kind of Lenin: not 'good' in a Sunday School way, but well intentioned, determined, refreshingly savage. But perhaps I'd got it wrong. Could it be that to Sophia we both seemed alike: insecure, self-doubting creatures: children who need to be hugged and spanked . . . ?

There again, perhaps she liked Gritz just because he was a great poet (or so everybody said in the Red Cabbage; I'm no judge of these things). His poems 'miraculously unite exalted and colloquial diction' (I'm quoting a review by Tolya in one of the monthlies).

Gritz was reciting, with declamatory gestures and sniffles:

Sleep little children, the wolf will eat you up
unless you eat your nice buckwheat pancake up
with a stewed cranberry topping. With a stewed cranberry topping
the wolf will gobble you, unless you listen to a lullaby
containing an ideologically sound patriotic reference. The Red
    Army
guards Russia's heroic northern frontiers. They will shoot

the wolf and cut its belly and pull you out. So
sleep, little children, sleep, I said, sleep.

(Sophia helped me translate it. Well, to be honest, she translated it
and I corrected her spelling.)

'One of your own poems?' I asked.
'It is a lullaby. It sends children to sleep.'
'Yes . . . I'm sure. Er, mightn't it . . . scare – '
'The world is full of scares! The Bagman is bagging Russia! The
Nepman is sucking Russia's lifeblood!'
(I should explain. The 'bagmen' were entrepreneurs who bought
hoarded grain from the peasants and sold it in cities. This was of
course illegal: every day in *Pravda* you'd read that another dozen or so
speculators had been captured and shot. Mothers used to frighten their
children: 'If you don't go to bed at once, the Bagman will pop you in his
bag!'
The Nepman was the same kind of monster, except that he stayed
within the law. You see, Lenin had just started the New Economic
Programme – acronym: N E P – which permitted certain kinds of capitalist enterprise.)
'But Lenin has said – ' I objected.
'Lenin too is decaying. The forces of counter-revolution are prowling
and growling!'
'I think if you read this monograph by Lenin, you'll find he makes it
quite clear that he never makes mistakes.'
I took a red booklet, *Principles of the New Economic Programme*, from
my jacket pocket, and handed it to Gritz.
Gritz bent the booklet double, then ripped it into halves. He folded
and tore it again: into quarters, eighths, sixteenths. The red, black and
white fragments scattered on a hawthorn bush, like blossom.
'Thus they are savaging the Muse!'
'That's my only copy of the monograph, you know.'
'The State Publishing House. They are not printing Gritz's poems.'
'I really don't think you should have – '
'Jealousy. Envy. Petty censorship.'
'Well, we can't always put our own interests first, you know . . . '
I stopped talking because I realised Gritz had vanished. I glimpsed
his black coat and hat through a gap in the trees.
I set off after him. (Well, he seemed more than usually eccentric; I

had a duty to look after him, if only for Sophia's sake.) He was elbowing through the forest at a cracking pace. I managed to keep him in view, or at least to hear his wheezing and sneezing. We pushed on through close clumps of birch, then high gorse.

I caught up with him in a brambly thicket. His trousers were hooked on thorned branches; red scratch marks stained his knuckles. I felt like a hunter cornering a trapped beast.

'Gritz shall stay here in the forest!' he said.

'Oh, really.'

'They have strangled the children!'

'What?'

'The poems are in their coffins.'

'For one thing, Sophia would be awfully upset if – '

'Ah, Sophia. She does not love Gritz. She loves only you.'

'Gosh, do you really think so?'

As I helped him detach himself from the thorns, he chanted the lullaby again.

He cried into his hat.

Then he recited:

Intellectuals need bears.
A seal would do, or farmed mink,
or fox, or even rabbit pelts stitched together.
But my favourite fur is bear fur.
I have a bear fur hat that keeps my brain cosy.

We're not Siberian peasants
who carve chess pieces from your teeth
and boil down your tail grease to make candles.
We're not after your rump to make goulash.

We are the intelligentsia.
We live in the effete city of Moscow.
We need your skin.

'Yes, have a good weep,' I said. 'You'll feel much better for it, probably.'

At this point I realised that: 1) it was getting late and it was time for us to return; and 2) I had no idea where we were.

I asked Gritz, 'Excuse me. Do you by any chance know – '

He atishooed ferociously.

Well, if I'd intended to perish of exposure in the midst of a Russian forest, Gritz wasn't the person I'd have chosen to perish with. But, oddly, the danger exhilarated me. Also, I felt a kind of affection for him: an almost fatherly responsibility. And I now had something else in common with him besides a shared love for Sophia. (Had she intended even this?)

He returned my handkerchief. It was encrusted with . . . encrustations. I dropped it behind me discreetly.

As I leaned over, my watch fell out of my pocket on to a tree root. Gritz, trying to pick it up, stamped on it. I retrieved the watch in the end: it was dirty but still ticking.

I tried to think my way out of this problem logically. The sun was visible through the trees. If we walked towards it, we'd reach the edge of the forest soon enough – wouldn't we?

My thoughts were interrupted by Gritz's shout.

'Gritz will find the car! There is an old Russian trick for tracking a bear. You growl like a bear, so . . . ' He made a bear noise. 'Thus the bear growls back at you, so . . . ' He did another bear imitation.

'But we don't want a – '

Gritz turned into a car. His mimicry was perfect. He was the roar of its engine, the clank of its chassis, the swish of its tyres, the honk of its horn . . . And, lo! in the distance, we heard the answering honk of the Renault horn.

We advanced towards that sound. At intervals Gritz would make his car noises – his big hands would rotate like wheels, he'd blink like a windscreen wiper – and the unseen chauffeur would operate the horn. We passed through dense gorse, and purple man-high heathers. We crossed the mudland where invisible birds chirped. We skirted a bush with white berries (Gritz grabbed a handful, chewed them, pulled a long face, spat them out). We traversed chill regions of thin birches . . .

At last we reached the Renault.

Having survived danger, we felt comradely, and sang together (he in Russian and I in English) 'Old MacDonald Had a Farm' (' – with an oink-oink here, and an oink-oink there') all through the drive back to Moscow.

5

I next saw Gritz a few weeks later.

The three of us, him, me and Sophia, were about to take a vacation together – heading south for the summer, just like migrating birds only the other way round. (Well, actually, it was a working holiday: I'll explain the circumstances in a moment.)

Gritz (according to Sophia) had promised to help me pack. I went round to the Red Cabbage Café to meet him.

I'd never seen the café before in bright daylight. The little painted-over windows at the back were open and shafts of sunshine streamed in. The place smelled of turpentine – a resinous, woody odour. A long ladder was propped near the entrance. Gritz was at the top of it.

I called up, 'Good morning, Gritz.'

'Gritz is installing a banana.'

'I beg your pardon?'

'The Red Cabbage Café was closed down. Political objections. So we opened the Red Tomato Café. Then it was the Red Pepper. And now . . . '

He was holding a large yellow plaster banana over his head, and attaching it to a chain connected to a hook on the ceiling. Then – using a pot and brush tied round his waist – he painted the fruit a purplish red.

Soon he wiped his hands on a rag, and climbed down the ladder.

He hugged me – in the traditional, over-affectionate Russian greeting. He seemed in a good mood.

'How are your . . . poems doing?' I enquired tentatively.

'What poems?'

'Yours. Has the State Publishing House yet – '

'Gritz doesn't write poems. Gritz is a painter.'

'Oh. Right.'

*

We went back to my place by a jerky troika (it was operating with two horses instead of the canonical three). Gritz's own luggage – bulky long brushes (more like a chimney sweep's than an artist's) and paint pots – was already stored on top.

This was the first time Gritz had come to my apartment. We climbed the flights of stairs.

The concierge poked her head out of her door as we passed by. 'Who is your friend, Comrade Fraya?'

'He is an artist, Comrade Nadia Gavrilovna.'

Gritz took her hand and kissed it.

She said, 'He certainly is an artist.'

I opened the door of my apartment. 'There!' I said. I was quite proud of the place – it was luxurious by Muscovite standards – and I expected Gritz to be impressed.

He looked round, eyeing the icons, grunting, not saying anything.

I waited for his comments. I blew my nose quietly. (I had caught a modest cold.) He nodded at the haloed saints and outstared the Almighty's oval eyes.

'Gritz thinks these are icons – '

'Oh, I couldn't agree more.'

' – which will shortly be surpassed – '

'That's certainly quite a suggestion.'

' – by the Futurist Movement.'

Instead of telling me about Futurism, he talked about the history of icons. He seemed very knowledgeable. It was all quite interesting stuff: apparently the faces were constructed according to rules of proportion – more like an engineering diagram than a work of art. First, you take a sheet of wood; you cover it with gesso to make it even, a layer of alabaster to whiten the surface, and you outline the saint in charcoal. You paint the figures with tempera (that's a kind of paint mixed with yolk or fig juice or something) and gild the haloes. Then you varnish the thing with linseed oil. Finally you burn it.

'Beg your pardon?' I said.

'Let iconoclasm reign.'

'Who?'

'The doctrine that any depiction of the human form is idolatry.'

I considered this point.

It turned out he was referring to events in the eighth century. He pointed at an icon of the Madonna with three hands. Apparently the Emperor had cut off the hand of an artist-saint, who'd prayed

73

to the Virgin, who'd restored it. Gritz was on the side of the Emperor.

'The iconoclasts ripped and burnt all the old paintings. Futurism says: destroy art again! Only when the Venetian palazzi are turned to rubble and the canals filled up, can Venice rise once more!'

'Do you think you could help me with my packing? We haven't got very long.'

I took my suitcase out from under the bed and laid it, open, on top of the desk.

'Only when the eyes of the Mona Lisa are stubbed out . . . thus and thus . . .', he was brandishing a lit cigarette, '. . . can she smile once more.'

I opened my wardrobe. 'Now, what do you think I should take? Of course, it'll probably be nice and hot down south, and I haven't really got much in the way of summer clothing . . . '

Gritz tilted the entire wardrobe forward so all the contents fell out on the floor. Then he scrabbled amongst them and, with his hands and feet, slapped and kicked a selection of clothing on to the bed.

'Yes,' I said, 'that's very . . . On my own, you know, I take forever to pick and choose . . . '

He laid my shirts on top of each other, and my trousers likewise.

'You want summer wear? You shall have summer wear!'

A penknife jerked from his pocket, flicked itself open, and – in four rapid slashes – cut off the lower arms and legs of the clothing.

'Er . . . thank you,' I said.

Gritz was often curt and too original for my taste – but it had to be admitted he did get things done. I began to understand how, beneath a surface eccentricity, he could actually be a good artist.

He stubbed out his cigarette on the frame of a Massacre of the Innocents.

He tossed the shortened clothes into the suitcase, shut it, sat on it to close it, locked it, carried it from the room. I heard his voice drift up the stairwell: he was telling the concierge some elaborate fairytale about monsters in a northern forest. Meanwhile I filled a net shopping bag with odds and ends for the voyage – my toothpowder, *Das Kapital*, a quarter of a salami . . . and followed him out. The cut-off arms and legs lay on the bed, jumbled. I imagined intertwining invisible hands, feet, torsos, faces.

I arrived at the St Somebody-or-another (well, it had some revolutionary name officially) railway terminus by cab. Gritz had stayed behind, planning to make his own way here, so I'd had to take charge of his luggage as well as my own. The cab driver, a sleepy-eyed man, was helping me carry all the stuff, in return for a modest tip. (I felt guilty about this capitalist enterprise.)

'Do you know', I said to the driver, as we entered the iron and glass building, 'that the reason Russians call a railway terminus a *vogzal* is that in the early nineteenth century somebody visited the London terminus at Vauxhall and thought that was the generic name?'

'Thank you, sir,' he said.

I gave him his tip.

'Thank you, *Comrade*,' I corrected.

The baggage was dumped in the waiting room, the attendant there was tipped to have the stuff delivered to the train, and the cab driver (tipped once more) departed.

I had three-quarters of an hour before the train left. Neither Sophia nor Gritz were around yet, that I could see. I strolled through the station, under the high roof echoing with chatter and chuff-chuffs – thinking about the journey ahead . . .

The three of us were setting out for the Crimea to accompany a tour of the waxworks. Sophia had arranged the trip because (so some man friend of hers in the All Russia Extraordinary Commission for Fighting Counter-Revolution and Sabotage had warned her) she was under investigation as a subversive. (It was alleged that her display of Romanovs was intended to glorify the monarchy!) Anyway she reckoned that, if she kept out of the limelight, the affair would blow over by autumn.

Gritz was coming along as 'Artistic Adviser' (whatever that means) – Sophia's doing. And I was the Technical Adviser. (Lev had got me authorisation: the metro planning stage was halted by a capital expenditure freeze.)

And talking of freezes . . . it was quite cold that June in Moscow. I thought of the Crimea – the sunny Crimea! – where oranges danced on the vine and humming birds blossomed in the azure sea . . .

The station was full of soldiers: smirking, smoking and rubbing things out with the heels of their boots. Most of the civilian travellers seemed to be elderly folk with frightened flickering eyes and chattering dentures. It was National Toothbrush Day. Posters with lots of teeth and pro-toothbrush slogans were pasted on the walls. One showed a girl whose gums were gushing blood: IF ONLY I'D BRUSHED REGULARLY! Another featured a young Red Army soldier sinking his teeth into a huge moneybag trailing from a capitalist's posterior: BITE THE ENEMY WITH

STRONG TEETH! I recognised the style – angular, bright-coloured shapes and bending words – like many of the paintings (Tolya's for instance, and Gritz's too) on the walls of the Red Cabbage Café. Half a dozen illiterate soldiers with Polish accents were pointing at the posters, trying to guess what they meant.

It was now only ten minutes till the train was due to depart. (They always left late, anyway.) I made my way to Platform 17. There was a blackboard there, chalked with: DUE TO COUNTER-REVOLUTIONARY ACTIVITY, DEPARTURE DELAYED TILL 15.00 HOURS.

I checked the time on the huge station clock, suspended in a wreath of steam. Two hours to go. There seemed no point waiting here.

I left the station, and strolled north, on this pleasant, cool day, towards the centre of Moscow. Wonderful how attractive a city (*any* city) seems just before you are about to leave it. The clamour of the traffic, the charcoal smoke, the rudeness of traffic policemen ... all that had once annoyed, now appeared quaintly characteristic. I peered through windows and watched: a boy oiling his hair; a girl painting her toenails; a woman cleaning a carpet with used tea leaves; an ancient man stirring a pot very slowly ...

I had a slight cold, which made the world fuzzy – yet somehow, also, strange and interesting. I fiddled with my handkerchief.

As I was half-way across a busy intersection, I suddenly realised: I had forgotten my toothbrush! There it was, in my apartment, on its usual ledge ... I could visualise the spot where I'd left it. Would I have to spend the next three months in the Crimea with dirty teeth? Or would I be able to buy a new one (there was a severe shortage)? Or would Sophia let me share hers (I'd like that)? Or would she insist I borrow Gritz's (yugh!)?

A bus honked. A horse neighed. I did a quick calculation: there would just be time for me to go back to my apartment, pick up my abandoned toothbrush and make it to the train on time.

I jumped up and down in front of a bus. The driver – grumbling – halted and let me in. I journeyed north through thick traffic.

'Nadia! Comrade Nadia Gavrilovna!' I hammered on my concierge's door. (I'd already packed my key in my luggage, I'd realised.)

She opened the door a crack – then wide. 'Oh, it's you, Comrade Fraya! How pleasant to see you so soon.'

'Door – key – open – toothbrush – train.'

'Would you like a little tea first?'

'Teeth – fall out – hurry – unlock.'

'Are you in a little rush, Comrade Fraya? Your nice friend came already and took everything?'

'Friend?'

'Your artist friend. Such a jolly man.' She said coyly, 'He promised me he'd paint me sometime. Said I had an interesting bone structure.'

The concierge was walking ahead of me up the stairs. We reached my apartment. She turned the master key in the lock.

At first glance, the room was unchanged – my toothbrush with the bakelite handle was on the floor, in the middle, next to the *burzhuika*; I picked it up and put it in my pocket – but, at second glance, it was totally changed. The walls, dappled with sunlight, were bare. *No icons!*

I was about to ask some pertinent question – in my shock, I couldn't think straight in Russian – when the deep bell in St Basil's rang the hour. Once, twice, thrice . . .

I checked my watch. It was 15.00 indeed.

I ran downstairs.

At the crossroads outside, a bus was heading south – but it was full and wouldn't stop for all my entreaties and palms-together prayer postures. An army fire engine was idling. I flashed my passport and my permit to visit the Crimea, mumbled some explanation. I was hauled on board, and – the big brass fire-bell clanging – they raced towards the railway terminus. The firemen clearly enjoyed the speed; they leaned out so the wind swept through their hair. They asked me what a toothbrush was for and why. I did my best to elucidate.

I arrived at the station ten minutes after the train was supposed to have left. Rushed to Platform 17. Of course the train was still there. The blackboard was now chalked: DEPARTURE DELAYED TILL 16.00 HOURS.

I wiped my brow with my handkerchief. Automatically I held the handkerchief to my nose – but realised then that I no longer had a cold. The shock must have cured it.

It's a Russian custom to sit down for a few minutes before embarking on a voyage. I perched on the edge of a semi-demolished horse trough. I thought about my arrival in Russia – at this very station, was it? – only a year and a half ago, but it seemed much longer.

I walked along the train to the front, right by the puffing engine, where the special waxworks carriage was located. The train was painted in Futurist style with patriotic slogans and health warnings.

The waxworks carriage could hardly be missed. It was decorated with the huge grand smiling bald bearded face of Vladimir Ilyich Lenin.

I approached closer. The locomotive whistled. The whole train slid forward. I ran. Now I could see the train decoration more clearly: it was a composite picture, made up of separate facets like a fly's eye. It was composed of a tessellation of polygons of gilt and painted wood which were (I approached more closely) chopped bits of icons.

A compartment door was swinging open. I sprinted. I grabbed the handle. I hoisted one foot on to the step, and – while I was leaning back, asway – the toothbrush leaped from my pocket and fell on to the track.

The train was picking up speed. I was hanging on to the door, lurching, trying to rock myself into the compartment.

I could see the face from closer up now. Two heads were poking out of Lenin's mouth: Gritz and Sophia.

With a final vast muscular effort, I shouted, 'Have you got a spare toothbrush?' and hauled myself into the train.

6

The main railway lines of the Soviet Union stretch out from Moscow like the spokes of a wheel. In olden times wars were fought by infantry, then cavalry. The Great War was a combat between mechanised land vehicles, but these were lumbering things. The Russian Civil War was the first truly modern war: it was a contest of armoured railway trains. Across the steppes sped flame-flickering trains with guns firing from every window.

Imagine that the railway lines under Bolshevik control were coloured red. From 1917 to 1921 these lines expanded and contracted like a huge crimson octopus. First a tentacle stretched out towards Finland, and retreated sharply. Another wavered far to the east, and withdrew. The southern extensions flickered rapidly – now being consumed by the white worms of the enemy – now devouring them. Not till the summer of 1921 did the octopus, bloated and static, control almost all the major territories of the former Tsarist Empire.

I was rather proud of the octopus simile. It had taken me quite a while to phrase it just right.

I told this to my comrades as we journeyed south by train.

'Honestly, Humph,' said Sophia, 'you're mixing your metaphors. A wheel can't very well be an octopus.'

'Hail the Revolution! Hail men with nerves of steel and steel with nerves of men!' said Gritz.

'Oh, Gritz,' said Sophia, running her fingernails down his shirt front, 'you're wonderfully poetic.'

'I wasn't *trying* to be poetic,' I butted in. 'I was making a serious point in military strategy. If it hadn't been for the centralised control of the rail network, the Communists wouldn't have won, and you and I wouldn't be here today.'

During the three weeks it took us to get from Moscow to the Crimea (the waxworks carriage was shunted to and fro, attached to one troop train or another; we were sent an incredibly long way round, as far as

79

Tsaritsyn on the Volga), I occupied myself by inspecting the railway facilities en route. I noticed several construction techniques and organisational methodologies which could profitably be employed on the forthcoming Moscow metro. I took notes.

Meanwhile, Sophia was applying rouge to her dummies, 'to befit them for the merry Crimean temperament'. And Gritz was writing an epic poem about the Civil War.

'Are there any railways in it?' I asked him several times.

'Gritz does not discuss his work in progress.'

'What about your Lenin-face on the carriage? That's to do with his role in rail transport, is it? What you poets call a "symbol"?'

'Gritz is *not* a Symbolist.'

'I certainly think you should include a reference to the marshalling yards at Rostov-on-Don. Jolly impressive. And vital to the war effort.'

'There may be some mention of modes of transport – '

'I could give you an idea or two.'

Gritz dipped his nib in the portable inkwell, and shook the pen. Drops of ink spattered: on the compartment floor, on the brass fittings and leather straps, on the track, on me.

Our relationships changed drastically during those weeks of travel . . .

Let me tell you about a game I played with my fellow engineering apprentices in New York. It's called Piggy in the Middle. Two participants toss something between them (any old thing: a ball, a book, an embarrassing love letter) and the third dashes about in the middle, trying to catch it. If he succeeds, then the last person to throw the thing becomes Piggy in his turn, and the former Piggy takes his place. The game continues until a tired Piggy walks off, yelling, 'Aw, hell, it's a kids' game, anyway.' This game shows how three people must always interact: one person is in the middle and two are on the outside.

So it was with the three of us. At first Sophia was the centre: Gritz and I vied to please her. And I honestly supposed it would go on like that for ever. But a triangle is not as stable as it may seem: it can crack at any of its vertices. To my (and the others', too, I think) surprise, Gritz became the object of attention: Sophia and I competed to gain his approval.

Of course I'm being clever in retrospect, making it all seem neat. At the time, I told myself I was being nice to Gritz: 1) to gain Sophia's favour; 2) because he was a great poet; 3) because I felt sorry for him; and 4) I was scared of him. And all these reasons were true, of course.

But my major motive was this: I was terribly afraid Gritz would kill himself. And what would happen to us then? Oh, I had no illusion that

Sophia and I could settle down to a blissful monogamy; I realised that she only loved me as an antidote to him (and him, me, to be sure). So I brought Gritz glasses of tea from the samovar at the rear of the carriage. I smiled my best smile at him a lot. I offered him information about the course of the Civil War (I'd made quite a study of the period). I did what I could.

Sophia was cruel to Gritz – that's how it seemed to me at the time. She was unkind to him in every way, from: 'I think it's *your* turn to lend *me* a cigarette,' to, 'If you don't wash your armpits, Gritz, you'll have to sleep with the dummies again and Humph will take your slot on the rota,' to, 'Stop sulking *this instant*, Gritz, or I'll smack your botty!' And just occasionally she was lovey-dovey and nibbled his chin and fell into his arms. But of course she was trying to jerk him from his self-obsessive melancholy. Hers was the best way: I accept that now.

Love means doing anything at all that will please the loved one – anything. Caring for a potential suicide is just like love. A single thought butts aside all others: *he must not die.* To ensure that his slightest whim is humoured, the shallowest grumpiness is teased away.

And yet, I wasn't at all sure that Gritz was suicidal. Yes, he grumbled about his 'Muse' deserting him. But that was probably just poetic hyperbole. Yes, he spoke about death at boring length. As we passed bonfires he talked about burning himself; as a power station sallied past on the far side of the tracks, he was all for electrocution; any hint of water – a river, the sea, even dew on the grass – and he would recite his list of famous poets who had died by drowning. But that could all be affectation. He never said in so many words that he was considering killing himself: he just implied it by his invocations of Thanatos. In fact I had a shrewd suspicion that Gritz's death wish was a style put on as deliberately as his black boots, docker's tunic, shaven head.

We crossed into the Crimea at the beginning of August. The train inched along a long narrow spit of land at no more than five or ten kilometres per hour, while soldiers scurried alongside, checking for mines, landslips or sabotage. This was the famous Perekop isthmus where the White and Reds had battled so fiercely in the Civil War. Sophia and I rushed to and fro in the waxworks compartment, stepping over the strapped-down dummies, to peer at the Black Sea on one side, the Sea of Azov on the other. Blue waves: blue waves. Gritz lay on his bunk in the sleeping compartment with a black handkerchief tied round his eyes, claiming to be seasick.

'It's so beautiful!' said Sophia. 'I want to have it all for myself.'

'Remarkable feat of military prowess', I added, 'for the Reds to have captured it so easily.' The Crimea had been liberated as recently as the end of 1920. Black burnt-out lorries, gun emplacements and an occasional tank rested beside the sea.

'Gritz smells fire!' Gritz called out. 'Burning! Smoke!'

'That's the locomotive,' I called back. 'I'm afraid they've shunted us to the front of the train again.'

A rolling thunder-grey smoke was pluming from the engine; our carriage and ourselves were flecked with smut. (At least the dummies were thoroughly protected with canvas covers: Sophia always took good care of them.)

Gritz called out again in a soft voice, 'I'm sick.'

When Gritz used the personal pronoun, this was often a sign of weakness. I went to investigate.

He was lying on his bunk, the black cloth clenched between his teeth. He spat it out. 'I'm not well.'

'Perhaps something you ate disagreed with you? That *piroshki* – '

'I am giving birth.'

'Want to come through to the other compartment and look at the sea?'

'I am giving birth to my epic poem: "The Civil War". By Gritz. In my agony, I come to understand the suffering of war. And your breath stinks.'

'I really don't think your tummy upset can compare with a Civil War,' I remarked jocularly, determined to adopt Sophia's technique of 'joshing' him. 'Besides, it's not my fault I can't brush my teeth properly.'

'Every little agony helps.'

I was shocked and puzzled. I determined not to let Gritz notice my dismay. I concentrated on a splinter of blue sea, visible through a crack in the wall.

Then I noticed, out of the corner of my eye, that Gritz was smiling. *He* was making fun of *me*.

As soon as he saw I was looking at him, he tautened his face again.

'I really must be getting along,' I said in my serious voice, and betook myself through the sliding door into the waxworks compartment.

The train speeded up a little, and we left the isthmus by nightfall. A balmy Mediterranean scene: a few crooked olive trees and a concrete fortification were silhouetted against the setting sun.

As soon as we entered the Crimea proper, Gritz became calmer. For one thing, his epic poem was going well. And I suspect he overheard this conversation between Sophia and me:

Me: 'I don't think Gritz really means to kill himself.'

Sophia: 'Kill? Kill? What are you talking about, Humph?'

'He's not suicidal. He'd want to be around to see what effect he had. Now I could imagine him destroying the entire world in his pique – but not even Gritz supposes the world consists of just himself.'

'Humph! You're morbid! Honestly you are. I don't know where you get these . . . ludicrous notions.'

'But you've been so kind to him lately.'

'I try to be kind to everybody. Gritz is his usual imaginative self.'

'You mean . . . you weren't trying to stop him – ?'

Sophia raised her hands in an X across her breasts. 'Humph. Shush!'

And of course, in retrospect, we were both right.

7

The Crimea was a curious place. Not at all like Russia. More like an anti-Russia, in fact – soft where Russia is hard, flabby where Russia is lean, easy-going where Russia is stern. And I'm not just talking about the climate and the oily, spicy foodstuffs; politically the Crimea was a mess.

Little boys and old men used to run alongside the train. They'd jump on to the running boards and rat-a-tat on the windows. They were selling things: sausages or oranges or little red flags to wear in the lapel.

These entrepreneurs accompanied us throughout the four months we spent in the Crimea. Gritz used to stomp up to them, make his monkey face, and feed them scraps of food – a slice of orange or a grape – through the bars on the window.

Sophia would sometimes buy a little item that took her fancy: a sprig of blossom, perhaps, or an enamel brooch. 'Ah, it reminds me of the old days.'

'I'm afraid I must disapprove on ideological grounds,' I used to tell the vendors. 'Lenin has referred to your activities as a "transitional stage" and I don't doubt it. But I must refrain from supporting this personally.'

As night fell, the sellers would become fewer, and be replaced by mosquitoes and big stumbling moths.

This quasi-capitalism was authorised by the NEP. As a result, I suppose, of the Petrograd food riots and the Kronstadt rebellion, Lenin had permitted small-scale enterprises to flourish. No doubt there were urgent economic reasons. But the policy stuck in my gullet – as I used to tell Sophia.

'Ah, Humph,' she'd say, tickling my throat, 'such a serious man.'

'I *am* serious.'

'I bought this charming thingumebob from a little brown boy this morning. Don't you think it's sweet?'

'The boy was not brown but "Green",' I'd retort wittily. ('Green'

84

was the slang for those lukewarm neutralists who refused to commit themselves to either the Red or the White sides.)

'Oh, he was brown all over, as far as I could see.' She'd dangle some bauble in front of my eyes, as if she were trying to hypnotise me.

It takes a lot to annoy me, but that would do it.

'Honestly, Sophia, you're nothing but a radish! A white vegetable with a thin covering of red!'

'I am teasing you, Humph! I am *teasing* you!'

'I nevertheless am of the opinion that – '

'We wouldn't *be* here if it weren't for NEP. How do you suppose my show is financed, Humph? No state subsidy. Our income derives from the sale of tickets.'

Eventually, one way or another, she'd mollify me. I'd let her tousle my hair. She'd let me bury my nose in her armpit and make squeaky noises. (The Russian for armpit translates literally as 'arm-mouse'.)

Sometimes we'd have to call in Gritz to adjudicate. Sophia would show off her latest item of costume jewellery, and I'd explain the political background. Then Gritz would agree with either me or her, according to his whim. The process calmed us all. Only by perpetual quarrels and making amends could the three of us get by.

I didn't see much of the 'real' Crimea. We were all too busy working. Every week our carriage would be detached at a different railway station and shunted to a siding. Then Sophia would unpack the dummies, dress them and arrange them. Gritz would set up the tent, and the lighting, and the fake blood (I'll explain about that in a minute) – he showed a surprisingly practical streak when he had some specific task to do.

And I was in charge of publicity. In the mornings, I'd put on an elaborate purple robe and a gold-coloured crown. I'd amble through the winding streets of the near-by town, up dirt tracks and down cobbled ways, dodging the clopping donkeys laden with baskets of fruit, and the bomb craters, and the gaily coloured clothes hung on ropes to dry. It was hot; I'd sweat. I'd shout, 'I am the Tsar and I will be executed this afternoon! Come and see me at the railway station!' Shy soldiers would nudge each other, and cock their guns at me jokily. Little children would dance after me in an impromptu conga, and they'd be joined by a chicken or two, a goat and a mad old man singing, 'Tsar, Tsar, Tsar!'

The waxworks were on display from noon till an hour after dusk. There were three separate Special Performances, for which we charged extra: at midday, afternoon and evening. The first one was for the children. Sophia would come up front and narrate, in her special story-telling voice, a tale about the bad old days before the Revolution. She'd introduce the Capitalist (a lean dummy with a hooked nose and a money bag), the Priest (pimply chin and bejewelled crucifix), and finally the Tsar himself (wearing the robes I'd had on earlier). Then she'd lead the children in a chant of: 'One – two – three – KILL!' Gritz, dressed as an executioner in the proper all-black hooded outfit, would axe the dummies' necks. A red gore – the consistency of *borshtch* – would flow from the wounds.

The dummies wore a kind of ruff made of oilcloth, so it didn't take too long to clean them up for the next show.

The afternoon performance was for the troops. Some officer from the CHEKA would deliver a speech, explaining how our dummies illustrate the fundamental principles of Marxism-Leninism. There would usually be an extra couple of dummies representing the local White commanders, Denikin and Wrangel (i.e. the old Kaiser Wilhelm and George V in new whiskers and costumes). Then chop – chop – chop – chop – chop.

We couldn't always get a permit for an evening session, but where we could, it was a rousing success. A premium entry fee, naturally. Off-duty soldiers would come in, and civilian couples too. Sophia would announce, 'I am honoured to bring you, Comrades, by gracious permission of the Supreme Soviet, THE FOULNESS OF RASPUTIN.'

Rasputin was the Kaiser dummy, re-dressed yet again, with a beard stuck on and a long tangly wig. A series of tableaux depicted events from his life. Gritz would illuminate each scene in succession (using candles or searchlights, whatever he could obtain), and I'd have to lug Rasputin from one to the next. Rasputin as a young capitalist in ice-bound Siberia. Rasputin as a devout Christian under an onion dome. Rasputin seducing the Tsarina. The penultimate tableau was Rasputin locked in a compromising position with Princess Anastasia (the only dummy with painted nipples). Finally, Gritz would stab the Mad Monk – gore everywhere.

At the end of October (on Hallowe'en, in fact) Sophia received an order from Moscow, direct from the Commissariat for the Nationalities, that she should 'show kulaks in a bad light'. Well, we'd all become rather detached from day-to-day politics and none of us knew what a *kulak* was. Sophia guessed it might be some variety of vegetable and Gritz said it was a colloquial term for a usurer. When we got hold of a copy of *Izvestia*, and read it carefully, it turned out Gritz was more or less right. There was a campaign under way against the more prosperous peasants, who were now said to form a special socio-economic class of their own: the kulaks. The campaign, sponsored by Stalin, only lasted about a week (at that time; it recurred later), but Sophia had to obey her orders.

'What does a kulak look like?' Sophia asked.

'Haven't the faintest,' I said.

'A tall figure with his nose tied to his chin,' said Gritz.

In the end, we used the old dummy of Woodrow Wilson, minus the Stars and Stripes top hat, He got executed in every show, from 5 November on.

By the middle of November it was time for us to return to Moscow. It was getting cold; there was frost at night, glistening on the cobbles, the beach, the bomb craters, the ruts left by the tank . . . I was glad we were going back. Granted that this jaunt had been pleasant enough, and that I'd become more considerate through having to deal with Sophia and Gritz on such close terms, nevertheless I wanted to return to the real world of Moscow and its metro.

Gritz was not altogether in his right mind. He'd got into the habit of making bubbling noises with his lips.

What had happened (I reflected) was that Sophia and I, just because we were collaborating in looking after Gritz, had become closer. So Gritz himself was excluded: the Piggy in the Middle.

I told him this.

He reacted by laughing out loud. 'Oy! Sophia!' He staggered after her. 'Humphrey says I'm a piggy!'

The upshot was that, that night, Sophia locked herself alone in the sleeping compartment, and we two men had to sleep among the dummies. Gritz kept me awake till the small hours with his cries of 'Oink! oink! oink!'

At the end of November, our carriage was attached to a train delivering arms and ammunition. It was scheduled, before heading for Moscow, to voyage right round the peninsula, dropping off supplies.

At Yalta, in the south of the Crimea, the train halted for a couple of days to deliver artillery and take on a load of machine tools. We were prevailed upon by the commander of the local garrison to put on one last show for his troops. Since the tent had already been packed away with elaborate care, we set up the waxworks in a windmill right by the station.

Naturally the windmill was not in use in winter. Its sails were tied in place. Oddly, sacks of corn lay all round the building, like sandbags around a fortification, and were riddled with mice.

Our carriage was shunted over to a siding only a few metres from the windmill. The Lenin-face made from icons – just a little battered by the weather – was gazing sternly at the octagonal mill, as if to say, 'I understand how small-scale primary goods processing plants fit into the overall economic strategic planning of the NEP.'

As we were setting up the waxworks in the morning – I was marching round the windmill in my robe and crown telling everybody I was the Tsar – I noticed a crowd of youngish soldiers on the waste ground by the station. They were paying me no attention, so I rang my bell and shouted my message louder. 'Oy! oy! oy! I am Tsar Nicholas – ' (etcetera).

Still none of them glanced round. I walked across to them. They were gathered in a ring, obsessively watching some spectacle. I looked over their shoulders.

The first thing I saw was a bottom covered in trousers made from what appeared to be sackcloth. Legs stretched beneath. A shaggy beard was dangling between the thighs.

I walked round. Now I saw the rest of the body: an old man was bent over with his hands on his knees, like a boy playing leapfrog. Every so often, a soldier would run up to him – as if to jump over his back – and kick his bottom hard.

'Excuse me,' I said, 'would you mind stopping that?'

The soldiers looked at me puzzled.

'The old man's an old man,' said one.

'He's crazy,' said another.

'He's got a green beard,' said a third.

What they said was true – as I saw for myself when I stepped closer – the victim was a wrinkled old thing who giggled constantly, all the more when he was booted, and whose beard was apparently infested with moss.

'I'm Tsar Nicholas,' I said to the soldiers, 'and I really don't think you ought to do that to him.'

But everybody ignored me so I gave up and went away.

That evening we put on our final performance. Gritz had put some stuff that smelt like rotten eggs into the artificial blood. The executed villains stank. The audience clapped and departed.

It was late when we finished. It was freezing cold: the first true night

88

of winter. We'd run out of fuel for the charcoal stove. The three of us, trying to get warm enough to sleep, put on whatever clothes were to hand. My own shirts and trousers lacked arms and legs, so they were hardly suitable. Since I'm rather tall, I could find little to fit me in the clothes trunk: I wore the Tsar's costume underneath, the Kaiser's over that. I jammed the *Pickelhauber* on top of the crown on my head. Sophia, with plenty of regal dresses to choose from, looked as majestic as ever, if rather plump. Gritz was in kulak disguise; he seemed comfortable. Both he and I vied for Rasputin's facial hair. In the end, I got to wrap the beard round my chin (warm but tickly) and Gritz wore the wig. The three of us curled up together on the floor of the wax-works compartment. We left the naked dummies in the windmill, being too tired and stiff to deal with them straight away – let them wait till morning.

We dozed.

In the small hours I was woken by – I don't really know what woke me.

I staggered up (uncoiling myself from open-mouthed Sophia and snoring Gritz), and peeked blearily through the barred window. The moon; the windmill; the silvery tracks – all was present and correct.

Then I saw a cylindrical object rolling out from under a sack of corn. It was the old man with the green beard. Mice scattered as he budged.

He was gripping a lighted taper. He chose a sack a little way from the rest, and held the taper to its corner. The sacking glowed; it caught light. The corn burnt slowly; its smoke smelled like a battery. The old man rubbed his hands together. He warmed his chin over the fire. I supposed he was just trying to keep cosy. Mice with flaming tails ran in every direction.

Suddenly there was a bang and flash, like a firework. The whole bag of grain flew up in a small explosion. I was reminded of popcorn (I'd seen it made in America). Glowing grains settled gently like luminous snow. The old man was alight.

'Help!' I cried.

I kicked Gritz and Sophia. I hurled down my spiked helmet and my crown. I stumbled out – encumbered with multiple flapping layers of garments – to assist the poor fellow.

He was wriggling on the frosty ground. His beard was aflame, stinking horribly. His coat was seamed with fire as if infested by fiery worms. I pressed my Prussian jackboot on his beard, trying to stamp out the flames. Bone crunched. I ripped off the Tsar's cloak and threw it over him, hoping to smother the fire. I listened for his breathing. I could hear nothing. Rasputin's beard was choking me: I spat it out.

Every minute the fire spread to another sack of corn, erupted in a little glittery explosion. The walls of the windmill were smouldering.

Sophia came tottering out of the carriage. 'The waxworks!' She charged at the mill door. It broke. She ran inside.

I yelled at her, 'Don't be a martyr for your dummies!'

Far from the Tsar's clothing putting out the old man's fire, he was kindling the Tsar. I stripped off the Kaiser's uniform and tried to choke the flames with that. Hopeless. That too was consumed.

At this point Gritz came to the door of the carriage. A horribly androgynous figure in Rasputin's wig, he was walking with arms extended like Lady Macbeth.

He banged his own chest. 'Gritz! What have you done?'

Sophia hobbled out of the windmill bearing a bulky human-ish figure: an unclothed dummy of the Tsarina, its face already softened and bland-featured. She dumped the figure on the tracks. She stripped away some of her own clothing – satin dress after satin dress – shrinking to smaller versions of herself like a Russian doll. Then she sprinted back into the mill again.

'Oy! Oy!' I said to the old man frazzling at my feet. I couldn't find an adequate response; my emotions had frozen. Surely by now at least he was dead and out of pain? I stood in my underwear, leaning over him, crying. A terrible desire overtook me to . . . do something . . . to remove my jackboots; I almost tripped as I hopped on one foot then the other, tugging each boot off by its sharp spur. It was very hot. I felt a queer urge to recite whatever it is people do recite at funerals. I muttered about the only religious bit I know. 'I am the Lord thy God . . . '

Sophia came out of the mill with a Grand Duchess under each arm.

'Thou shalt not make to thyself any graven image . . . '

Gritz was hysterical. He was leaping up and down, shrieking.

The rope binding the mill sails caught fire, and, like a wick, rapidly shrivelled to a long black charcoal. The sails tilted this way, then that; they began to turn anti-clockwise.

As he burnt, the old man quivered.

'Honour thy father and thy mother that thy days be long . . . '

Soldiers were arriving now. They formed a line stretching from the well to the mill, passing buckets of water from hand to hand and pouring them on the flames. Hissing steam rose, but the fire was unabated.

Sophia lurched out of the mill. Her face was blackened and her dress was charred. 'I can't save any more.'

She joined the front of the line of soldiers and chucked water hopelessly.

'Thou shalt do no murder. Thou shalt not commit adultery . . . '

Gritz was screeching, 'Gritz is to blame for everything!'

'Thou shalt not bear false witness . . . '

The soldiers – and Sophia too – were shouting at me to run back.

A strong wind had risen. The sails were rotating with a grinding sound as if corn were being crushed. The windmill was leaning, teetering towards me.

Not rushing, I stepped backwards to the tracks. Meanwhile the windmill bowed like a flunkey; it cracked at its waist. The whole upper portion, aflame at the core, toppled on the poor old man.

I remember I was weeping yet my tears were instantly evaporated by the fierce heat. I only wished I could somehow die in place of the victim. 'Thou shalt not covet . . . anything that is his.'

I walked farther away from the fire across the sidings. Sharp hot objects pressed into the soles of my bare feet. I wandered over rails, sleepers and intersections until I was standing in the countryside not far from the sea, with grassy sand beneath my feet.

Now that I was away from the death place, not in view of any living person, my emotions unfroze. I felt a ferocious, unfocused sympathy. Compassion streamed out of me; it flooded the railway and the land and the sea and the whole ridiculous world . . .

Somehow I was alive. All I could see was a glow, and the silhouette of the train, and the glinting, shining face of Lenin over everything.

8

'Actually,' said Sophia, as we lay in my bed together in December 1921, soon after our return to Moscow; she was smoking a post-coital cigarette and dropping ash on my eiderdown.

'Would you not do that, please?' I said.

'What? Oh, *that*.' She flicked the ash on to the floor. 'Actually . . . '

'I love you, Sophia,' I said in a rush. 'I mean, I don't want you to think that when I asked you not to do *that*, what I meant was I didn't want you to do *that*. Because I didn't. Not that. *That*. That was all I meant.'

For a minute, we lay quite close together (my bed's rather narrow) and gazed not at each other but at the oriel window glittering with frost like an icon.

I kissed the mole on her chin thoughtfully.

We both began to speak at the same time.

I said, 'About that fire in the Crimea . . . '

She said, 'Actually, Humph, you remember that poor old man you saw getting himself burnt?'

'Ah, Sophia, I've been meaning to talk to you about that,' I said loudly. 'No, Sophia. No, you listen to me. I think your attitude in rescuing the dummies rather than the old man was simply disgraceful. The only word for it is wicked. Of course, none the less, I still love you.'

Sophia smiled. 'You certainly know how to compliment a lady.'

'This is not a joking matter.'

'Humph,' she said softly, 'nobody died in that fire.'

'But I saw – '

'The old man was standing right in front of me in the line; I passed him buckets of water to toss on the flames.'

'That's impossible!'

'He was no ghost. He smelled of mice.'

'But I distinctly remember – '

'It must have been a burning dummy that scared you so, not a human at all.'

'Oh, Sophia.' I touched her arm. 'Why did you wait so long before telling me?'

'Ah, Humph, you were enjoying your misery so much. It would have been a crying shame to disillusion you.'

I gulped. I was close to tears. It seemed so unfair. Not that I wanted the old man to die, of course; but given that people die as a direct and indirect result of the Revolution, surely I was entitled to observe at least one such death at close quarters? My former emotions were revealed as pointless; I felt like a hypocrite.

'Why can't I have a bit of tragedy in my life?' I asked Sophia.

'Oh, I expect something tragic will happen to you sooner or later, Humph.'

Nothing was said for a while. She read a romance set in the Napoleonic Wars (I can never see the point of putting love stories in the past, it just makes them harder to understand), while I searched for my bookmark in *War and Peace* (if you must read novels, it's best to pick one which teaches authenticated historical facts). We put our books down. Our breaths misted in the cool air. On the window-pane, the frost was developing in an intricate fern-like pattern.

I murmured, 'Jack Frost.'

'What?'

'That's the frozen condensation of our breath,' I said. 'Also known in English as hoar-frost.'

'Jack/Hoar. Jack/Hoar . . . ' said Sophia. 'I think I prefer the former designation.'

'About Gritz . . . ' I said. (I'd been looking at the icons, many of them stained and torn, having been used for Gritz's Lenin collage.)

'Why is it', said Sophia, 'that whenever we are in bed together, you always wish to discuss Gritz?'

'I bet you and Gritz talk about me,' I said slyly.

'As a matter of fact, Humph, no. Gritz and I find alternative ways of passing the time.'

'Well, anyway. What do you see in him? I mean, he's not even altogether right in his head?'

Sophia thought for a while. She said, 'Gritz is a – ' She used a Russian word I didn't understand. She translated, 'He is a goblin, an imp.'

I wasn't sure whether she was praising or disparaging him. I visualised Gritz's stick-out ears and pendulous lower lip.

I recalled some Russian fairytales that Alla had told me. 'You can't trust them,' I said. 'They steal milk from the dairy and rape the maids.'

'As you must understand, Humph, trust has very little to do with love. Love is a question of mutual power.'

I didn't really follow. 'You mean . . . like Lenin's love for the Russian people?'

She lit another cigarette. 'Gritz really admires you, you know.'

'Oh, does he?'

'In fact, he's written a poem inspired by you.'

'The "Bear" poem?'

'No, not that one. This one.'

She recited the following poem with smoke rings between the stanzas:

I have been learning English
to read Shakespeare in the original.

In English, even the stupidest characters
speak fluent English.

In the sonnets, people stay still.
In the plays, they are always off to somewhere.

In England, they use the one verb
to mean 'going' regularly, or to 'go' just once –

marvellous sea-faring imperialistic nation!
In Russia, we have many different words for,

and considerations concerning, and hesitations preceding,
and restrictions to be taken into account in advance of . . .

'Pardon?' I said.

'Of course, you have to replace "Shakespeare" by "Humphrey" throughout.'

I was still baffled.

'That's what we Russians like about you foreigners . . . you Englishman . . . American . . . German . . . Jew . . . so free, so unbridled . . . '

She stubbed out the cigarette on the bed frame.

I bit my thumbnail pensively. 'I suppose, if you think about it, there's a kind of tragedy in not having a tragedy.'

She held me very tight.

Outside it was the kind of winter that is ashamed of being wintry. Clouds hurriedly dumped great loads of snow, then suddenly seized up. Short

94

icicles crystallized on eaves, dripped as heat leaked out from the human activity within, then refroze. Famine was afflicting thousands or perhaps millions in the countryside. Even Petrograd ran out of grain for a while, according to *Pravda*. Moscow was insulated against the worst of it. We had to put up with the condescension of capitalists, though. On the streets of the city, we saw them often that winter, the American so-called 'relief workers' wearing their queerly cut furs, inspecting our socialist achievements with a mixture of abashedness and patronage. Hollywood movie stars (by name, Pickford and Fairbanks) posed for publicity photos in the mouths of the Kremlin cannons. I was stopped by an American once, near the Kremlin, and asked for directions in halting Russian. 'No speakee American,' I replied, and strode away fast.

I recalled my own adolescence when I'd worked on the New York subway. How spotlessly clean it was, not like Russia. There was no spitting or litter in the carriages because all New Yorkers were proud of their city and their public transport . . . As the American disappeared from view, I felt a colossal unfocused yearning.

Russia was in danger. Yet, all through the worst of this, Lenin was in charge! He was in the heart of the Kremlin, planning the future of our country. He even gave it a new brave name then: 'The Union of Soviet Socialist Republics'. When things were going badly, at work or in my relations with Sophia, I'd think about Lenin. Somebody, somewhere, loves and controls us. We have to believe that.

9

Three men in black leather overcoats had taken Sophia from her studio in March and driven her through numerous security checkpoints into the centre of the snow-messed city and directed her along a stone-flagged corridor, a steel stairway through an oak door and an iron door into the heart of the Kremlin. She'd found herself in a dim study furnished with bookshelves, filing cabinets; on the wall, a large map of the Soviet Union stuck with coloured pins. The only light had been an electric table lamp covered with a frilly orange shade. On a desk behind that –

'Get on with the story!' I'd urge Sophia every time she narrated these events. 'I'm not interested in frilly lampshades! Tell me what he looked like!'

'Humph, *please*,' Sophia would reply. 'I am keeping up the suspense. Since you insist . . . Lenin was most impressive. His huge domed head, like something carved out of – '

'Granite?'

'Don't be silly, Humph. Granite is black. Lenin is not a Negro. No, no . . . And his solemn limpid eyes. And his voice – '

'What did Lenin say to you, Sophia?'

'We discussed politics, naturally. He told me about his – '

'Does he think the State's going to wither away in a hurry?'

'Humph! I'm a busy working woman. I really haven't got the time to answer all your petty – '

'I'm sorry, Soph, I really am. Will you forgive me?'

'Lenin is most sympathetic to modern artistic movements. "I'm something of a Futurist myself," he has more than once remarked to me.'

'Why did he invite you?'

'Ah, Humph . . . this is a secret – '

'Oh, *yes*, Sophia!'

'You won't chatter to your colleagues at work? Or at the Red Cabbage? Yes?'

'Oh, *no*, Sophia! . . . I mean, that is, oh, *yes* . . . no . . . *yes*!'

Sophia would press my hand. I'd gaze into her emerald eyes and she'd tell me anything I wanted to know.

Not till the summer of 1922 did Sophia permit me to see the concrete result of her closetings with Lenin. She invited me into her studio at the back of her house. I followed her through; my shoe soles made a sucking sound as they skidded over the wax drips on the floorboards. At the far end of the work bench sat an object the size of a goldfish bowl or a pumpkin. It was covered with a sort of tea cosy made of orange towelling material. Dramatically Sophia lifted the cloth. Underneath was Lenin's head in wax.

'Well, Humph? Your opinion, please.'

'It's . . . big. Isn't it?'

'Certainly. Lenin has a remarkably capacious skull.'

'And white.'

'Lenin is scarcely a devotee of the "sun bathing" fad.'

'He doesn't look very . . . human.'

'Lenin is superhuman . . . The head is made to be viewed at a distance.'

I stepped back as far as I could go in the studio – among the stock of wire armatures, which clinked and tinkled as I backed into them. I admired Lenin from that position. He certainly looked impressive.

Sophia tilted the head back a little. 'Thus he will appear seen from below.'

As she did so, the features changed shape almost imperceptibly: the thin lips quivered, the nose twitched, the hooded eyes narrowed – Lenin seemed to spring to life.

'Bravo!' I applauded; my claps echoed across the long room.

Then the obvious question struck me. 'Er, Sophia . . . *why* does Lenin want his head copied?'

'To stand in for him, of course. How many times do I have to explain that, Humph? Lenin is extremely busy and – at certain formal occasions – meeting foreign ambassadors, listening to whingeing capitalists and so on, he is adequately represented by a dummy.'

'I see. You've chatted with him a lot, have you?'

'Lenin is so . . . *sympathique* . . . ', Sophia drifted into a Gallic accent and intonation, as was her custom when gossiping about *amours*, 'such a ladies' man, too. His wife . . . and his mistress . . . I tell him how *magnifique* his head is, what strong cheekbones, what a powerful forehead . . . and he smiles and, "Oh, Comrade Sophia Arkadievna, I wish I could believe you. My hair has been receding since I was sixteen. They nickname me *Starik*: the old man." And I say, "But your bald dome is a sign of virility, Comrade Lenin!" And he says, in his Germanic accent – he is a lover of all things German, his family comes from there, did I tell you, no? "When I was hiding in Finland, I wore a wig. Those were the best days of my life." "No, no," I say – '

I interrupted her reminiscences. 'Do you really think, Sophia, a bald head is attractive?'

'Lenin's head is such a – '

'I looked in the mirror, this morning, but I couldn't . . . see it properly. Would you still love me if I had a bald spot, Sophia?'

'Humph! Don't be silly. "No, no," I said to Lenin – '

I was standing quite close to the waxen head now. 'I think I'm going thin – can you see it, Sophia? – right here on the top.' I tapped the summit of the skull.

'Humph! You've dimpled Lenin's pate!'

The thing I most admire about Lenin, I think, in retrospect, is that he kept on devising and experimenting even after the Revolution. He's famous as a man of action: he was also a man of thought.

It was much the same with the metro. Although the tunnelling and track-laying was well under way in 1922–3 (the sector to the north of the Kremlin was built first), the Planning Section remained in force. Naturally, it wasn't the top priority. Apart from Lev and myself, there was only one other engineer in the Section: a Sicilian-American named Mario. He was a short dark fellow with teddy-bear eyebrows and a broad horizontal mouth; when he smiled, his lips would widen but not curl.

In fact, I'd met Mario back in Manhattan, when we'd both been apprentices on the subway engineering works. We'd been – in so far as adolescents can have any deep emotions – 'friends'. (Well, I'd known hundreds of acquaintances in England and America. I was bound to bump into one of them sooner or later. A 'coincidence', to be sure – but it would be more of a coincidence if there were no coincidences.)

To begin with, I was delighted to see Mario again. I hugged him in the Russian manner (which rather puzzled him) and said what an unbelievable coincidence it was that we should find each other after all these years.

Mario agreed. He told me his story. He'd been conscripted into the US Navy, and sent out with the task force to Vladivostok in 1919. (The United States then had been half-heartedly helping the Whites.) He'd deliberately surrendered (he'd always been a keen Communist, I remembered), then been imprisoned by mistake for several months. He'd been released when the Americans withdrew, and he'd volunteered to join the Red sapper units. Now that the Whites in Siberia were neutralised he was relocated in Moscow.

'You haven't changed one bit, Mario!' I said to him.

'You have. You're fatter and your hair's falling out.'

'No, I'm not!'

'Oh, yes you are!'

We danced round each other with boyish glee.

We discussed old times. We reminisced about the fun we'd had working on the New York subway; he and I (and a third apprentice engineer whose name neither of us could recall) used to play poker and Piggy in the Middle till late at night.

'Remember', I said, 'how we fantasised about extensions to the subway network? Subways stretching across New York City . . . subways protruding far upstate . . . subways to California . . . subways across the Atlantic, linking the entire world by hidden underground routes and bringing unity and peace to all mankind . . .'

Lev, who was working at the back of the office at the time, growled, 'I want a revised copy of the central signals map before you go home tonight. Humphrey: check the triangle of forces calculation. Mario: check Humphrey's arithmetic.'

How pleasant to meet Mario again. Yet . . . now I had Sophia, some of the old affection and trust I'd invested in Mario was assigned to her. Also, I was no longer the clear-minded idealistic youth Mario had known, but a muddle-headed, worried adult.

In the spring of 1923 the Planning Section was expanded; we were commissioned to design all the stations. About a dozen new engineers and draughtsmen – mostly Russians, all looking about fourteen years old (gosh, I was twenty-four already!) – squeezed into the office. We sat next to each other, elbow against elbow. Whenever I wanted the table of logarithms or a thermodynamics reference text, somebody else was sure to be using it. Lev quite enjoyed being in command of so many people, I think. Mario worked away, ignoring his surroundings. I was the misfit.

The differences between Mario and me came to a head then. The so-called 'Scissors Crisis' was troubling the State. (The mean peasant income was declining and the price of their net purchases was increasing: the graph was a scissors shape, whence the name.) I suggested to Mario that the government should raise the price paid for agricultural products.

'What *is* this, Humphrey? Lenin's wrong, you're saying?'

'Well . . . not exactly . . . well . . . yes.'

'Uh huh.'

'I beg your pardon?'

'You're anti-Leninist. I got to report you to the appropriate authorities.'

I thought he was joking. I said, 'Ha ha.'

He called over to Lev. 'Hey, Comrade! Humphrey's saying Lenin's mishandling the Scissors Crisis.'

'I didn't exactly – ' I tried to interrupt.

'So?' said Lev to Mario.

'So I'm reporting him to you. You're the boss.'

Lev thought about this for a while. Then he patted Mario's shoulder tentatively. 'Thank you, Mario . . . Now, about those Young's modulus estimates . . . '

In March we had a public ceremony to celebrate the completion of the first kilometre of track. It began in the usual fashion, with a march round Red Square. (In those days, the Square was always hosting groups of enthusiastic celebrants. We had to synchronise our demonstration carefully to avoid colliding with the Youth Pioneers and the Campaign for the Socialist Elimination of Culinary Waste.) Flapping red flags came at the front of our convoy, borne on long poles by manual workers. Next: clerks, catering workers, cleaning women. Behind them: managers and engineers. The Planning Section (in an inverted logic, I thought) took up the rear.

How proudly we paraded! Lev swung his arms; he smiled (which he hadn't been doing much lately) and made punning gags which I couldn't understand. I told him an English joke, about what is black and white and red all over (the answer is *Pravda* – 'red'/'read', you see), and he thought I was making a serious point and complimented me on my acumen. I stepped out with pride, and fixed the little Soviet flag which Sophia had bought for me in the Crimea in my buttonhole. Mario was walking wonkily (he was trying not to step on the cracks between the paving stones) but with a swagger.

En masse we marched northwards. We swerved to the left – once we had passed the wired-off triangle of war-ruined houses and shops – over to the metro site. It hadn't yet been covered over, so to the layman it probably looked much like all the other trenches and pits in Moscow – remnants of fortifications or bomb sites. But to us it was beautiful.

Three workers – selected for their enthusiasm and ideological purity – descended the ladder. The rest of us remained on the ground, peering down at them. The snow had been cleared in advance from the track, which looked strangely dark against the banking white drifts. The workers climbed into the prototype train (in fact, a Model 'T' Ford, altered to run on rails) and operated the controls.

A coughing rumble. The train slid forward!

'Ah!' we all said, like admiring relatives around a cradle.

As the train passed below us, we saw, isolated in glorious contemplation and the rear compartment, Vladimir Ilyich Lenin. His big bald skull, dimpled slightly on top, rocked.

I had to tell *somebody*.

'Mario. Can you keep a secret?'

'No.'

'What would you say if I told you that figure there wasn't Lenin?'

Mario shrugged.

I explained everything. I passed on the gossip Sophia had told me (with, perhaps, a few elaborations of my own) about *Starik*.

'This is just between you and me, Mario,' I added.

'Oh yeah?'

'You wouldn't tell . . . would you?'

Mario ignored me.

'Me and my big mouth, ha ha.' I was terrified Mario might innocently pass on my idle chatter. He didn't seem to notice my fright.

He turned to Lev, and had a long serious discussion with him about the pros and cons of different track gauges.

The ceremony ended and we all went our separate ways. The Swiss excavator machine, massive as a prehistoric monster, tusked with a rotatable array of pneumatic drills, was pummelling into the hard earth. Labourers in striped clothing (looking to me like some species of beetle) hunched behind the machine, shovelling and heaping dirt, and tramped in and out of a network of tunnels. Up on ground level, gawpers were gathering and peeking through the barbed-wire fence; I joined them. A military detachment was idling near by.

One evening in November, I was at Sophia's, grumbling to her about my fellow engineers, when I thought of a terribly apt quotation: a bit of a poem by Browning. (I'd been forced to learn it at school.) It's not often I recite poetry to Sophia – more often vice versa – so I cleared my throat and elocuted:

The high that proved too high, the heroic for earth too hard,
The passion that left the ground to lose itself in the sky,
Are music sent up to God by the lover and the bard:
Enough that he heard it once: we shall hear it by and by.

Sophia pressed a finger to her lips. 'Shush, Humph . . . I'm cold . . . '
'Oh. Are you?'
We were in bed at the time, with our clothes off.
'I'm *very* cold indeed.'
Then I got the point, and started warming her.
I got bored of that after a while. I said, 'That's by the famous poet, Robert Browning. I heard him recite it.'
'Don't be silly, Humph. He died before you were born . . . I'm really quite chill . . . '
'No, Sophia, I heard him on a phonograph.'
She sat up with a start. 'Phonograph?'
'Nnn. My cousins in New York. We had one of them. It kept on breaking down, and we had to fix it – '
'Humph! You're just what I was looking for!'
'Thank you, Sophia. You, too, of course . . . They used to play Scott Joplin and – '
'You're a Soviet hero, Humph!'
'Me? Really? Why?'
'I'll tell you very, very soon . . . Now heat me up again, Humph . . . here.'

Two days later I was walking alongside Sophia and in front of two guards through a short dark corridor beneath the tower known as the Nameless Tower in the Kremlin. The government wanted to make use of my skills in mending phonographic equipment – Sophia had told me this much but no more. I could hear, somewhere in the distance, a quiet voice saying, 'Union of Soviet Socialist Republics', over and over again, but always mispronouncing the words in one way or another.

We entered a bright high chamber. The walls were whitewashed panelling. A very long, very shiny mahogany table stretched almost the length of the room. I gazed down the perspective: there, at the far end, was the familiar domed skull with the red beard.

Thrice I bowed. I stepped nearer to my hero. His face was big and white and unnaturally static. For a moment, I thought . . . But then the forehead wrinkled. The skin over the right eyebrow was stained with a purplish comma.

'Honoured to meet you, Comrade Lenin,' I said.

Lenin's mouth moved, but no words came out.

A sheet of ruled paper lay on the table in front of him. Using his left hand, with a fountain pen, he scrawled: HELLO. (The letters were in English, and the right way up from my point of view.)

'Er . . . hello,' I said. Then, feeling something else was required of me, 'How clever of you to write upside-down. I wish I could do that.'

Lenin's lips wobbled.

'Are you all right?' I asked.

Lenin scribbled: NO.

'I'm afraid Comrade Lenin is not in the best of health,' said Sophia. 'He's had a little accident.'

'Accident?'

'An assassination attempt.'

'Assassination?'

I could tell my echoing was irritating Sophia. She said, 'Some madwoman shot him.'

'When?!'

'Two years ago.'

Lenin's eyebrows moved up in amusement or pain.

'And you've been like this ever since?' I asked him. 'You can't talk?'

Lenin said nothing, pointedly.

'Comrade Lenin has suffered a series of strokes.'

'But . . . Sophia . . . all you *said* to me . . . '

I was peeved at Sophia for having told me the gossip about Lenin. She must have made it up, given that he couldn't communicate – or not very much, anyway. I made a mental note to tick her off when we were next alone together. I really was jolly annoyed.

I said, 'Oh.'

At last, Lenin was about to speak. His jaw struggled. His lips parted, and a queer breathy word came out. 'Pho . . . no . . . graph.'

Sophia nodded. From a shelf at the side, she carried across a tray containing some electronic equipment, and placed it on the table in front of Lenin. I recognised the machine – the rotatable cylinder, the bakelite exponential horn, the tangled wires and cables – as a recording phonograph.

Lenin made a gesture at her; it resembled a wink.

She beckoned me over. 'Comrade Lenin wishes to record his speech. He prefers not to strain himself on public occasions. His dummy will say whatever needs to be said.'

I examined the thing. It was an old Edison model, rather battered. I spun the cylinder: the bearings seemed fine. I checked the crank: the friction wasn't excessive. Then I shut one eye and peered along the edge of the waxen recording cylinder. It was heavily scratched. No wonder the machine wouldn't record properly: the playback would be drowned in random interference.

I explained this to Lenin and Sophia.

'Can you mend it?' she asked.

'Well, we need a little wax . . . '

Sophia took another item off the shelf. It was covered in that orange cloth I had seen before at her studio. It was Lenin's head. She lifted it with one hand, and, with the other, scratched some wax off the base of the neck.

Lenin raised one eyebrow.

Sophia came across to me. I ran my fingernails against hers, scraping the wax on to my fingertips. This was a tickly process, and rather erotic. I smeared the wax on the recording cylinder. Then I turned the crank slowly to make the cylinder rotate. Meanwhile she rubbed her warm palms over the slim pinkish cylinder, up and down, round and round, till it was perfectly smooth and scratchless.

Now we could test the phonograph.

Sophia put a sheet of paper in front of Lenin, typed with a sentence.

I was feeling pleased with myself because of my success in getting to the root of the problem, so I said, 'Here, let me try it out first.'

I leaned over Lenin's shoulder, and – while turning the crank – read out: 'The Union of Soviet Socialist Republics will defend itself against counter-revolutionaries by every means at its disposal.'

I reset the recording arm and switched the machine into playback mode. I heard my own voice say: 'The Union of Soviet Socialist Republics will defend itself against cow-cow-cow . . . '

I jogged the phonograph with my elbow and it completed the sentence.

I was rather proud.

'Now *you* try, Comrade Lenin,' I suggested in a bold tone.

Lenin spoke hoarsely. 'The Union of So-so . . . ' He ran out of breath.

The guards stepped forward on either side of him.

Sophia scowled at me.

I was afraid that my brashness had disturbed Lenin. I felt ashamed. I shifted from leg to leg.

Sophia leant over Lenin and, with the tip of her lavender-scented handkerchief, wiped a drop of spittle from the corner of his mouth.

'Repeat after me,' she said. 'The Union of Soviet Socialist Republics . . . '

Sophia was even ruder to our Leader than I'd been! She was patting His forearm! She was speaking to Him like a nursery school teacher!

I tut-tutted.

Lenin's mouth quivered. No words came out.

'Not quite, Comrade Lenin,' said Sophia. 'Now, we'll try just once more, shall we?'

We laboured for a full ninety minutes, but Lenin never did say that sentence completely and coherently.

In the end – as the bell of St Basil's was striking the half-hour – the bodyguards strode forward on either side of the table.

'It is time for Comrade Lenin to leave,' said one guard.

'Leaving is what it is time for Comrade Lenin to do,' said the other.

Each hooked a hand under Lenin's armpits. They lifted him (his head seemed to levitate above the shiny table top). They carried him from the room, his little withered legs dangling.

Sophia and I were left alone in the room.

We said nothing for a while. Idly, I turned the phonograph crank. It emitted – in my voice, but slowed and cracked like that of an almost paralysed man –

The Union of Soviet Socialist Republics . . . '

'Honestly, Humph! You should be ashamed of yourself.'

'It was a bit your fault too, you know. If you hadn't been so – '

' . . . will defend itself . . . '

'I don't know how I can bring myself to be associated with you, Humph!'

There was a bit of wax on the thumbnail of my left hand. I rubbed it against my trousers.

'Well, perhaps, Sophia, if you'd not been so . . . bossy with Lenin – '

' . . . against counter-revolutionaries . . . '

Sophia's face flushed. She drew herself up to her full height (and extra too: she stood on tiptoes). She wrinkled her nose as if something stank. 'You ridiculous little creature! You baby! Go and find some other woman to be your Mummy! I never want to see you again! You're as silly as the proverbial hare!'

'Er . . . Do you mean "hare" or "hair"?'

'You rabbit!'

'Well, I don't like you very much either!'
'. . . *by every means at its disposal!*'

After that incident, I avoided Sophia. And vice versa. Of course some-times we bumped into each other by accident, in the street or at a café, and instantly walked off in opposite directions.

I'd let her down. I was so ashamed. I was hoping against hope she'd forgive me. I daydreamed about our reconciliation; perhaps, for instance, Lenin might want to have another go on the phonograph, and he'd insist, 'Make sure you bring that nice young foreigner who knows so much about machines,' and she'd have to invite me then, wouldn't she?

I sank into complete anti-sociability. I avoided our common acquaint-ances at the Red Cabbage; they were more her friends than mine, really. I didn't get on with my workmates, either. The only person I could still trust was Vladimir Ilyich Lenin.

Yes, he was physically paralysed, but that showed his mind was yet more powerful and his heart even braver than I'd known before.

And we were *friends*, Lenin and I . . . well, sort of. He'd written HELLO and I'd said hello back.

I imagined his huge white face in front of me wherever I went, as if postered on a giant hoarding. (His face often *was* depicted on hoardings – which was rather confusing.) His heavy eyes would scrutinise me. His deep ears would listen out for information from all over the Soviet Union, including my most secret thoughts.

'Vladimir,' I'd say to him, 'do you think we should put loyalty to Soviet principles before our own petty affections?'

'Funny you saying that, Humphrey,' he'd reply. 'I couldn't have put it better myself.'

'Even if that means being cruel to the ones we love, Vladimir?'

'That's just how it is, Humphrey.'

'Even if it hurts us too, Vladimir?'

'Ah, Humphrey, life is full of hurt. It's full of pain. Think of all the innocent ones who have perished in the Civil War. Think of the guilty, who have suffered unduly too. Think of my big heavy head and my big agony which I can't express! Humphrey! Humphrey! Think of me!'

And his big tearful face would fade from my imagination . . .

His triangle of red beard, the flabby pouches beneath his eyes . . . would turn into a vision of Sophia, naked.

10

The world was a huge white mound of snow.

Thoroughly muffled, I strolled through the city of Moscow, relishing my self-pity.

Near my apartment building, on the corner of Salt Cabbage Alley and Milk Lane, children were building a snowman. They were clustered around the white bulk, patting it into shape with numerous mittened hands. They were granting it an icy neck by dint of determined squeezing. Two coals were its eyes. A stalk of red cabbage was its mouth.

I stood very still: flakes fluttered on to me. Little icicles formed on my eyelashes. I only wanted the children to come and pat me too.

Nobody loved me, I told myself, and nobody ever would . . . I wasn't altogether convinced of this, so I wandered round Moscow in search of . . . well, I didn't know what exactly. Statistically speaking, I reminded myself, 54·3 per cent of the population of the Soviet Union was female, versus 45·7 per cent male; surely one woman out of the 8·6 per cent surplus might do for me?

I recalled how I'd met Sophia: I'd just been dithering and she'd appeared out of thin air and taken charge of me. Working on that principle, I meandered in and out of places where women might be found. I even wandered into chapels and coughed hopefully amid the fumes of incense. Whenever I went to get my cheese ration, for instance, I'd make some pleasantry to the rather nice-looking raven-haired lady operating the cheese wire. 'I can't help but notice your cream cheese is smelling exceptionally fragrant today.' She'd smile politely, but that was that.

I did have social intercourse with one woman. I was by a lingerie shop for no particular reason, window-shopping at a display of unclothed mannikins (they reminded me of Sophia's dummies) when I saw, superimposed on a row of busts, the reflection of Alla's thin profile.

We got talking, more or less. I asked her how Poetry was doing. She said something sympathetic about me and Sophia and remarked what a pity it was that neither of us turned up at the Red Cabbage any more.

I couldn't think of any reply. She didn't seem to mind.

Well, she wasn't exactly my type – too skinny and too young. Her clothes sense was disconcerting: she wore white furs in winter and brown ones in summer, permanently camouflaged like a stoat. Still . . . she was kind. A cotton thread was trailing from the edge of her muff and curling on her bared wrist.

'You're wearing a muff, I note.' (She always wore it: I cursed myself for my inept comment.)

'Ah, the snowflake no more opts to fall from the sky than we may decide our future.'

'Yes,' I said. 'I couldn't agree more.'

Then, just as our conversation was buzzing along merrily, I decided that I didn't really want an intimate relationship with anybody at all.

For several minutes, Alla stayed beside me, facing the window, letting her breath turn to fog. Then:

'Perhaps I will see you at the Red Cabbage again?'

'Perhaps.'

'You won't have to meet Sophia there, you know. She hardly ever comes in now, except on Saturdays to set up her art . . . Unless, of course, you *want* to meet her . . . ?'

She turned to leave.

'Excuse me,' I said, 'there's one thing I've been wanting to do to you all the while we've been talking.'

I leaned close to her, and, with difficulty, using my gloved hand, tugged the loose thread from her muff. It snapped off cleanly. The curlicue of white cotton settled on the snow.

I had one other point of contact with my former Sophia-centric life. Gritz was having an affair with my concierge. (Evidently, he'd split up with Sophia soon after I had.) Anyway, he was being fussed over by my concierge, and in return he was supposed to be painting her portrait. Their romance was a confounded nuisance (or so I selfishly thought); besides, if I was lovelorn, everybody else should be too. I only had myself to blame: it was thanks to me that the two had met when Gritz had come round to assist with my packing for the Crimea.

To his credit, Gritz did his best to avoid me. But he was no bashful tiptoeing creature. As often as not, when I'd be entering the apartment building on my return from work, crossing the hallway or the landing, I'd hear his voice close by and have to dash into a dark corner until he had passed. Later, in the small hours, I'd be awakened by his bawled endearments to the toothy concierge – 'Oh, suck Gritz's life blood with your fangs, my precious!' – and her response in the same vein. Then I'd have to listen to them making love, audible through five solidly built storeys.

Even when I muted the sound (I stuffed torn bits of *Pravda* in my ears), I couldn't forget about Gritz. The icons on the walls of my flat were – many of them – slashed and dirtied like Old Masters, having been used by Gritz for his Lenin collage.

I was sleeping badly. I'd nod off an hour or so before dawn, and soon be woken by the concierge. She'd set down the bucket of hot water with a thump; then clean the stove with a poker ringingly.

She'd say, 'He's a chum of yours, isn't he, he was saying, Comrade Fraya?'

'I wonder if the water could be a little hotter in future, Comrade Nadia Gavrilovna.'

'A very famous poet, too.'

'The *burzhuika* doesn't heat up like it should, sometimes, Comrade Nadia Gavrilovna.'

'Such a genius! He's painting me in oils. And, do you know, he's promised to make it look just like my soul.'

I didn't spend all my waking hours moping. I hadn't the luxury. I went to work. The young Russian engineers swapped hearty jokes in an argot I couldn't understand, or played endless games of chess. Lev was too busy to talk.

The only one who spoke to me (apart from essential work-related communications) was Mario. He'd say things like:

'Say, you know what they're saying?'

'No . . . no, no . . . Who?'

'About Lenin. They say he's a – '

'Oh, really?'

'You bet!'

'Oh . . . quite.'

Then he'd tell me some anecdote that I'd told him that Sophia had told me. (In particular, the triangular relationship between Lenin, his wife and his mistress fascinated Mario.) I couldn't tell whether he was deliberately teasing me or had honestly forgotten the tale's source.

It was unnerving. I couldn't very well tell him to shut up. Lev made him and me sit at neighbouring desks and co-operate on projects: I'd calculate the friction forces in a system and he'd be assigned the reaction forces. There he'd be, working away, with his mouth open and his teddy-bear eyebrows jumping, when he'd come out with another Lenin story. My most effective tactic for changing the subject was to bring up the 'overt/covert' controversy.

This was the grand issue dividing us engineers. Me, I favoured covert tunnelling: you dig a hole straight down, insert your equipment and expand sideways underground. People on the surface don't even realise what's going on beneath their feet; at most they hear a rumble or feel a low vibration. (This was the technique I'd learnt in New York.) Mario and Lev were overtists: you dig a long open trench, build the track in it, then cover it over afterwards. I used to argue, 'Overtism means taking stuff out and putting it back in again,' and, 'Overtism is a nuisance while it's being built,' and, 'Didn't Lenin himself favour keeping the Bolsheviks under cover before the Revolution?' but I was in the minority.

The metro itself was advancing daily. It was comforting to know something was getting bigger and better. It was being constructed in the overtist style: a trench was dug along the north side of Red Square – as if Moscow were the front line in a battle – and the track was laid in it. The first station, beside the Kremlin, was completed infrastructurally by the end of 1923. It was boarded over against the weather, and surrounded by barbed wire to keep off intruders.

Now and then, when there was some question about, say, the interpretation of the blueprints, Lev used to send me over to the work site. Well, I was more experienced than most of my colleagues, and Lev thought the fresh air would do me good.

I remember standing beside the part-built archways of the Kremlin station. They began twenty metres underground and leapt up to ground level, like the flying buttresses of a buried cathedral. The chief site engineer had some question about the stress limit for the underpinning struts, so I descended with him to the bottom of the workings. There – while I was saying serious things about stress-strain ratios and the importance of staying well within the safety limits – I saw in the background labourers in striped clothing shovelling the hard earth. Armed overseers were prodding them. Obviously these were penal workers – no doubt thieves, Whites, capitalists, who deserved to be enslaved. Of course, I'd known that forced labour was a traditional Russian punishment, and I'd read that these criminals were employed on major construction projects; I myself had often argued (with Jock, for instance) that it was entirely proper that selfish individuals should compensate the State

110

in this way; but I hadn't realised before that they were being used on the metro. So be it. But it was not a pleasant sight: those hunched figures worming in the frozen ground. I had bad dreams.

I had bad dreams. Lenin would hiss at me: '*The Union of Soviet Socialist Republics will defend itself against counter-revolutionaries by every means at its disposal.*' His huge white skull would chase me round and round the room.

Just before the New Year, I went to the Red Cabbage. (I took care not to go on a Saturday, when – according to Alla – Sophia might be expected.)

The place hadn't changed much. It was now officially named the Red Raspberry Café – but the old plaster red cabbage still hung over the doorway, with a stencilled sign beneath it: THIS IS A RASPBERRY. The cabbage was surrounded by portraits of Marx and Lenin and assorted quotations from their writings. (Presumably the café-goers were pre-empting any charge of political dubiousness.) Quite a number of the people there I didn't recognise even by sight – a younger, more conventionally dressed crowd.

'We are entering an era of convervatism with a small c,' I said to Alla, who was sitting at a table by herself, scribbling in her elegant twirly handwriting on pink paper.

She looked up. She smiled.

She read out:

'The sun asks me, "Where are you?" and I say to the sun, "Where are you?" The clouds ask me, "Where are you?" and I say to the clouds, "Where are you?" – '

'Very interesting,' I interrupted – fearing she could go on like this for hours.

'I say to the sun, "The clouds are between us." I say to the clouds, "The sun is hidden from us." And all the while the sun is riding on the clouds' golden mane.'

'Yes,' I said. 'Would you care for a drink?'

She shook her head.

Efim shambled over and sat down at our table. I'd never known him well, and, to be honest, I'd never quite understand why this unintellectual (not to say stupid) taxidermist should spend his spare time in an artists' café. I noticed he had a mauve dormouse tucked behind his left ear.

111

'Stuffed,' he said, as he extracted the animal and rapped it on the table. 'A little hobby of mine.'

In a habitual gesture, he wiped his hands on his leather apron.

'How . . . original,' I said.

'Efim has an exhibition of his *oeuvre* here,' Alla informed me.

The three of us walked to the back of the café. Three Pekinese, a poodle, half a dozen rats and a mongoose, dyed in assorted pastel shades, were arranged on straw in a naturalistic tableau.

'It symbolises the colourfulness of nature in the Soviet Union,' Alla explained.

'That's right,' said Efim. 'Got to tan the skins, you see. The chemicals get up my nose something awful.'

'Where did you get the *mongoose*?' I asked him, using the English word because I didn't know the Russian.

'What?'

'That animal. Where?'

'My bad ear, that is.'

I moved round Efim, and shouted in his other ear, 'Animal! From where?'

He still didn't hear. He shrugged and pointed across the room. 'That's my friend, Vadim, there. He sometimes buys me a drink.'

I'm not a very inquisitive man, but once my curiosity has built up I do like to satisfy it: I wanted to know about the mongoose.

My hand was twitching in my trouser pocket, fiddling with the edition of the *Communist Manifesto* I always keep there. I took it out and flicked through the booklet, hoping by some kind of bibliomancy to chance on a useful line of advice. The *Manifesto* opened on the blank flyleaf.

Inspiration! I tore out the page, rolled it into a cone, stuck the sharp end in Efim's ear and called through it, 'Where's the mongoose from?!'

Efim grinned. 'That's lovely, that is. Every word, I heard. Every tiny word. Mine's a vodka, thanks very much.'

Efim got his drink. Alla began to narrate some fairytale about a deaf princess who fell in love with a frog – but I wasn't listening; when she asked me, 'What do you think she heard, Humphrey, when she regained her hearing?' I could only croak incoherently.

I never did find about the mongoose.

Around the New Year, I went to a rally in front of St Basil's . . . well, to be honest, I was ordered to go there. Every office and workplace in Moscow had to appoint one representative to the League of the Militant

Godless. Nobody from our section had volunteered, so Lev sent me along.

We processed to Red Square. We all stood in a circle around a candle-lit display of anti-god leaflets, as if around a Christmas tree. We wore hammer and sickle pins in our lapels. The snow was falling thickly, and the candles kept flickering out and having to be relit. Our assembly point (I noted) was just where Sophia's waxworks tent had stood.

Some squeaky-voiced man gave a yearning speech about how dialectical materialism can comfort us in our time of sorrow. Then we sang atheist hymns – full of imagery of water, light, fire, blue skies – to the effect that godlessness brings clarity into one's life. I didn't know the words, so I had to mime mostly.

Somebody else – a woman with a gruff voice – gave a lengthy speech about the good works the League was doing throughout the Soviet Union. They were retraining priests, demolishing synagogues, taking peasants on aeroplane flights to show them Nobody was up there. They planned to dispatch emissaries to less civilised peoples. She exhorted us to assist the League in its valiant efforts. A shoe box was passed round, and we all had to drop a few coins or notes in it.

Finally the male speaker announced that, as a special treat, an honoured comrade would be saying a few words.

A searchlight shone on the Kremlin walls. Dramatically, like the opening scene of *Hamlet* (or do I mean *Macbeth*?), the tall pale figure of Lenin appeared on the battlements. His electronically amplified voice boomed: '*The Union of Soviet Socialist Republics will defend itself against counter-revolutionaries by every means at its disposal.*' It took me a while to recognise my own voice because the recording had been slowed and hence deepened in pitch. The faithful atheists stared at Lenin in wonder, with palms pressed together.

I felt silly.

Meanwhile, Gritz was, more often than not, staying overnight with the concierge in my apartment building. Of course I'd have liked to move to a different place, but that's easier said than done.

One morning in early January, after an exceptionally noisy night – Gritz and the concierge had been shrieking joyfully and banging into each other till the small hours – she crept into my apartment.

She gave me a bucketful of hot water (as always in the mornings) and I, bleary eyed, mumbled a word of thanks and began brushing my teeth.

'Comrade Fraya . . . '

I turned round and frothed a little at the mouth.

The concierge was squeezing her fists together as if gripping an invisible rod. She had a black eye.

'Could you do something, please, Comrade Fraya?'

I swilled out my mouth. 'What?'

'I don't think he's quite right in the head. And seeing as you're such a friend of his, like he's always saying . . . '

I tried to explain that I wasn't exactly a 'friend' of Gritz's – more of an enemy, really – so I wasn't the right person to ask . . . and anyway, speaking from my experience, love is a complex business. It's a matter of establishing hidden subterranean connections, not just building an open link and concealing it.

She was holding some large object behind her back. She showed it to me. It was a painting on canvas, an abstract design.

She said, 'He says it's a portrait of me.'

I crouched to examine the painting. It consisted of polygons in primary colours, juxtaposed to create the effect of a crashed rainbow. I said slowly, 'I think this is what they call . . . modern art.'

Her eyes moistened. 'Gritz is complaining . . . '

I snapped the lid back on the tin of tooth powder.

' . . . that they're censoring his poems and he can't buy good paints and . . . and now . . . ' Hot tears flowed down her cheeks and dropped on the picture frame.

I shifted from leg to leg, feeling extraordinarily useless.

'I'm sorry,' I said. 'I prefer a nice Botticelli, myself. But what can I do?'

The snow continued to fall throughout January. A white screen blurred the city. The snowman by my apartment building was covered with fresh snow and lost its features. Finally it vanished inside a huge snow drift.

11

I used to wander across Moscow after work, with my coat collar turned up and my hat pulled down, relishing the gloom, the snow and my self-pity. This was around the time of the Orthodox Christmas and the churches were quite full of old people nostalgic for the Christmases of their youth. They used to wander out after the service, their greatcoats fragrant with incense.

Once I strolled into the House of Unions for no particular reason. A non-Christian version of Santa Claus called Grandfather Frost plus his Snow Maiden was installed there (one of the many Germanic traditions that Lenin had introduced). He had a long white beard and chuckled at children (Grandfather Frost, I mean, not Lenin). I said hello to Grandfather Frost but he didn't chuckle at me. How pleasant it must be to hide behind a beard, I thought. I retreated into the bad weather.

Soldiers would be marching past. Snowflakes would settle on their convex caps in a kind of halo.

As I meandered, I often talked to myself. Russians do this a great deal so hardly anybody would give me a second glance. On the few occasions when someone did, I pretended I was reciting some verse I'd learnt at school, 'The Lady of Shalott' or *Hiawatha*.

I worked. I slept. I didn't eat much. I often used to lunch at a semi-legal restaurant near my office building, run by a group of Hassidim. I didn't understand the Yiddish chatter in the background but it made me feel at once comfortable and sinful, which suited my mood. (My father, a devout atheist, had never permitted anything kosher in the house, so I was rebelling against him, I suppose.) I usually ate *kishka* (whatever that is). To my surprise, kosher food didn't taste much different from the usual kind.

When I felt the need to punish myself further, I'd go to the *banya* on the Arbat. Gritz always used to claim that Russians are centaurs: they rationalise like Europeans but from the waist down they lust like Asians. (Sometimes he'd reverse this saying.) The *banya* was surely of Oriental

115

origin. It consisted of three large brick chambers: a dressing room, a fearsomely hot steam room and a cold bath. Only senior Party members could gain admittance there, plus a few foreign experts such as myself.

I'd sit on the slatted bench in the steam room. Steam would rise from a grille in the floor, eddy, condense on the ceiling and drip on my head. I'd listen and watch. Grunting groans of responsible *apparatchiks*. Patches of sweating, ruddy skin. An old peasant in a very worn grey – almost translucent blue – robe used to hand out bunches of twigs, and the men would rhythmically hit their own paunches and buttocks like flagellants.

Amid the steam and the smack of stick on flesh, nobody noticed me conversing with imagined figures: Lenin, Papa; Jock, Yuri . . .

Mostly, of course, I spoke to Sophia.

'Love', I used to say, 'is a kind of sharing, a Communist ideal?'

No reply.

'Karl Marx has explained everything. In the beginning, each of us is a feudal lord surrounded by serfs who have no function but to wait on us, deliver our rusks, our talcum powder, our nappy-rash cream. Next, we enter the capitalist stage of adulthood, we accumulate as much as possible, exploit or are exploited. Finally, nearing our deaths, we convert to Communism, we assign our remaining worldly goods, "from each according to his ability, to each according to his need" . . . do you follow me so far?'

No reply.

'And human relations also obey the Marxian tripartite scheme. Every love affair begins with one person dominant. That was you, Sophia. Then there's an epoch of fierce competition. We're in that stage now. Finally, the happy couple settles down to a perfect equality, a give and take. Will that happen soon?'

She still wouldn't respond.

'You know I'm right, Sophia. And I can prove it!'

Out of the swirling mists, a beard would manifest itself, then the rest of Karl Marx's head would nod in agreement with me and vanish.

Sophia would float away in a wisp of steam. Only her laugh would remain, in the sound of shaking twigs. I'd stay in the steam till I could bear it no longer. Then I'd walk through to the next room and jump in the ice-cold tub.

12

The Red Cabbage was rather empty; just a scatter of artists along one side, beneath a mural depicting what might have been a battleship or an elephant. I was sitting two tables away from the arty crowd, angled towards them in such a way that I'd have the option of joining in their sociable chatter or, there again, not. For the purpose of being lonesome, a crowd of acquaintances can be every bit as perfect a setting as a steam bath or a snowscene.

I meditated on tunnel construction techniques.

Alla waved at me – with her little circular gesture as if polishing a clock face. 'Care to join us, Humphrey?' She always stressed my name on the second syllable 'Hum-*free*.'

I felt a twinge of claustrophobia.

I said, 'No. No.'

How peaceful and timeless it was. The café-goers were doing typical things, like those iconic saints who always stand in a furnace or carry a representative instrument of torture. Alla was narrating the legend of Daedalus updated to 1917, Petrograd. Katya was manicuring her nails. Efim and Vadim were singing a very slow, very mournful drinking song.

Tolya – whose turn it was to be waiter – delivered a jar of *kvas* to me. 'It's on the house.' I inspected it. A little cigarette ash was floating on the dark fluid, like snow fallen on to a river by night.

'This *is* rather pleasant,' I said – à propos of nothing in particular – to no one in particular.

'Ah, what does the sun know that the firefly does not?' said Alla. She came and sat next to me.

'I give up. What's the answer?'

Now everybody else moved over to my table too. Efim and Vadim set their hands on the *kvas* jar. 'Have a drink,' I said. They had several.

They linked arms and swayed from side to side. They began to sing again, to a deep repetitive tune like the tolling of a bell,

The rooster has golden hair, alas!
In the village of my youth.
My beloved has tuberculosis, alas!
In the village of my youth.
The rooster has big blue eyes, alas!
In the village of my youth.
My beloved has diphtheria, alas!
In the village of my youth . . .

They seemed to be making it up as they went along; there was no obvious reason why they shouldn't go on – inventing new physical features of the rooster and diseases of the beloved – ad infinitum.

I began muttering my goodbye excuses, 'Thank you for the very nice evening but . . . ' when I noticed the singing had stopped and everybody was looking towards the café entrance.

Gritz was posing on the steps. He was wearing unseasonally light-weight clothes. His tunic was dotted with snowflakes, and his black cap, topped with a column of snow, looked like a chef's hat. I was reminded of the first time I'd seen him: he'd been standing in just that place and posture, declaiming some brave nonsense. Now his lips wobbled and little bubbles of saliva came out.

He shook his head and the piled snow plopped on to the floorboards. With a tired lope he made his way into the body of the café. His boots clattered. He heaved one of the packing-case-cum-chairs into the space between my table and Katya's, and sat (surely most uncomfortably) with his legs astride it.

'Gritz is here,' he said. He was – by his standards – speaking quietly. 'Gritz will read you a poem.'

A sheet of paper appeared in his hand. He peered at it. 'This is my manifesto. It is a poem. The poem is called – ugh! It's all snowed on . . . '

He nodded sharply: his cap, lining side up, tumbled on to the edge of the packing case between his thighs. He folded and tore the paper five times. The thirty-two pieces drifted into the cap.

'This poem is called . . . ' he repeated; then picked a bit at random, and read it, 'THE CENSORSHIP OF THE.'

He dug his hand into the cap and scooped a fistful of paper scraps. He threw them down on the table near me, and arranged them in some mysterious order. It was like watching a player at patience when you don't know the rules.

I peered over his shoulder and read what he was reading out:

HOW MANY TIMES DO I HAVE TO TO THE ONLY ONE I HAVE
EVER LOVED LET ME SLEEP IN YOUR UNION OF SOVIET
SOCIALIST REPU I LOVE YOU I LOVE YOU I LOVE DEATH TO
THE BETRAYERS OF THE ARTISTIC REVOLUTION WHAT IS
CENSORSHIP BUT YOU ARE THE ONE DEATH TO WHY WON'T
THEY PRINT MY POEMS AND MY DEATH TO THE ENEMIES OF
YOU YOU YOU I WANT TO LIVE ONLY WITH THE WITH THE
THE SOVIET UN –

I was pushed out of the way. Somebody in a bulky fur coat hugging (or possibly fighting) Gritz from behind was putting his/her hands over his eyes. 'Guess who?'

Gritz said, 'Gritz never guesses!'

I recognised the voice. 'It's my concierge!'

'It's me!' Her cheeks were blotched and her mouth was twitching in and out of smiles. She whispered to Gritz, 'I've brought you your thing.'

'What thing?' he asked.

She seemed to split into two: she was taking a big black coat from underneath her own one and draping it like a cloak around Gritz's shoulders. Underneath, she herself was wearing a Mother Goose-ish dress with a ruff collar (which was probably supposed to be whatever the Russian equivalent of Elizabethan is).

She wagged her finger at Gritz. 'You could've caught a nasty chill, going out in that skimpy thing, turns into double pneumonia, you drop dead, and then what would you do?'

I realised that I was the only one there, apart from the participants, who knew of Gritz's affair with my concierge. This superior knowledge gave me a tickly, cosy feeling – the way Lenin must have felt when he surveyed the development of the Soviet Union. I began to make introductions. 'Comrade Nadia Gavrilovna, please meet – ' She and Gritz were tussling or hugging; their coats were fusing into one large furry lump.

It was really only to be expected she'd come to his favourite café now and again, but at the time it struck me as decidedly improper. In memory and imagination, characters from different arenas of one's life are often juxtaposed, but in reality it's rare and disturbing. I was reminded of the occasion when Jock had come to the café. I contrasted his ordered passion with Gritz's chaotic jumble of desires.

Gritz shrugged off his coat. He undid Nadia's and pulled it off too. Then he biffed the small of her back. I couldn't tell if this was erotic playfulness or violent assault. Nadia groaned and enthusiastically bit his neck.

The crowd began to disappear. It was rather like a scene in an opera when two characters decide to come downstage and do a duet together, so everybody else has to either slope off into the wings or freeze where they are and try to look inconspicuous. Tolya, assisted by Katya, carried a tray of dirty glasses back to the kitchen. Vadim lowered his grey eyelids – and when I looked a few seconds later, he'd gone. Alla and I shuddered and retreated, table by table, to the rear.

Gritz pushed Nadia away. She slipped and fell softly on the two fur coats. She fluttered her arms balletically. Her boots pedalled an imaginary bicycle. She was winded. She giggled breathlessly for some reason, which hurt her.

Gritz stuck one arm out like a skater – he was in the process of slipping on a wet patch on the floorboards – he thrust his head to one side, tipped forward in a hybrid somersault-cartwheel, and landed next to Nadia. He and she panted. The furs curled about them.

He climbed astride her and started pummelling her breasts. She shrieked.

'Excuse me,' I murmured, 'might there be anything I could do?'

Nadia sunk her nails into his cheek.

He banged his elbow on her nose two or three times.

She squeezed his throat.

He kicked her belly.

She kneed him in the groin.

I turned and muttered to Alla, 'Do you think, just possibly, they're . . . making love?'

Alla backed up the stairs and I followed her. We left the Red Cabbage Café.

Ten, nine, eight . . . Numbers flashed rapidly on the screen . . . *seven, six*
. . . Alla squeezed my hand and I smiled at her. We were seated in the
front row at the cinema annexe of the Hall of Unions. We'd come here
direct from the Red Cabbage. 'I'm so glad you invited me,' I said, 'I
really enjoyed that interesting travelogue about tractor production in the
Caucasus and, as for the funny film, well, when that stupid hare tripped
over the whatsit . . . it had me in stitches!' . . . *five, four, three* . . . I put
my hat on and stood up. Alla tugged me down again. 'There's one more
film.' . . . *two, one* . . . White flecks blizzarded diagonally across the
screen.

The pianist launched into something patriotic and dramatic (Glinka, I
think, or Chopin – all Russian music sounds much the same to me) and
on the screen lots of infantry marched past. Then some cavalry. Gun
carriages rolled along. Tanks. At this last sight the audience (mostly
workers who'd never seen a film before) chattered approvingly and some
of them clapped. I liked it too – but then I like all films (it's such a
clever invention: the film is made of lots of separate photographs taken
at intervals of 1/16th second or less, giving the illusion of continuous
movement – well, not quite: the carriage wheels always appear to rotate
backwards). Then, suddenly, the camera leapt high into the air (some
lens trick, surely?) and we saw the procession recede into the distance.
Everybody applauded.

The pianist did a sort of drum roll on the keyboard. The audience
quietened. The camera focused on a podium – drifted up to a lectern
– a face: Lenin's! The lips were moving so presumably he was orating,
but his voice was audible only after a second's delay. It was like hearing
a thunder-bolt and waiting for the lightning – only the other way round.

I should explain that although the 'talkie' as such didn't exist in 1924
(not in the Soviet Union, anyway), it was already quite the thing to show
a silent film along with an appropriate phonographic recording. The
sound and the picture were never quite synchronised, though.

'Long live . . . ' mouthed Lenin's lips (these words became audible while the picture switched to an aerial view of the procession), ' . . . the Union of Soviet Socialist Republics. The Union of Soviet Socialist Republics will defend itself against . . . ' (shot of a vast, waving red [well, it looked grey] flag) ' . . . rural hooliganism . . . ' (close-up of Lenin's jaw) ' . . . by every means at its disposal.'

Lenin stayed in the foreground while an army choir serenaded him with the Internationale. The cinema pianist harmonised with little trills and flourishes. Those in the audience who knew the words – and some, including me, who didn't – sang along.

As we tramped from the Hall of Unions into the snow, I tried to explain to Alla how films work. 'For instance,' I said, 'you think you just saw Lenin address a vast rally, but you didn't. What you really saw was Lenin's head, plus bits of his voice.' And the little we did hear him say was made up mainly of the snippet that I'd recorded on his behalf – though I didn't tell Alla that.

Then we went to her place and talked for a long while. (We avoided my apartment building in case Gritz and Nadia had returned there.)

Please don't misunderstand: Alla and I weren't planning to have an affair or anything. We were just good friends. We found each other very restful. I told her all the problems I was having at work, and she nodded at me. Then she narrated some Greek myth or Slavic folk tale, or said something poetic about the weather, and it was my turn to nod back.

'Let's meet again some time,' I said.

'Yes.'

'Sophia says . . . ' said Alla. She tilted her head first one way then the other.

I'd been sitting at home, quietly warming my feet at the stove and drinking my breakfast cup of tea (made in the English style), when the concierge (this happened a week after Alla and I had gone to the cinema) had knocked, opened the door with the master key, said coyly, 'A lady to see you, Comrade Fraya,' and ushered in Alla . . .

. . . who was now standing on my mat, twirling her muff.

'Yes, yes,' I said urgently, 'Sophia, what about her?'

'Sophia . . . ' she repeated.

It struck me I was a fool. I'd known, of course, that Alla and Sophia were old chums – they'd palled up back in Petrograd during the Great War – what more natural than for Alla to act as a go-between. Perhaps it had been Sophia all along who'd persuaded Alla to take me to the movies? Why hadn't I thought of it before?

'She says: meet her downstairs.'

'Downstairs where?'

'Here.'

'Good. Fine. Splendid. *Here*. Here, it is! When shall we – '

'Now.'

'Now?'

'Now.'

'Sophia . . . oh!'

I brushed my teeth and combed my hair simultaneously, taking especial care over the wisdoms and the bald (well, baldish) spot at the top. I glanced at my reflection in a gilt icon case – I looked jaundiced. I tried a silver one instead. I smiled at myself: a friendly but not obstreperous smile.

Then I dashed downstairs. I wriggled past Alla, past Nadia (who was standing by the door of her flat, arguing with somebody inside), and sprinted through the hallway and the front door.

'Will you ever forgive me?' I cried.

The two soldiers looked at me, then at each other, then shrugged. A black open-top Packard touring car – as used by very senior politicians – was parked on the pavement. Sophia was nowhere to be seen.

The soldiers strode towards me. They made me walk to the corner of Milk Alley, where they inspected my passport in a narrow shaft of sunshine. Sophia appeared out of somewhere and vouched for me. Her hammer and sickle brooch flashed. It was several minutes before the guards were satisfied.

We returned to the Packard. It was angled down at the back, as if about to shoot off into the sky. Sophia and I sat together in the rear. But there was a yard of leather car seat and an awkwardness between us. The soldiers jumped in the front and, with some difficulty, got the car going. They drove along the Kremlin wall as far as St Nicholas's Tower.

'Oh, Sophia, why – ?' I asked.

She pressed her finger to her lips.

The car turned right. We drove bumpily over a mixture of ice, sand and gravel: we were approaching the metro workings. I glimpsed, past Sophia's head, the long deep trench where the track was being laid; the few hundred workers at the bottom of it were from my perspective no larger than the beauty mark on her chin.

We turned right again, heading for the boarded-up semi-built metro station. The part above ground, fashioned from steel girders and concrete walls, looked like a row of blocks of different heights, giving a crenellated effect. It was ringed by a forest of barbed wire. I thought of Sleeping Beauty's palace.

Onward the Packard sped. The rush of cold air made my eyes water. A queer croaking noise, apparently from the rear suspension system, irritated me. We accelerated towards a wall of the metro station – faster, faster – and, at the last moment, braked sharply and (I was jerked against Sophia; she detached herself from me with little pats as if I were an over-affectionate St Bernard) swung left into a tarmacked space.

Security police sentries opened a steel double door. Up a ramp, through a corridor, into a long low space. At last the car stopped in a big square room containing (in the order I noticed them) lots of little electric lamps, a samovar, a gas cylinder, a crying middle-aged woman whose face was queerly familiar, a recording phonograph, a white sheeted bed, Comrade Vladimir Ilyich Lenin.

When I recall that scene, I think of a whirlpool. Lenin's big face was in the still centre. His wife, Krupskaya, was clutching his wrist; her head was circling around his. Everybody else in the room – the guards, Sophia, I – was spiralling out to the perimeter or in towards our Leader. And beyond this room was the Kremlin. And beyond that the vastness of the Soviet Union and the whole busy world.

Lenin was silent. Krupskaya mumbled to him in a low voice, and he responded by fingering her wrist, tapping out some sort of (Morse?) code. Every so often he'd gasp, and she'd lower the oxygen mask over his mouth and nose for a few seconds. The mask looked like an inverted funnel, as if he were pouring himself out into the universe.

Krupskaya was ugly with grief, scarcely recognisable from the photographs I'd seen of her in her prime. Her face was taut. She shifted in creaking movements. It seemed so unfair that her misery should destroy her beauty as well as her peace of mind.

Sophia and I were standing at the perimeter of the room, near the Packard. Krupskaya nodded to us. 'Comrade Sophia Arkadievna,' she whispered, 'Lenin thanks you for your valiant artistic efforts. You have copied him well.' Sophia crouched in a minimal curtsey.

'Comrade Humphrey Veil, Lenin desires you to record his message to the workers of the world.'

'What, me?'

Sophia rapped me sharply between the shoulder blades. I stepped forward three paces.

'Excuse me . . . er . . . madam. You want me to operate the phonograph, do you?' I couldn't understand why Lenin was so keen to have *me* do it. Granted, I'd mended the machine before, but surely there was somebody in the Kremlin who knew how to work the thing?

Krupskaya shook her head. Her voice was very flat and jerky, perhaps holding back tears. 'He wishes you to speak his Last Testament. He is dying. Your recorded voice is similar to his.'

'Hnn hmm,' I said, in nervous agreement. *Lenin dying?!?* It was impossible! I wanted to say something dramatic, such as: 'Lenin can never die so long as he lives in the hearts and minds of the struggling proletariat!' – but I felt it was hardly my place.

'Comrade Sophia Arkadievna, you may leave now. Lenin thanks you for bringing your . . . friend.'

'No!' I shouted. I bit my lip. Was I going to be parted from Sophia without even speaking to her? 'I mean . . . no, I need Comrade Sophia to assist me in . . . setting up the machine.'

Krupskaya nodded.

I advanced over the dove grey carpet towards Lenin. There was no colour in the room: as if everything had been shot in black and white. I slid forward in tiny steps with my arms held out, as if I were manoeuvring over slippery ice. I turned right at his knee (well, maybe his hip – the bump in the off-white sheet anyway) and made my way towards the phonograph.

I checked the recording cylinder. I blew a speck of dust from it. I held it up to the light of an electric lamp: its waxen surface seemed unscratched.

'Sophia,' I said. As the windy *f* in the middle of her name blew past my lips once more, I felt a queer happy-sadness.

As in my dreams, Sophia turned her face towards me and approached.

I wanted to whisper words of love, but instead I had to put as much passion as I could into instructions for assisting me in setting the phonograph in the recording mode. 'Hold this . . . while I hold this. Now this . . . And lift that, there. No, no, not that . . . and this, and . . . yes, that's right. Yes, that's lovely. Yes, yes, *yes*.' How odd it was to be in charge of her. While she was lowering the recording arm and I was adjusting the tension spring, our hands very nearly brushed.

Out of the corner of my eye, I noticed Krupskaya glancing with a strange slit-eyed look at me and Sophia. I recognised that expression. I too, in the weeks I'd been parted from Sophia, had peered in the same way at happy couples strolling arm in arm through glittery snowscenes. I'd sipped a cocktail of one part envy, one part admiration, one part hatred. Krupskaya supposed Sophia and I were happy lovers!

And then I thought of Krupskaya's sorrow. I wanted to say something comforting to her – but Sophia jumped in before I got round to it.

'All Russia will mourn with you,' said Sophia.

'Rightyo. I'm ready to record,' I said.

Krupskaya gave me a sheet of typescript entitled THE LAST TESTAMENT OF VLADIMIR ILYICH LENIN.

Reading out the testament into the recording horn, I made a mental note to remember as much of it as possible. *Now*, I kept reminding myself, is the high point of my life. I must forget nothing. Unfortunately, what happened straight after the recording session (which I'll tell you about in a moment) drove the memory of it from my head. I vaguely recall Lenin had something praiseworthy-ish to say about Trotsky . . . and something or another about Stalin, along the lines of: *Stalin has much power, he may not use it well* . . . and – oh! I remember – he concluded his Last Testament with: *Workers of the world unite: you have nothing to lose but your chains!*

Just as I was finishing, Lenin gasped. I thrust the recording cylinder into my coat pocket. His wife pressed the oxygen mask in place.

I heard a queer croaking rumble, like a death rattle. It was coming from somewhere behind me; I turned; the big black Packard was groaning. It was static, though. A wing mirror reflected a bare light bulb. It was absurdly out of place – this shiny foreign vehicle in a bedroom.

Lenin struggled under the oxygen mask as if trying to shake it off. The bodyguards came forward to help his wife hold him down.

At that moment, there was a clicking sound from the Packard's rear. Its boot swung open. Something jumped up like a jack-in-the-box. I thought some internal black tubing had sprung loose – then I recognised an uncoiling familiar shape.

Gritz was grinning.

Only Sophia and I saw him and we were too shocked to speak. Sophia lifted her hands in surrender or entreaty and opened her mouth.

Gritz hopped from the automobile and skipped across to the bed. He hugged – not Lenin but the oxygen cylinder.

'Gritz wants life!' he said. 'That's all Gritz needs! Just the freedom to write poetry, publish it, O grant me the oxygen of freedom!'

The guards pointed their guns at him. They didn't shoot – for fear the noise would shock Lenin, I suppose, or lest Gritz's collapsing body would break the oxygen tube.

I was dizzy with wonder and terror. I recall Gritz and Lenin locked in each other's arms, spinning in an aerial *pas de deux* (but I must have imagined that).

I definitely heard Gritz's quiet shout, 'Tell me you are against censorship, O Lenin! Reveal *that* in your Last Testament! . . . Oh, just one word is all I ask for . . . Oh, just . . . '

Lenin's mouth fell open. He seemed to be trying to say something.

His wife was bent double, her head on the bolster next to his. Her eyes were screwed shut.

Sophia and I instinctively moved side by side. We held hands.

Slowly the bodyguards approached Gritz. They moved cautiously, as if closing in on a vicious animal.

'Now, don't you move . . . ' said one.

'Moving is what you don't do now . . . ' said the other.

Their hands reached towards Gritz's shoulders.

Gritz dipped his right hand in his waist band, fumbled for something dark and shiny – a revolver – a little click like a very distant firework then a huge bang – and shot himself in the head. A thick stain developed on his cap; red liquid gushed.

Lenin jerked. The oxygen mask fell from his face. His head and shoulders swung from right to left, up and down. His wife tried to hold him down, but she was thrown about too. The pair of them tossed as if they were making love. At last, the whole of his torso heaved up and she was thrown on to the floor. Lenin fell back and did not move any more.

I realised I was crying. So was Sophia. Krupskaya was cradling her dead husband in her arms as if he were her baby, and feeding him tears instead of milk. The weeping bodyguards were leaning on her shoulders, trying to support her in the manner of flying buttresses.

The corpse of Gritz was shedding tears too. I smelled a turpentine-ish odour which reminded me somehow of the Crimea – and then I identified the sticky crimson stuff leaking through Gritz's cap as the fake blood he'd used in the mock executions there. 'O my darling Lenin,' Gritz yelled – and, pushing Krupskaya out of the way, he kissed the top of Lenin's skull.

Gritz was shot through the heart by both the guards. His skull writhed back in a reflex and his cap was hurled up to the ceiling, where it stuck.

Sophia and I hugged.

The guards pointed their guns at us.

127

We separated and began to raise our hands above our heads.

The cap fell on the phonograph.

Whereupon a door in the rear wall opened and a small man with a yellow, pockmarked face trotted forward. He chewed his moustache thoughtfully.

He spoke to me in a quiet provincial accent. 'I believe you possess our former Leader's Last Testament. If I may have it, please?'

I handed him the wax cylinder.

'Thank you, Comrade.' He didn't smile.

I recognised the man from newsreels. It was Comrade Stalin.

He nodded at me and Sophia, then spoke to the guards. 'These two may go free.'

THE EAR OF THE NEEDLE

In Russia, all needles have ears.
– Sophia Arkadievna Bellechasse

1

After the deaths we went back to her place, Sophia and I. We made love on the polar-bear rug. There seemed no other rational human response. The bed/the rug/the bed/the rug – 'love' had nothing in particular to do with it. Lenin's and Gritz's non-existences were colossal; they bulked everywhere – the more we tried not to think about them the more we did . . . so we grabbed bits of each other and squeezed hard.

When we were exhausted – it was some time in the small hours – we lay on the floor, panting, sweating, shivering, hugging the polar bear for warmth.

Sophia stretched out an arm and switched on a pink-shaded Pompeian-style electric lamp. The rug was dotted with irregular stains which, in the rose lamplight, looked black as scorchmarks. Sophia tilted the lampshade to see the blotches more clearly. They were rust red.

She emitted a swear word with lots of *m*s in it. 'It's my monthlies. How the hell will I remove the stains?!'

Nobody can accuse me of being prudish about such matters, but I do think women should keep that sort of thing to themselves.

Sophia groused about her menstrual cycle multilingually. She said in French, 'The English have landed' (some allusion was intended to the traditional red coats of the English soldiery, I believe), and she mumbled some Russian idiom which I couldn't understand.

I did my best to be practical. 'Try salt. It works with spilt wine.'

Then both of us simultaneously drew back, startled. There jumped into our minds a vision of Gritz's death – of his cap blowing up like a champagne cork and his gore spurting across the room.

'Bloody Gritz!' I shouted.

'It's my curse!' Sophia cried.

2

Artists are prescient. They – unlike the rest of us – were instantly aware that the Age of Leninism had passed and a New Age (which was to be the Stalinist era) was opening. Artists are always obsessed with ends and starts – unlike engineers, who are professionally required to assume they exist in the middle of long-term projects.

A couple of weeks after the deaths, Sophia came round to my place and we walked to the Red Cabbage Café together. By then it was spring (or so I convinced myself); the snowdrifts in Milk Lane were ablossom with little gold flowers (which turned out on second glance to be urine stains in the snow).

Sophia and I were not lovers. What we'd done on the night of the deaths, we had done – but it established no precedent. Not that we quarrelled much: it wasn't worth the trouble; nor did we bother avoiding each other, in fact we met quite often and chatted about this and that; the one activity we avoided was making love. It was quite one thing to betray Gritz when he was alive, quite another to cheat on a ghost.

We strolled along in silence. Finally I said something because I felt I had to say *something*. 'Stalin is forming an alliance with Kamenev and Zinoviev to isolate Trotsky.'

'So what?'

We entered the Red Cabbage. It was now officially renamed The Socialist Heroism Café. The plaster red cabbage was stowed under the steps. The place had been given a lick of white paint. The abstract art and the pointy sculptures (Katya's and Tolya's work, especially) had been thrown out; in their place, the walls were hung with neatly framed landscapes and portraits of muscular coal miners. The artists too, many of them, had changed their appearance. Katya was wearing lipstick on her lips instead of her cheek; her elegant tresses had been snipped off by a hair thief. Tolya was in a dark suit.

There was a general feeling – I can't pin it down more precisely – that it was time for the revolutionary exhilaration to end and be replaced

132

by a stern discipline. Yet . . . I can't help wondering if I imagined this mood in response to my lovelornness, or perhaps I'm just being wise after the event. After all, everybody knows that it wasn't till the late 1920s that Stalin took complete power and regimented the arts . . . Sometimes I think the entire Stalinist era was a figment of my melancholy.

Sophia and I settled down near the back of the café on packing cases – they at least survived from the old days. We chattered of this and that; we gossiped – who's-sleeping-with-whom or who's-been-arrested-and-why talk. I glanced around: plenty of café regulars waved or nodded at us. No doubt we seemed to them like a typical quasi-married couple: not head-over-heels in love but getting by. I watched the groups gathered around the low tables; they were nudging each other and saying the things that are said: 'Oh, Humphrey and Sophia are happy enough in their own way.' We were not.

Alla joined us. She was thin and her muff was in the process of disintegration (the hem stitches at one end were loose). Nobody said anything for a while.

Then we talked about Lenin's death, of course.

Alla said something to the effect that death is supreme, and may strike us down at any moment. (It had been reported that Lenin had died of a stroke, which was more or less correct, I suppose.)

I said I thought she was probably right.

Then Alla said that no poet was fit to write about Lenin's death, the only one who might have done so, who had had the colossal verve and courage to compress such a tragedy, was himself dead. (According to the press, Gritz had committed suicide – which was not untrue.)

Neither Sophia nor I disagreed.

'What is happening to our Art?' Alla asked. Her hands were pressed together inside her muff.

Sophia shrugged.

'I don't know,' I said, determined to keep the conversation chugging along. 'What about you, Sophia? Do you know what's happening?'

Alla was watching an oil painting of a birch forest as if she expected something to happen in it. (Personally, I quite liked the picture; it was a nice bright green.) She shuddered. 'I believe in nothing – '

'Well, negativism is – ' I interrupted.

' – except the flowers on the hedgerow.'

'Oh *yes*,' I said. I was drinking only tea but I was tipsy with marriage sadness. 'Hedges are nice, aren't they? And the birds live in nests there and go *tweet tweet*.'

133

Sophia threw me one of her special looks. She said, '*Tweet tweet*.'

Nor far from our table, along the back wall, was a tableau constructed jointly by Sophia and Efim. A wax-headed worker was 'carrying' (actually supported on wires) a steel girder, and a dummy of Sophia herself, plus assorted stuffed dogs, pigeons, and a carp, were assisting him by bearing bits of metal in their hands, muzzles, beaks and gills respectively. The thing was entitled: ALL NATURE APPLAUDS THE MOSCOW METROPOLITAN TRANSPORT RAIL PROJECT.

'Now I like that,' I said, pointing at the railworker with my thumb, and gulping the hot tea.

'It's hack rubbish,' said Sophia.

'Ye-es. But I do like it.'

Katya and Tolya joined our conversation.

Tolya: 'It's what's known as Russian Naturalism.' (I.e. what came to be called Socialist Realism a decade later.)

Katya: 'It's Stalin's taste. He is a provincial, dear, let's face it.'

'I don't know what you've all got against Comrade Stalin,' I said. They all shook their heads, dissociating themselves from my stricture. 'He's a dedicated worker. I know he looks hideous, what with his pockmarks and his jaundice, but that's no reason. And he's got a funny accent, but then, who doesn't?' I looked around. Efim and Vadim had come to sit with us. 'Who here doesn't, eh?'

None of the artists and poets were talkative, so I made a pleasantry. 'I mean, take me. Sophia's always telling me how badly I speak Russian. And I'm no beauty. My hair's thinning on top and I've got this funny little wrinkle above my nose, but it doesn't follow I'm politically unsound!'

Nobody replied.

'Eh?' I said. 'Eh?'

A bottle of vodka was being passed round; I took a drop in my tea.

'And you have to admit,' I said, 'Stalin's been very nice about poor old Gritz.'

Soon after Gritz's death, Stalin had delivered a speech to the League of the Militant Godless in which he'd quoted a whole stanza from Gritz's epic poem on the Civil War, 'Death to the Radishes'. He'd declared, 'Gritz is the Voice of the Soviet Proletariat.'

Tolya snorted, 'Stalin is making Gritz compulsory, just as Catherine the Great forced the peasants to eat potatoes!'

At this point, everybody (except for Vadim, who'd just knocked over a salt cellar and was superstitiously throwing some glittering crystals over his left shoulder in the direction of the tableau) stared straight ahead. An official-looking person in a dark overcoat and homburg hat was entering the café.

He sat down at a table near the entrance. He snapped his fingers. 'Comrade waiter. I would like a glass of plain water, please.' A pair of pince-nez rested on his nose. He clicked open a briefcase and took out a thick wad of documents.

Soon Alla, who was on waitress duty, was bringing him his water. About half the people in the café joined a queue snaking away from the man and coiling around him in a semi-circle.

Without looking up, he said, 'First applicant, please.'

'Who is he?' I asked Sophia.

She leant close to me and said, 'He's a Very Important Person.'

'Yes, but . . . '

The official was interviewing a red-haired fellow, who was responding with earnest hand twiddles. Soon that interviewee slouched off and was replaced by Alla. I listened carefully: her soft voice didn't carry across the room so I only heard his half of the conversation.

'Now let me see . . . now let me see . . . Ah, yes. I note that we in the Commissariat for Culture, Writers' Section, awarded you an increased clothing ration on the fourth of February last, why was that exactly? Ha . . . ha. That's discontinued, I'm afraid. And you're requesting now . . . ? Ha . . . ha . . . I'm sure you appreciate, Comrade, that our quota of extra food coupons is decidedly limited. We might stretch to some . . . now let me see, let me see . . . cheese. We could only award it, you understand, on the strength of your poetic achievements. You have a sample here? Good, good. A lyrical ballad-cycle, fine . . . Ah hah. Ah hah . . . A definite fault in the trochaic hexametric scheme, just there . . . No, I really cannot accept the mis-stress is deliberate. We do insist on metrical regularity, as an absolute minimum requirement . . . And over the page . . . now, let me see, let me see . . . Ha, that's better. Your anapaestic tetrameter is perfectly competent . . . one dubious rhyme to be sure in the third stanza down, but I think one may overlook that on this occasion . . . Very well, Comrade, you are permitted to receive an extra cheese ration on a temporary basis, but take better care of your hexameters in future . . . ha . . . ha . . . Next, please!'

I had another reason for favouring Stalin. He often used to be quoted in *Pravda* as having stated, 'Socialism in One Country is the way forward. Major infrastructural projects contribute to National Solidarity,' which was interpreted as fervent support for projects like the metro. Its construction was receiving extra funding and a huge influx of penal workers.

What's more, he published a policy statement (it was pasted on the wall in the metro Planning Section office) giving clear backing to covertism. It said that all overtists were saboteurs and monarchists in the pay of France – well, it didn't actually *say* that: the relevant sentence ran: 'Is it a coincidence that at this very moment the Paris metro is being expanded in accord with so-called overtist principles?'

I was jubilant. 'Look here, Lev. I told you so.'

'You told me *what*, Humphrey?'

'I insisted that the metro tracks should be laid in hollowed-out tunnels, not just dumped in trenches and covered over. I said so all along!'

Lev put on his serious face. He looked me up and down. 'Of course you did, Humphrey. Of course you were a keen covertist from the beginning. So was I. So were we all.'

'But Lev! You were the one who was always telling me that overtism was . . . '

Lev was staring hard into my eyes. He repeated, 'So were we all.'

'Actually, Lev, now I come to think about it, you too have been a covertist all along.'

This conversation took place while we were strolling by the banks of the Moskva river during our lunch break. A wild duck honked.

I was pleased that Lev had changed his mind, of course, but rather surprised.

Mario had been an even keener overtist in the old days than Lev. I'd never spoken to Mario about it (I wasn't as close to him as I was to Lev), but surely he knew that I knew that he knew that I knew, which gave me a hold over him.

I asked Lev, 'Is Mario a secret overtist? I've noticed that he often says things like, "Let's get this out in the open," or, "I want to be clear on this."'

'Did you do that estimate in your head or use logarithms?'

'Pardon?'

'Never mind.'

I flicked pocket-fluff to the duck. It gobbled it all up.

'Just suppose,' I said to Lev, 'for the sake of argument, that you – I mean – that one – were an overtist, would you – er, one – change one's mind because the Politbureau said so?'

Lev thought a while. Then he crouched on the bank and spoke to the duck rather than me. 'Truth only exists in the context of what the Party says. It's ridiculously egotistical to suppose one's own ideas should count for much. Remember Jock . . . '

Then he stood up and brushed the knee creases on his trousers frenziedly. He talked about his wife and children.

Meanwhile, the first section of the first metro line, a shuttle across the Kremlin for the sole use of troops and police, was coming into operation. Simultaneously, the north–south line construction was begun on covertist principles. In fact twenty metres beneath our office a tunnel was being dug. Penal workers were employed in large numbers.

'Funny to think of all those prisoners scratching away down there,' I said to Mario in the first week of February.

'Where?' He followed my gaze to the floorboards.

'No. I mean, deep underground. Honestly, we're allotted seven thousand forced labourers – I didn't know there *were* that many criminals in the Soviet Union!'

He seemed unconcerned. This (in retrospect) was the first indication I had of his unfortunate condition. He was working on a different project from me so I seldom spoke to him. I wish I could trace his development and perhaps so come to understand him, but all I remember are a few scattered incidents.

For instance, in the second week of February I noticed Mario was in the habit of holding his pen between thumb and little finger.

During the third, I detected him playing a counting game before selecting one of the nine volumes of *Elements of Engineering Thermodyamics* from the shelf.

In the last week, he began to complain about the light in the office. He said it was too dark and the ceiling was being secretly lowered, millimetre by millimetre, every night. Or else, it was blazingly bright and a harsh wind was blowing through. Already, he said, his colour vision had gone.

On the Leap Day, he didn't turn up at the office, and it was a week before we heard he'd been taken away by the psychiatric section of OGPU. He'd been declared insane and an American spy.

I tried to make sense of this. I imagined white-coated gun-toting orderlies simultaneously arresting and confining him in hospital. I was young then and felt that every life had an internal logic in it, like that of a character in a novel, and could be understood if only one were perspicacious enough.

'Perhaps', I said to Lev, 'it was his experiences in Siberia, his shell shock and imprisonment, that broke his mind.'

Lev shook his head. 'There's *no* explanation.'

'Anyway,' I said, 'there's something odd. Surely the Americans wouldn't pick a spy who was crazy.'

'I don't know.'

'And Mario'd never work for America, anyway. He's lived in New York. He knows what it's like! He'd have to be off his head to spy for them!'

'I don't know. I do not know.'

3

I got down on one knee and said, 'Sophia, will you marry me, please?' And she said, 'Very well, Humph, but don't be silly.' And since we didn't have a ring, I made my finger and thumb into an O and slipped it over her nose.

This proposal took place just after Mario's disappearance.

Everybody was getting hitched then (Tolya and Katya, for instance). It seemed for the best, in a time of fear and uncertainty, to be linked to somebody else.

In our case, there were more practical reasons. An anonymous (but known to be authorised by Stalin) letter in *Izvestia* had denounced foreign technical experts as 'extortionists' who should all be expelled. I had to marry Sophia to gain Soviet citizenship and guarantee my right to stay in the country.

As for Sophia, she'd fallen on hard times. Most of her formerly highly placed men friends were suffering in the Trotsky–Stalin power struggle and were no longer able or willing to help her with extra rations and allowances. Her art, which was on the boundary of bourgeois élitism versus Socialist Realism, was not exhibited in the larger galleries. She was in danger of losing her Moscow residence permit. As my wife, she'd be entitled to live in the capital and use the foreign workers' canteens and shops.

I tried to cheer her up. 'Marriage will probably be quite fun.'

'Possibly.'

'Anyway, we haven't got any choice.'

'True.'

'We're both of bourgeois origin and it's only to be expected we'd suffer in a proletarian revolution. Marx predicted it all! I do think that's some consolation.'

'Humph.'

'What do you mean, *Humph*? You remember what Marx wrote about – ?'

'Yes.'

'What?'

'How can I know exactly what – '

'What? What did he write?'

'He wrote: "It is as difficult for a bourgeois to enter the proletarian consciousness as for a camel to pass through the ear of a needle."'

'No, he didn't! . . . And anyway, needles have eyes, not ears. At least, that's what we say in English.'

'Of course, Humph,' she said pointedly, 'you are *such* an expert on sharp objects . . . nevertheless, I assure you, in Russia all needles have ears.'

The ceremony took place in the middle of March. We had to get up early that day to arrive outside the House of Trade Unions annexe by six in the morning and secure a good place in the queue. It was chill. Sophia vomited in the evergreens (she'd eaten something which disagreed with her, she surmised). The Marriage Department opened at ten. We were sent from office to office to have forms filled in and stamped. By late afternoon we finally reached the last stage of the process.

A sickly looking man with a League of Militant Godless badge pinned on his lapel peered at us. He inspected our forms shortsightedly.

'Splendid,' he said vaguely, 'absolutely splendid. Now, we do just need one more little piece of paper.' He opened a drawer with difficulty, looked inside and shut it. It slammed, which made him start. He examined other drawers. 'Oh dear. Just a teeny weeny form . . . All I seem to have left in the marriage certificate line is the . . . what do we have here? . . . tum te tum . . . the Jewish kind . . . atheist version, of course. Might that do?'

'Well . . . ' I said.

'Yes,' said Sophia.

'Good. Good.'

He guided us through the ceremony. I had to put a ring on Sophia's finger. (I'd borrowed it from her; it featured a rather resplendent fire opal.) Then we stood under a canopy – a red flag actually – which symbolised (so the official informed us) the protection provided by the Party. Finally, in a peculiar ritual, I had to break a glass (well wrapped in brown paper) underfoot, which served to remind us that the 'internal contradictions' within capitalism lead inevitably to its downfall. The official read out, 'You are hereby married according to the laws of Marxism–Leninism and the Soviet Union.'

And that was that.

'Surprise! Surprise!' said everybody. The reception was at the Red Cabbage. We'd expected just to drop in for a quiet drink – but the regulars had put on quite a party. The tables were pushed together and loaded with assorted mismatched crockery, cutlery and food. The latter was mainly what Katya (who'd organised its preparation) called 'canapés', i.e. geometrically cut pieces of brown and white bread covered with bits of fish paste or fragmented vegetables. Somebody had got hold of a pot of caviar (which tastes better than you might think). Vodka a-plenty. It was all very seemly and friendly – what the Russians think of as *Kultura*.

'Congratulations!' said somebody, waving a bottle of spirits. 'You two make a lovely couple.'

Sophia said, 'Do you think so?'

I said, 'Er . . . not at all. Don't mention it.'

We were hugged and kissed by all and sundry.

Then everybody burst into a mournful song whose lyrics were something about, 'May you have a thousand-and-one great-great-grandchildren . . . '

A rhythmical clapping and banging: Vadim and Efim linked hands and did a crouching dance on the tables, spinning together, kept upright by centrifugal force, till Efim fell over backwards and bruised his ear.

Tolya pressed on me a whole packet of cigarettes. Vadim breathed on my wife's opal ring.

'Speech! Speech!'

Sophia raised her arms to invoke silence. She delivered some operatic aria to the effect that her lungs were riddled with consumption but her heart beat strongly with a pure passion.

Then it was my turn. The only parlour piece that sprang to mind was a ditty that had been all the rage in London in my youth: 'I'm Gilbert the Filbert, The Knut with the K, The Pride of Piccadilly, A blasé roué!' . . . but I didn't think the Russians would understand it.

So instead I recited one of Gritz's poems. It seemed appropriate that he should be commemorated on this occasion.

I have said that cold is hot,
that snow is a white sand,
that our poor Moscow is bleached

by the December heat, that we have
to hide in stone houses
away from the drifting dunes, and
to wear thick overcoats and felt boots
against sunburn and sand-itch.

I have said that the Sahara
pops up in Red Square,
that the Gobi floats down the Moskva river.
I have said that St Basil's –
its cranky twisted domes –
is a variegated cactus.
Repeat everything after me.

I shall say that camels
are limousines for the Politbureau,
that the Bedouin are Muscovites
really, as are
the tiniest sand-flies, and nothing at all.

All the glasses were filled to the brim with vodka. Everybody drank,
and shouted something I couldn't understand.
    'What are they saying?' I asked Sophia.
    'They're celebrating our marriage.'
    'Yes, but what are they *saying*?'
    'It's a word that means "bitter": *gorko*. It signals that the couple should
kiss.'
    'Why?'
    'It's traditional at weddings.'
    'Why?'
    'I don't know.'
    'Why?'
After drinking the toast, everybody, all together, hurled their glasses
back over their shoulders. A giant hissing crash. Glittery splinters
bounced off the walls and twinkled on the floorboards. A smithereen
embedded in the ear of the dummy steelworker gleamed like an earring.
Sophia and I formally and tiredly mimicked a kiss.
    Again, again – and once again:
    '*Gorko!*'

4

'I crave a moon of honey,' Sophia said in Russian, a fortnight after the marriage.

I'd been reclining against the plinth of the Marx–Engels monument near the Bolshoi, on my way home from work by a very long route, browsing through the *Communist Manifesto*, when she'd come sauntering past, by chance. For an instant, I'd said to myself, 'Just look at that beautiful lady!' and then I'd recognised my wife.

I didn't tell her this. I don't know why not. Perhaps because I feared intimacy, or because I was married, after all, and it would have seemed like a quasi-adultery. There is a kind of closeness between a couple which becomes impossible after marriage.

So we were chatting about this and that.

'You crave *what*?' I said.

'My desire, Humph, is for a *lune de miel*.' She twirled her wrist busily in frustration at my thickwittedness. 'A honeymoon.'

'You mean, go somewhere with me?'

'With*out* you, Humph . . . Actually, I've been offered a display space in dear old Petropolis – '

'*Petro*- . . . ? . . . Oh . . . yes, there . . . '

'I am leaving tomorrow with my waxworks . . . I shall spend one month there, one honeyed month. Perhaps longer.'

'That's all right,' I said, flicking my chin with the *Manifesto*, 'no need to tell *me* your plans in advance.'

I wasn't very experienced at irony so I probably didn't do it right. Anyway, Sophia didn't appear to notice. She snatched the *Manifesto* from me and walked off towards the Bolshoi. Not that I particularly wanted to go to Leningrad with her (I wouldn't have got the time off work, anyway), but I did think she might have asked. She left Moscow the following day.

*

A week later I dreamt that Marx and Engels, their beards swaying, asked me in chorus, 'Why hast thou abandoned us?' So I decided to go to Sophia's house to retrieve my *Manifesto*.

Of course that wasn't the real reason. I thought that if I spent some time at Sophia's while she wasn't around to irritate me, if I gazed in peace at the familiar sights, smelt the old-time smells, and fingered the textures of yore, I might be able to summon back the early days of our love.

After work I caught the tram northwards. They'd just re-installed the tram system – it had been out of action since 1917 – and Muscovites were gazing fondly at the gliding electric carriages. The older citizens were tearful with nostalgia. 'Ah, but you should've seen the horse trams. They were magnificent!'

Me, I'd never seen the trams before (they'd broken down before I'd arrived in Russia) but in imagination I shared the collective memory. As an engineer developing a rival means of transport, I was ambivalent. Would the people of Moscow one day speak of the metro so tenderly?

I leaned on the back platform of the tram, watching the city unroll as in a film. I saw: oil lamps winking behind small windows; a platoon at ease; a shaggy cart-horse whipped by a boy; a greengrocer's displaying onions speared with green shoots, potatoes with big bruised eyes, and no red cabbages . . . The moon was full.

At the nearest stop to Sophia's house, I jumped off. The tram continued its journey. I thought it looked like a stag beetle; its antennae were plucking fireworks from the overhead cables.

I didn't have a key to her house, so I entered the back way. I climbed a few steps up the rusty fire escape, dug my fingernails into the frame of an unbolted window, opened it and prepared myself to jump through into her studio.

From where I stood on the fire escape, I peeked through a crack in the wall into the room above. A vision of decay. That entire floor had been wrecked during the Revolution and was uninhabitable. I saw, by filtered moonlight, splintered angled boards, a tilted doorframe.

I landed in a crouch. The studio was quite cold. I turned on the electric light. The place was neater than I'd remembered it: the limbs had been put away in cupboards and the floor had been swept clear of nodules of multi-coloured wax. I sniffed nostalgically: the dominant odour was the caramel and grease stench of wax, tinged with turpentine-ish paint.

I walked around the L-shaped room. No dummies were on show. I stood in the alcove where I'd once posed in the guise of Kaiser Wilhelm, and froze in that position for a few minutes.

Then I went through into the kitchen. I was hungry. There wasn't much there, just some dry grains. I made myself a gritty porridge from oats, wheat and buckwheat.

I returned to the sitting room. I sat on the pink satin sofa, the round black thing, and the tetrahedral yellow pouffe, and said, 'Sophia!' out loud several times. The pouffe flattened under my weight and deposited me on the carpet.

Next, the bedroom. I closed my eyes and opened them suddenly. Visions of Sophia covered the walls and ceiling in a kind of patchwork . . . and faded.

I examined the polar-bear rug: it was spotless. I lay down on the big square bed in the centre of the room. I took off all my clothes. I climbed under the sheets. I closed my eyes. I smelled lavender and the sour spiciness of Sophia's sweat.

'Gritz is here!' said Gritz. He was coated in sheeny armour. What puzzled me was that his head was in one piece; the only sign of his injury was a little red spot between his antennae.

'What have you done with your head?' I asked.

He didn't reply.

Fearing I might have been too brusque in my questioning, I added, 'If you please, Comrade Gritz?'

No answer.

'Who's been eating *my* porridge?' asked the polar-bear rug.

'Who's been eating *my* porridge?' asked the Kaiser, who looked just like me except his face was less wrinkled and he didn't have a bald spot (so the dummy was physiologically correct after all, I noted with surprise) – not to mention his furry brown body and wagging tail.

'And what about Gritz's porridge?' said Gritz.

The same line of questioning was applied to the topics of who'd been sitting on chairs and lying on beds.

Finally, 'Who's been sleeping in *my* bed and *is still there?*' growled Gritz, who had meanwhile become a black bear.

I was determined not to be browbeaten. 'It's not *your* bed. It's Sophia's. And I've just as much right as – '

The three bears roared menacingly.

Although I was frightened, of course, I was rather enjoying myself. You see, I'd never liked Gritz much (he coated his self-pity in so much

145

bluster and artifice) but I did like quarrelling with him. He was very good at it. And I'm not bad at a tiff myself, in my steady patient way. Yet it's no fun arguing with the dead: it's too easy . . .

Which reminded me.

'By the way . . . don't mind my mentioning this, Gritz, but aren't you supposed to be . . . deceased?'

'*All* the best poets are dead. Homer, Shakespeare, Pushkin, Lermontov, Gritz . . . They all perished in duels.'

'I don't think that's quite correct . . . ' I said cautiously.

We had a vote on this issue, but the Kaiser and the rug sided with Gritz.

'Choose your weapon!' said Gritz.

'Pardon?'

Gritz was holding a tray of armaments at waist level, the way *kvas* sellers carry their tin cups. Unfortunately the weapons were invisible. I groped. I clutched a hilt.

I got the Kaiser as my 'second' and Gritz was assisted by the polar bear. My opponent and I stood back to back. We marched ten paces in opposite directions, so were both hovering a few feet off the floor.

My weapon was difficult to handle: quite apart from its invisibility, it was long and so heavy I had to hold it at thigh level.

I feinted at him, then thrust – but he parried, and shielded himself with (an unfair advantage, I thought) a copy of the *Communist Manifesto*.

I managed to wound the *Manifesto* front cover. There was a red fleck on the booklet. I roared, 'So much for your Marx and Engels!'

But at that moment Gritz cut open my heart. Its blood-purple frilly leaves unfolded . . .

. . . and Sophia was leaning over me, hugging me, saying, 'I love only you, Humph . . . '

. . . but this too was a dream.

When I awoke it was morning. The world was cold and bright. I knew I'd lost something but I didn't know what.

5

Efim's workshop was in a slummy area in the east of the city. As we crossed the threshold of the grey building, the acrid odour of the chemicals hit us. Melted snow dripped from the eaves down my neck. Efim reminded us at length how secret this all was and how I mustn't tell anybody. Which had me wonder if I were doing something wrong. Which made me feel guilty. Which led to thoughts of my marriage . . .

My wife and Efim were striding in front. She was talking busily at him about technical matters. Soon after her return from Petrograd, he'd come round to my place seeking her out, wanting her advice on cosmeticising his stuffed creatures, and had insisted she come to his workshop immediately. I tagged along, because I had nothing better to do and because I was, after all, her husband.

We entered the operating theatre (or abattoir, or whatever the right word is). 'Look here,' he said to Sophia. He was pointing with his thumb at a carcass in a long enamel tub. I couldn't see it clearly at first because the room was windowless. Efim fumbled for a match to light the gas lamp. The first match flickered out, and he dropped the second.

Meanwhile I was enjoying the suspense. What was being taxidermatised? I imagined all sorts of creatures: a mouse; an elephant; an elderly badger with grey hair and a saintly expression (I'd say to it, 'My, you don't look a day over fifty, you're very well preserved!' That's a pun, you see.) I chuckled at my little joke.

Another match jerked into flame; it burnt Efim's finger; he dropped it, cursing.

At last he lit the fish-tail gas lamp. He turned the knob to make its flame fan brightly.

The thing in the tub resembled a giant slug. It was as tall as a bookcase and swathed utterly in bandages. It stank of vinegar and acetone. 'It's very delicate,' Efim said as he peeled away the bandages from one end of it, revealing a bumpy bruise-coloured thing. 'There! Isn't it a beauty?'

'No,' said Sophia.

147

'It's somebody!' I said. 'That's the head of somebody! Who is it?'

Sophia told me.

'Not *the* Lenin!' I gasped.

'I have the special commission', Efim said proudly, 'from the Polit-bureau itself.'

Of course. Often, passing through Red Square, I'd seen the red granite mausoleum under construction. It had never occurred to me, though, that Lenin would be mummified (one doesn't do that sort of thing in England or America), but it was perfectly in accord with Russian tradition.

I winced. The skull really did look nasty. It was purplish-brown and bulged in the nasal region. I turned away and stared into the gas flame, determined to visualise Lenin as he was when alive, not this slab of pickled meat.

Meanwhile Sophia and Efim were fingering components of the face and mulling over the possibility of painting or skin-grafting it. Their discussion was all Greek to me. I clasped my hands together and contemplated all that Our Leader had meant to me and the workers of the world.

'Lenin's head's coming out all bumpy,' said Efim. 'It's the blood in the brain does it. Can you make him look respectable?'

'You're asking me to manufacture a wax prosthesis?' said Sophia.

'What?'

'He'll need a new jaw.'

'Umm,' said Efim.

'Plus a new nose. I have quite a range of noses in my studio . . . plus a new . . . No, to be quite honest, Efim, if you wish to me redesign Lenin, I will do so, but the resultant head would be more wax than flesh. He wouldn't stand up to close scrutiny.'

Efim made a dubious hum.

Sophia smacked her palms together as if brushing off some dirt.

'Excuse me,' she said, 'is there somewhere I could wash my . . . Lenin *is* rather sticky, isn't he?'

Efim gestured through the door. Exit Sophia.

The lamp hissed. Efim folded his hands behind his back and bowed over the body. He smirked like an obsequious valet.

'Frankly,' I said, 'embalming seems to me in bad taste.'

'I've stuffed a saint or two in my time,' he said.

'Pardon?'

'Before the Revolution. Old women, mostly. Taxidermy . . . '

148

'I know. You do a very nice mongoose . . . '

'They call me in when a holy lady pegs out, get me to tan her skin and replace her vitals with sawdust. Then they display her in a big silver box in the church. Sometimes, gold . . . '

A single scream. Efim and I rushed to the source of the noise. In a workroom at the end of the corridor, Sophia, open-mouthed, was sinking to her knees – whether in (secular?) prayer or to have a closer look, I didn't know – alongside a basin containing another corpse.

'Not a bad job, eh?' Efim said to me. He patted his leather apron in a modest gesture.

This body, stretched out as if relaxing, was completely naked except for its feet. These, protruding over the rim of the tub, were encased in grey woollen socks and big black boots whose soles were reinforced with horseshoe-shaped copper bands.

Efim followed my gaze. 'I couldn't get the boots off,' he said. 'I tugged very hard, but they're stuck at the ankles.'

I recognised the cadaver's footwear.

'It's Gritz!' I said.

'Hmm,' said Efim. 'It was his last request to me, before he went and did himself in. "Taxidermatise me", he says, "just like your squirrels." He paid me in advance, of course, a whole tin of roll your own.'

The face was barely recognisable as Gritz's. It was stubble chinned and its pate was coated with a thick layer of black hair. (Well, they say it grows after death.) The skull was swollen at the top and shrunken around the cheekbones. The mummy's mouth was set in a wry pout.

Sophia was sobbing.

I spoke to Gritz in my imagination: *You cheat! You swindler. Trying to steal Sophia off me again, are you? You were never one to turn down an unfair advantage.*

Meanwhile, Efim was barbering the skull using what looked like a pair of garden shears. He snipped off the stiff hair in bunches.

'He'll be good as new', said Efim, 'when I've soaked him in alum salts and tanned his skin. Give him – I reckon, another three days in the vat.'

A memory jumped back: Gritz in the Crimea shaving his own head. Without using a mirror, he'd managed, by a sense of touch and instinct, to raze every hair on his skull.

'What are you going to . . . ah . . . do with the corpse, when it's been tanned?' I asked.

Efim looked surprise. 'Bury him, of course. In a proper coffin. What else?'

Sophia stood up. Her mascara had dripped, making her look old and haggard. 'There's really no choice,' she said coldly. 'Lenin is patently unsuitable to adorn the mausoleum. Gritz will have to substitute.'

'But . . . ' I said, 'b-b-but . . . '

'Ah, Humph, I know *just* what you're thinking – '

'But . . . '

'We'll have to give him a little red beard, of course. And shave off most of the hair.'

She wiped her hands on Efim's apron.

'That is settled, then?' She examined her eyes with a pocket mirror and wiped away the misplaced make-up with the corner of a scented handkerchief.

I wanted to comfort her, but I couldn't think of anything to say which mightn't be misinterpreted as gloating at my rival's death or jealousy at his promotion to the Mausoleum. So I talked about the weather instead. I said, 'The ice on the Moskva river is breaking up.' I realised too late this sounded like one of those profound remarks characters are always saying at tragic moments in Chekhov plays.

Efim nodded.

Sophia blinked.

Gritz did nothing.

Two weeks later the mausoleum was declared open by Stalin. Selected dignitaries paid homage to the corpse of 'Lenin'. The metro Planning Section office was required to send a representative to the ceremony who – at my fervent request to Lev – wasn't me.

6

The thing about arty people, I've noticed, is that they never say what they mean. They always use 'similes' and 'metaphors' instead. Gritz, for instance, used to compose endless poems consisting of 'A is like X, B is like Y', etc., and I'd accuse him of *kakophony*! (That's a pun, because in Russian *kak* means 'like'.)

So when, at the beginning of July 1924 I wanted to persuade my wife to love me more, I decided to do this metaphorically. I asked her – and she agreed – to let me guide her round the Tukhachevskaya metro station complex, which was almost completed then and very impressive. We would descend to the depths and stare, beyond the soaring arches, at a patch of blue sky. We would watch the Swiss tunnel-drilling machine – that gigantic earthworm – bore into Mother Earth. And, without my having to say anything explicit about passionate creative urges and idealism, Sophia would get the point.

We'd arranged to meet outside the station on Sunday afternoon at half-past two. I was there a little early. It was quite hot. I climbed on a dune of golden building sand and looked at the horizon of Moscow – red stars and gilt crosses – and a corner of Red Square (I could just see the tail end of the crowd queuing for the Mausoleum) and further down into the metro workings. Engineers I knew by sight were descending and ascending; I waved to them.

The bells of St Basil's rang the half-hour and played the *Internationale* on the automatic carillon. Still no Sophia.

A foreman told me to get off the sand heap because they wanted to use it for building. He made a rude remark about my personal appearance. I dismounted. I watched the workers filter the sand and gravel through giant sieves.

Still no Sophia.

'Gather ye rosebuds while ye may' – to quote Shakespeare or somebody. The same could be said of quick-set concrete. White lime was spaded on top of the sand and a little water was poured on that. The

151

mixture was stirred till it thickened. Then the gravel was added, and the whole goo was mixed together like fruit-cake dough. The damp concrete was taken away in wheelbarrows hurriedly, because if you leave the stuff lying around it soon turns hard and is unusable. Which (it occurred to me) was a very good metaphor for not postponing love. I tied a knot in my handkerchief to remind myself to tell Sophia all about wet concrete. What a pity she wasn't here.

A familiar figure was shambling towards me over the hillocks of gravel – a balding, middle-aged man with a twitchy smile. It was a moment before I could put a name to the face – thingumebob, what's his name, that fellow from the Red Cabbage, chum of Efim's – *Vadim*.

Vadim offered me a low-level wave which looked like shaking hands at long distance. He approached.

I tried to remember what he *did*. I knew it was something artistic – painting, sculpture, music – one of those. I'd always vaguely supposed he was quite good at it – whatever it was – because (now I came to analyse my thoughts) he looked just like William Shakespeare in that engraving you always see: the same unnaturally symmetrical domed forehead, the same mounds of hair above the ears. Also, his face was curiously colourless, more like a black-and-white photograph than a human.

'Hello, Humphrey.'

'Hello, William – I mean – '

'Well, well, well.'

'Fancy meeting you here, Vadim!'

'Yes, isn't it?'

'Yes.'

'Yes.'

'Yes.'

'Well, well, well. Actually . . . '

'Yes?'

'Actually, Humphrey, I followed you here – '

'Oh, really? Had a nice walk?'

Vadim took a deep breath.

'Suppose, Humphrey, just suppose, I'm a . . . I mean, we all have to get a living, haven't we? And my novels aren't selling too well. The critics say my historical details are wrong, my narrative is too sketchy and my characters are frankly unbelievable. Maybe they're right . . . Well, what else can I do? So, to be totally frank and not beat about the chest and get it off my bush, I'm a civil servant. For OGPU, that is. I have to seek out enemies of socialism and report them. Only, I don't know many enemies of socialism. Any, really. Most of my friends, at the Red Cabbage and so on, are writers. And – although I mayn't be much good as a novelist myself, in my own little way, I do try to . . . well, I wouldn't want to get writers shot. Naturally. But you, Humphrey . . . seeing as you're a . . . and a foreigner, too . . . I mean, I've got my quota to fill. I hope you don't mind?'

I didn't know how to react. A desire to trample Vadim to a pulp flared and burnt away. I was alternately angry/calm; concentrating with desperate clarity/distracted by every little incident.

I felt a powerful *déjà vu*: I realised I'd expected this to happen to me sooner or later. How often, arguing with Jock about revolutionary justice, had I protested it was better that innocent people should suffer than that guilty subversive elements should go scot free.

I said, 'No. Er . . . yes . . . no.'

Vadim patted my shoulder. 'I knew you'd understand.'

Where his fingers had rested, my skin ached.

'Oh, I reported the usual thing . . . Humphrey . . . I mean, if you'd rather I hadn't . . . ?'

'Well, actually . . . '

'It's too late to change it now. The report's been submitted.'

'Yes.' I felt a queer relief that my fate was settled.

Vadim breathed out. The puffs of hair over his ears shook. 'I was so nervous about telling you . . . You're a brick, Humphrey! . . . By the way, the arrest's tomorrow at noon . . . Oh, hello, Sophia.'

My wife was standing behind me. She was wearing her voluminous midnight blue satin dress and a matching picture hat. She was beautiful.

We stood in a triangle. Vadim pecked Sophia's cheek, Sophia pecked mine, and I felt duty bound to complete the symmetry by pecking Vadim's, but I didn't.

Sophia delivered a monologue about how sorry she was to be late but one thing had cropped up and then another and wasn't it a simply gorgeous day and how pleasant it was to chance on Vadim but goodbye and the two of us really ought to be going into the metro station.

Vadim nudged me. 'Er, Sophia. Humphrey has something to tell you.'

'Yes,' I said, 'I . . . yes.'

'Honestly, Humph, it's really getting quite late and I – '

'They're going to arrest me.'

'Humph?' Sophia was holding my arm and dragging me towards the metro elevator. She didn't seem to be listening to me.

153

'I'm a traitor and they're coming for me at dawn. Well, actually, I'm not a traitor, but – '

The three of us climbed into the works elevator, a wire cage supported by a pulley system. I operated the controls, and we descended.

What I recall of that interminably slow descent is absurd details. I remember the criss-cross of the cage wires, the twin sliding elevator cables, the rivets in the iron girders outside. I remember a workman, suspended by a rope sling, coating the girders with red anti-rust paint. I remember Sophia's feet: she was standing in the one spot where there was no trampled wet concrete underfoot. (She always did take good care of her shoes.)

'Do you understand?' I said. 'Sophia? I'm going to be – '

'I heard the first time, Humph,' she said in a low voice. 'How could you do a thing like that to me?'

I said, 'But I'm *not* a – '

' – a covert capitalist and German spy,' Vadim interpolated.

I explained, 'Vadim is employed by OGPU. He informed – '

Sophia swore a vast potent oath incorporating Christian terminology and anatomical functions at Vadim. He cowered against the cage wall. Accidentally, he bumped into a control lever, and the elevator began to rise again. He hit it a second time, and the cage once more descended.

Then Sophia turned her attention to me. 'Humph, you nincompoop! How could you let him do this? Why didn't you betray him first?'

'But . . . '

Sophia thought furiously. Her hands clenched and unclenched; her scarlet fingernails flashed.

'Humph, there's only thing to be done. We must accuse Vadim here, this worm, of himself being a spy and traitor and – '

'It won't work,' Vadim said quietly. 'They'd just shoot us both to be on the safe side.' He looked from me to Sophia and back again. 'I'm sorry, but it wouldn't work.

'And there's another thing I forgot to mention . . . ' He turned to Sophia. 'As the wife of a traitor, you get arrested automatically. It's just one of the rules. I'm sorry, but it slipped my mind earlier.'

Sophia shouted, 'Don't keep saying you're sorry!' She began to cry. She raised her hands as if to scratch Vadim's eyes out, but clawed empty air instead.

'Fortunately,' said Vadim, 'there's a way out. Provided you accuse your husband yourself, they'll let you go free. Probably.'

'Oh,' I said, 'that's good news, then.'

I was in a kind of dream. It wasn't that the news hadn't 'sunk in', rather it was as if I were standing outside myself, watching my reactions with a bewildered detachment.

Sophia stopped crying and hugged me hard. She smothered my face with wet kisses. 'I will never betray my darling Humph!'

I was rather enjoying this, *but* . . .

'Oh, but you must betray me, Sophia. I would lay down my life for you.'

The elevator reached the base of the metro workings. Vadim unlocked the door. Sophia and I, still in each other's arms, stepped out. (I had to turn backwards, which was awkward, like that tricky bit in a *schottische*.) Vadim shut the wire door after us, and shouted through it, 'If you want to get hold of me, I'll be waiting in the Mausoleum queue for an hour or so.' The elevator ascended.

Sophia and I kept hugging each other for a while, and weeping, and saying how much we loved each other. Getting imprisoned and perhaps shot seemed almost worth while, if it made us realise and declare how much we were in love.

Sophia repeatedly told me she'd never betray me, and I insisted she must. I got quite upset because she wouldn't take my advice, so I bumped her belly.

'Oh, Humph, how *can* you?'

And then I made amends with lots of kisses. For a few seconds, we had no thought except for the present and each other: we were blissfully happy.

I held her at arm's length. I saw her wet eyes and smeared lipstick. I forced myself to think in a longer perspective. Behind her, wheelbarrows were being steered, spades were dragging on the ground with a horrid screeching noise, the rear of the giant drilling machine was vibrating and penal workers were scraping curlicues of mud off its bit while singing a work chant in (I think) Ukrainian. 'You *must* do what I say,' I said.

I thought of a stronger argument. 'Look, Sophia, if *you* betray me, and I get imprisoned, at some later date you can always say you were wrong – mistaken, or something – and I'll be released. Perhaps.' I wasn't convinced.

'They'd never believe me, Humph. What reason could I give for having been mistaken about *that* in the first place?'

'Oh . . . you could say you'd accused me . . . er . . . maliciously . . . '

Sophia burst into tears.

I wiped away her dripped mascara with my handkerchief. It had a knot in it: I remembered I'd put it there to remind myself of something, but I couldn't remember what.

'Very well, Humph, I'll betray you.'

'Oh, of course! "Gather ye rosebuds . . . "'

Nevertheless I was defiantly loyal. As we exited from the station, arm in arm, we passed the damp concrete metro wall. I scratched on it with a stick: LONG LIVE THE SOVIET UNION!

We passed through Red Square on the way back to my flat.

We spotted Vadim before he saw us. He was about half-way along the queue to enter the Mausoleum, sandwiched in the midst of an Old Believer bridal party – the men in long beards and tall hats and the women wearing headdresses embroidered with beads in a floral motif.

He waved to us. 'What's your decision?'

I gulped. 'Sophia has decided to inform the police that I am a traitor.'

'Oh, that's good, good . . . ' He spoke to Sophia. 'I submitted a detailed account of your husband's crimes to the police this morning, signed in your name . . . Just as well you agreed, isn't it?'

She spat in his face. 'Vadim, you're nothing but a *novelist*! You deliberately hide your own personality. You manipulate other characters just for the hell of it!'

In my bedroom we undressed rapidly. My terrible fate was in one compartment of my mind, shut off from the rest of my thinking. I was unnaturally calm. When we were naked, I asked tenderly, 'Sophia, there's another reason why you must betray me, isn't there?'

'What *do* you mean, Humph?' She was the one who was nervous.

'Isn't there?'

'What?'

'You're pregnant, aren't you? You think I haven't noticed the signs but I have. The baby must be . . . ' I did a quick mental calculation, '. . . past four months by now, half-way to birth. You couldn't be imprisoned and risk the future of our darling son! Or daughter, as the case may be.'

'What are you gibbering about, Humph?'

'You *are* . . . '

A long silence. She gazed at me in . . . regret, sorrow, maternal satisfaction . . .

'I am,' she said.

156

I climbed between her breasts. Then I curled up, rotated and pressed my ear to her rounded belly. I heard a sort of intermittent rumble, which could well have been the baby.

We caressed and whispered sweet nothings. That night was the horriblest and happiest night of my life.

Meanwhile, the Moscow metro system was being enlarged. The elevator in the Tukhachevskaya station was rising and falling. The drill bit was turning. The concrete was setting. The socialist State was establishing itself.

7

I awoke early the following morning, 4 July 1924. I knew that today was special, but I couldn't at first remember why. Then I turned my face and flickered my eyelashes against Sophia's body – my head was tucked in some squishy part of her – and I remembered vaguely our reconciliation of the night before.

Second, I heard what had woken me: children's voices outside were chanting the Cyrillic alphabet. Today, I recalled, was officially Red Letter Day (I know it sounds odd in translation), a celebration of the national literacy campaign.

Third, I remembered I was to be arrested at noon.

Under the circumstances, it seemed ridiculous to be lounging in bed. I jumped out and got dressed. Then I returned and lifted the sheets a little to peek beneath. My wife's warm naked body rolled over.

Given my impending doom (which I both feared and desired), every little thing I did was awfully special. It would be a shame to waste one second. What activity should I accomplish first? I raised my arms and yawned. Well, I might as well begin by cleaning my teeth. I took the toothbrush from its place on the ledge of the Jesus icon, dipped it in toothpowder, and brushed with great thoroughness, paying special attention to the wisdoms. I swilled out my mouth into the tooth mug.

I said out loud, 'I have brushed my teeth for the last time.'

What next? I could have shaved and combed, and all that, but it seemed rather pointless. Surely I was obliged to carry out a once-in-a-lifetime act, something grand and reckless.

I gathered all the odds and ends I could find: brushes, combs, pencils, string, beans, candlesticks, socks, etc. I arranged them on the floor beside the bed to spell out, in big capital letters: I LOVE YOU. When I'd done this, I still had quite a few bits left over, so I repeated the message in Russian. I surrounded the words with a ring of toothpowder.

I glanced at my watch. It was later than I'd thought: I had to hurry to get to work on time. I kissed my wife on the cheek. Her arms stretched towards me and she babbled something which could have been my name; then she turned over and slept. I whispered, 'Goodbye,' very quietly. Then I crouched to the mound in the sheets and goodbye'd my unborn baby.

I wanted to wake Sophia and I wanted not to. I desired a tearful farewell scene, yet, to be honest, I didn't care for passion and drama so early in the morning. In the end – I know this sounds cowardly – I tiptoed to the door and let myself out. When Sophia awoke she'd understand, surely.

As I was stepping over the threshold of my apartment building, I heard the sound of weeping.

I looked behind. It was my concierge.

'Nadia Gavrilovna,' I said, 'is something the matter?' To be honest, I'd been avoiding her ever since Gritz died, not wanting to get involved in her bereavement. And I certainly didn't want to have a long conversation with her now.

'You!' she cried. 'I know all about you.'

'Yes.' I'd long suspected her of peeking through my keyhole and listening at my door – but this was neither the time nor the place to reprimand her. 'I'm rather busy just now.'

'She betrayed you! That stuck-up Sophia. I always knew she would. Your fancy woman!'

I said, 'It's not exactly like that . . . I really must dash.'

I tried to sidle past her into the street, but she hooped her arms round my shoulders. Her cheeks were blotchy and her eyes were bloodshot. She said, 'I love you.'

'You're exaggerating, aren't you? . . . Your lover is Gritz. Was. I mean.'

'No, no!' She pressed her wet face next to mine. 'I never loved Gritz, I loved you! *He* loved you. He was obsessed with you. He thought of only you. *You* were what we had in common. *You* were all Gritz and I ever talked about, you, you, *you!*'

She pushed my head against hers. Her fingers squeezed my nape. Her tongue forced itself between my lips. She shut her eyes tight and rocked her head from side to side while she kissed me; her damp eyelashes slithered over my cheeks.

At last she let me go. I broke away. I dodged past her into the street, and then jogged round the corner. It saddened me that the last hug before my imprisonment – perhaps the last one in my life – should come from poor old Nadia.

Infants were thronging Salt Cabbage Alley. Some were gurgling cheerfully, some were crying, some were wriggling on their backs, some were investigating the gutter contents with immense absorption. They surrounded me as I turned the corner; I didn't dare to move for fear of crushing them. The official in charge, a pretty flapper wearing the red beret of the Young Communist League, was holding a bunch of placards, each stencilled with a different letter of the alphabet. She set about assigning one letter per child. Then she pointed at me and told the toddlers, 'Now just you all stand near that big man there.' They clutched my knees and waddled around me. I felt like a lighthouse.

A lock of auburn hair curled rebelliously from the front of her beret. She had one dimple when she smiled. It occurred to me that I might not see any pretty women – any female at all – for a very long time. I felt a huge sadness. And then a tremendous sense of freedom: there was nothing worth worrying about any more.

How beautiful was Moscow, now that I was about to leave it. The red-brick walls shone like blocks of fire. Even the infants were exquisite: the moistnesses on their faces were diamonds, rubies, emeralds.

I saw, beyond the mob of children, the bus I regularly took to work idling at a stop. I tried to ease through the crowd – impossible. Then a daring thought struck me: *Why go to work?* Of course I had to be at my office by noon in order to be arrested (presumably they were expecting me there, and I didn't want to cause any awkwardness) but in the interim I could do . . . anything!

I had a freedom of choice. I decided to stroll round the centre of Moscow in an anti-clockwise spiral. I estimated that should take me to the office by the noon deadline. Having made that decision, I was disburdened: now I had a freedom of no-choice.

The toddlers closed in on the placards – leaving just enough space for me to scrape past.

I headed south, through busy purposeful crowds off to work or school or the Red Letter Day demonstrations. As I sauntered away, leaving my apartment building perhaps for ever, I muttered a poem Gritz had composed not long before his death.

Goodbye to you. Goodbye to you. Goodbye to
you. Goodbye to him and her and it and goodbye to

160

everybody I haven't yet said goodbye to.
Goodbye to (why not?) the lions in the zoo.
Goodbye to the people in the zoo watching
the lions about to go home for a nice
good strong drink and fall asleep. Goodbye to
dust in sunshine in a cage in a second.

I reached the river.

I perched on the high point of the bridge for a while. The water was a flickery blue-brown, like the eyes of that girl in the beret. I realised I was being mentally unfaithful to Sophia already. I felt guilty at first — but, I argued to myself, if I were never to see my wife again, it didn't matter what adulterous thought I had. A freedom.

Maintaining a south-westerly course (in the general direction of London and New York, I teased myself), I crossed on to dry land; traversed a further bridge near the Church of the Resurrection; picked my way along the bank and saw, over the crest of a ruined factory, the turrets and domes of the Kremlin. I named the towers to myself: Water Tower, Annunciation Tower, Secret Tower, First Nameless Tower, Second Nameless Tower. They looked like an array of thimbles and reels in a sewing box.

I re-crossed the river. My route so far was circular, keeping at a constant distance from the Kremlin, as if I were tied to it by a string.

A bunch of youngsters in Komsomol uniform tramped by, chanting the alphabet in a slow sing-song. I remembered myself at their age. I was a London schoolboy, experiencing class distinctions and prejudice at first hand. Then I was working on the New York subway and acquiring a basic knowledge of the tenets of Marxism. I waved to them but they didn't wave back, as if I were already removed from Moscow.

I went as far north as the Marx–Engels monument. I leaned against the plinth. On the opposite side of the square, between the Corinthian columns on the neo-classical façade of the Bolshoi Theatre, a dozen earnest trade-union officials were hawking dictionaries with enthusiasm and experience. 'Buy every word everybody ever wrote! Literacy is power! Hurrah for the alphabetical order!' They were doing brisk business.

I strolled eastwards. I passed the Chinese Teashop (it was decorated in Oriental style a century ago, on the occasion of the state visit of the Chinese Emperor to the Tsar). Now it served as a workers' canteen. I entered the chipped gilt mouth of the dragon door. The waitress ignored my waves and cries of, 'If you would be so kind, Comrade!' as if I were a ghost. In the end, I took a glass of tea left behind on a neighbouring table. How delicious was the lukewarm straw-coloured infusion – given that it was perhaps the last tea I'd ever drink.

At the back of the teashop a party of elderly Mongolians(?) were sitting in a way that gave the impression they didn't use chairs very often. They were unwrapping parcels of soft brown and green stuff, and eating the contents. They were chatting in high cracked voices. Occasionally they'd all sing together, humming a melody through their mouths while simultaneously emitting a harmonising whistle through their nostrils. They too were evidently taking part in the Red Letter Day celebrations, for each wore a cap to which was pinned a letter. I couldn't read this! For a moment, I supposed that, in my hope and despair, the Russian language had erased itself from my memory – then I realised they were displaying a different, exotic alphabet.

I checked my watch. It was half-past eleven. I had to rush to reach my office in good time to be arrested.

I caught the bus. It was diverted round Red Square to avoid the celebratory crowds, so I didn't reach the Metropolitan Transport building till a quarter past noon.

I rushed upstairs. Lev, ashen-faced, was blocking my path.

'Lev? Have . . . has anybody called for me?'

'They came. They went.'

'Oh. You mean I missed them? Oh.'

Lev said nothing.

I said, 'Er, sorry I missed work this morning. You see – '

'Get the hell out of here!'

'Lev, I really am sorry that – '

'Humphrey! Out!'

'Lev, you used to be such a jolly person when I first . . . I don't know why you're – '

'*I* don't know why. I don't know what you've done. I don't know you. I never did know you. I don't know anything except that I have to take care of my wife and children.'

I thought of a legend Alla had told me about Alexander the Great. Apparently he was on his way to conquer China. The canny Chinese sent a boat to meet him, laden with extraordinarily antique fellows. 'Excuse me,' said Alexander, 'am I going right for the Orient?' 'Ah,' replied the ancients, 'we left China when we were youngsters and look at us now! You will never reach the land you seek.' So Alexander gave up and went home.

I felt much the same about jail. I'd supposed it would be straight-forward: on the dot of noon I was to be arrested, and by now (nearly one in the afternoon) I should have been properly locked up. It seemed that getting incarcerated was going to be a messier affair than I'd expected.

I plodded back towards St Basil's. My life seemed aimless. I even began to wonder why I'd ever come to this damn city . . . but that was absurd.

I tried to convince myself that my forthcoming arrest would serve some useful purpose. To be sure, I myself was innocent, but perhaps news of my incarceration might frighten off some genuine counter-revolutionaries?

Besides, this was the end of the Leninist era so it seemed proper (if illogical) that keen Leninists like myself should vanish from the scene. Katya, for instance, had already been arrested. Ma Gold was in Siberia. Tolya had recently purchased a salt herring wrapped in a sheet of newspaper which had turned out to contain a vituperative denunciation of himself.

I analysed my state of mind. I realised that I was holding two contradictory axioms. On the one hand, I didn't really expect to be imprisoned for long: no doubt I'd soon be able to establish my innocence. On the other hand, I expected to be shot or jailed indefinitely, which saved me from having to contemplate my future. Both assumptions were comforting. Reluctant to abandon either, I focused my mind on little details instead: a smile of rust on a drainpipe . . . the stench of cabbage or charcoal . . .

Red Square was crammed with people. A chorus of elders was singing the Literacy Song. A fraternal delegation of Italian Communists was displaying the Roman alphabet. I stood at the end of the Square (on that round thing with the twisty railings where the Tsars used to execute people) and watched.

Banners stretched in front of the Kremlin. Boys were reading them out for the benefit of the illiterate. They were inscribed with maxims, such as: 'The most powerful weapon against ignorance is the diffusion of printed material – Lenin.' The longest banner stated: 'All happy families resemble one another, each unhappy family is unhappy in its own way – Stalin.' This was accompanied by two posters in red ink: 1) a family group arranged as for a photographic portrait, fronted by *The*

163

Collected Works of Marx and Engels, versus 2) a disorganised tumult of tall and small people failing to cling to an upside-down *Pravda*.

I decided that I ought to turn myself in to the security police. But I could only see the regular kind of policeman, and it would just cause confusion if I surrendered to that sort. (Of course I could have made my way to the OGPU headquarters in Lubyanka Street, but I was too tense to think logically.) I blinked repeatedly.

The crowd was bustling and chanting. I squeezed through, muttering my excuse me's, as far as the Mausoleum. It was quite an impressive building, constructed of reddish granite; the yellow cement stripe that ringed it like a hat band bore a notice: THIS IS TO BE PORPHYRY. Evidently, the building was open to the public: an S-shaped queue was snaking from the entrance.

I thought I might as well see Lenin before I was sent to prison. I pushed my way to the front of the queue, murmuring, 'I'm a personal acquaintance. He raised his eyebrow at me several times.'

A pair of guards stopped me.

'Show your identity card at once.'

'At once is how your identity card must be shown.'

I slipped between them and scrambled up the slippery steps. My way was blocked. Sightseers, gawpers, awestruck babushkas. I darted through the mêlée and came up against an oblong glass box. It contained a person – no, a mannikin – no, a corpse – no, a peculiar dummy with gaudily made-up cheeks and lips. I twisted my head to see the figure face to face.

The creature had a beard and a bald pate like Lenin, but the rest of his face belonged to Gritz. I checked the ears and the nostrils against my memory. There was no doubt.

I was outraged by the substitution.

'Why are you all worshipping this dummy?' I said out loud, drawing courage from the knowledge that I was bound to be arrested soon anyway. 'This man didn't help the Soviet Union much! Most of his work was fake, if you want *my* opinion! He used up his energy sleeping with my wife!'

I saw the funny side of the deception. I chuckled. I guffawed. I wheezed and choked with laughter. I bent over double. I slapped my thighs. I rolled on the floor, giggling helplessly among the high heels and jackboots . . . till the guards hauled me away.

As I was dragged out of the Mausoleum and into a waiting police van, I saw the woman with the beret and the dimple. She was lining up her

164

charges in alphabetical order. Each was carrying a letter placard. One little boy, the smallest of them all, was clutching an upside-down placard inscribed with the letter *yat*, which had been abolished in the new Soviet orthographical system. He was hunched on the pavement, weeping helplessly.

8

'Now just repeat your . . . story nice and slowly,' said the policeman. He was a (war?) cripple with a wooden leg and a friendly smile. His accent was quite posh, considering. 'My assistant here will write it all down.'

I sat up straight on the hard chair. 'Well, as a matter of fact,' I said, 'actually . . . '

He leaned forward and spoke quietly. 'Are you comfortable, Mister Veil.' He pronounced my surname in the English manner, as if spelt *Vale*, which always irritates me.

'You're supposed to say it like "*File*", actually,' I said. 'It means a kind of flower in German.'

'Aha! So you admit it!'

'I beg your pardon?'

'How long have you been spying for Germany, Herr Veil?' (He got the pronunciation right.)

'I've never spied for Germany, in fact.'

'Oh? Which country have you spied for?'

'None. None at all.'

'If you were a spy, would you deny it?'

'I suppose so.'

'So you admit your denial corresponds in every single detail to that which would be furnished by a trained German spy?'

'Yes, but . . . '

'Ah! How come you know so much about the dissimulation techniques of German subversive agents? Come, come, "Comrade" Herr Veil, there is no point maintaining this pretence.'

'But . . . but . . . '

The policeman smiled at me again. He ordered his assistant, a young, studious-looking fellow, to bring me a glass of tea from the samovar.

'Of course, Humphrey, of course. You are completely innocent and free to leave here – '

I rose from my chair.

166

' – but first you might care to examine the evidence against you.'

He extracted some handwritten papers from a file. I gulped the scalding tea.

'Ah yes,' he said. 'Ah yes. Here we have – what is it? – affidavits furnished by concerned citizens, patriots, who inform us that . . . ah, ah . . . One of the accusers is your wife.' He glanced up at me. 'You're not surprised at that? How odd. Well, wives often do . . . Husbands also, of course. To be frank, Veil, we usually ignore such marital accusations. In the old days, soon after the Revolution, we were more ruthless, of course . . . and they say the subversive arrest quota is due to rise again . . . but just at the moment we are behaving with remarkable tolerance. However, your extraordinary behaviour at the Mausoleum – you don't deny you insulted Lenin, do you? – gives us no choice but to pull you in.

'And I have here . . . '

He pushed a photograph across the table. It showed the slogan I'd scrawled in the damp concrete by the metro station: LONG LIVE THE SOVIET UNION!

'Yes,' I said, 'I'm very patriotic.'

'Indeed? How dare you characterise the Union of Soviet Socialist Republics as a vegetable!'

Now I looked more closely, the initial letter of the last word did appear to be an O.

'Ah, well,' I said. 'Ah. You see . . . just like an onion . . . Russia has many layers . . . and when enemies attack it, they inevitably cry . . . '

He frowned. He handed me another photograph. This showed a dummy formerly in Sophia's waxworks, the one for which I had been the model.

'This isn't me!' I said.

'It looks like you.'

'But it's wearing full German dress uniform!'

'Indeed?'

'It's Kaiser Wilhelm!'

'Who just happens to bear a remarkable resemblance to Humphrey Veil?'

'Well, that's because – '

He grabbed my glass of tea and threw it back over his head. It smashed. The dark tea leaves spattered on the pale wall.

He yelled, 'You liar! Kaiser Wilhelm was a short dark man. This is the most ludicrous – '

Meanwhile the assistant was setting a phonograph on the table. He lowered the playing arm and wound the crank. The machine said, 'Stalin is not to be trusted with much power . . . '

'That's what Lenin said!' I exclaimed. 'In his Last Testament.'

'It sounds like your voice.'

'Well, our accents are similar, so – '

The policeman breathed in and out several times. 'Let's get this straight. The photograph of you in German uniform isn't really you at all but the Kaiser, who just happens to look like you, and the recording of you denouncing Comrade Stalin is really spoken by Lenin, who just happens to speak like you?'

'I'm sorry,' I said. 'I know it doesn't sound very convincing.'

The interviewer nodded to his assistant, who left the room.

'And in conclusion,' said the policeman, 'to wrap up our case against you, our *pièce de résistance* . . . '

He beckoned to his assistant, who stood up and moved round to my side of the table. The assistant lifted me up by my lapels till my eyes were an inch from his chin. He took off his glasses and tucked them in his handkerchief pocket.

The phonograph was playing the denunciation of Stalin over and over again, and the picture of the Kaiser dummy was projected on the wall.

I will not describe what happened next. Suffice it to say that I soon stated a complete and elaborate confession.

Editor's Note

Parts IV-XLVII of the memoirs have not been published in this volume, since the manuscript is not altogether legible, and the subject matter is of little general interest, and is in any case factually unreliable, given the author's limited viewpoint, and is besides well known from numerous previously published accounts.

Professor Heinz Deutsch,
Department of Anglistics,
Friedrich-Engels Universität,
Berlin, DDR

HEIL HUMPHREY

An autobiography can never be
completed.

          – Humphrey Veil

1

This is a happy ending, I suppose. Back in my youth when I read English bourgeois thrillers, they always used to conclude with the hero safe in his armchair, surrounded by fleecy slippers and mugs of cocoa, gazing smugly into the middle distance. And indeed my slippers are fur-lined; my valets will supply me with any drink I want (within reason); I'm looking at nothing in particular.

I'm writing the last few bits of my autobiography. The pad of paper is propped on my knee. At my side is a heap of five hundred pages – the chapters describing my experiences in the Siberian *gulag* – which you, presumably, have just read. I don't know about you, but I'm exhausted. It's evening. Big moths batter at the bars on my window.

Oh well, I'd better polish off my Life. Here goes . . .

2

About a fortnight after I'd been released from Siberia, in the spring of 1939, I turned up on the quayside at Yalta. Just that morning, for the first time in fifteen years, I'd been shaved, barbered, sprayed with disinfectant, sprinkled with delousing powder and eau de cologne, dressed up in the clothes I'd been wearing on the day they'd arrested me (wherever had they stored them, and why on earth did they bother?) which were naturally now too baggy so I had to keep my hands in the pockets of my trousers to stop them slipping down. The balmy air of the Crimea massaged my cheeks. I smelled citrus blossom and the sea. I had a view of a glowing sunset, a hill with a twisty olive tree, orange and violet reflections in the harbour. 'Isn't this pretty and where are you taking me?' I asked the guards on either side who were pointing their machine-guns at me. They didn't reply.

Well, obviously they weren't going to execute me – not after all the trouble they'd taken – but I was scared anyway. I made polite nervy conversation with the guards. 'Do you come here often? . . . Do you approve of the suppression of the kulaks? . . . Nice weather, isn't it? . . . '

We moved down the concrete slope towards the quay. A big ship was being unloaded of its cargo of military equipment. Dockers shouted and manoeuvred wooden cases. A crane was lifting an armoured troop carrier from the hold; a tank was being lowered on to the dock. A sheet of steel plating, the size of the wall of a house, was suspended in mid-air. In it, Yalta was duplicated in blurry reflection. The red sun shone from its upper edge. A platoon of the Red Army was marching down its middle. A familiar figure, shabby and skinny, was staring straight out of it. Me! I could scarcely recognise myself: it was fifteen years since I'd last looked in a mirror. Most of my hair had gone missing; my nose was broken; my face was so wrinkled it looked like a portrait which a child had scrawled over with a crayon . . . A pulley rotated and the steel plate turned through a small angle: my reflection slipped out of sight.

The commanding officer barked an order; one of the guards poked me with his gun. Dutifully I trotted after the officer, and the rest of the platoon marched behind me along the pier.

A destroyer was moored here. Its near side was camouflage-painted in dark blue and grey; the tips of sun barrels stuck out from the deck far overhead, like surf. I advanced shakily through the soft air, like swimming far underwater.

A steel gangway projected from the destroyer on to the pier. There was some bustle inside the ship; then a dozen foreign soldiers marched on to dry land. They were followed by a pale thin man, dressed not unlike myself. He stared at the dock and the sunset. He looked bewildered and very ill.

The Colonel who was in charge of me stepped forward and shook the pale man's hand. 'The Soviet Union salutes your heroism!'

I waved at the newcomer and tipped my homburg – then rapidly thrust my hands back in my pockets.

The foreign troops formed lines on either side of me. Their commander gestured I should mount the gangway.

'Why, sir? Where are you taking me to?' I asked him in Russian then English. He didn't answer.

The pale man turned to face me. He addressed me in queerly accented Russian. 'You are my *doppelgänger*, it seems. I have you to thank for my freedom, and vice versa. How odd that our respective countries should wish for better relations after all we two have done to promote enmity!' He smiled drily. 'They are exchanging us. I am being returned to the Soviet Union and you are being sent back to the country you spied for.'

'But . . . ' I said, 'which country's that?'

A distant ship blew its steam horn, so I didn't hear what he replied.

A foreign soldier tapped my shoulder with the butt of his gun. I trudged up the gangway into the destroyer. I passed beneath a flag belonging to no nation I recognised: it bore a crooked cross.

3

Well, here I am, three months later, in my commodious room in a suburb of Berlin. It's furnished with solid, nobbly, middle-class furniture. The wallpaper is mud coloured. The ceiling lamp is a very bright bare electric bulb. My two valets lounge on my bed, chatting to each other and pointing their guns at me. I'm seated at my desk, putting the finishing touches to my autobiography (though an autobiography can never be completed, really).

My valets are under orders to give me anything that doesn't cost too much. I have quite a collection of Sherlock Holmes stories and packets of cigarettes. A vase of fresh-cut flowers stands on my desk.

I'm even permitted to gaze through the barred window at the street below. Women in triangular hats hurry to market. A car rumbles over the cobbles. A boy whips a hoop . . . If I pretend the advertising hoardings carry revolutionary slogans and the swastikas are hammers and sickles instead, I could be back in . . . but I'm bored with make-believe . . .

The valets say little to me, but I often talk at them anyway. I say, 'I am glad to be back in the Fatherland.' (You see? My years in prison have taught me irony, if nothing else.) I remember, when I was a child, Papa's toothless mouth hovering over me and whispering a sentence that Karl Marx had declaimed at him when they'd been working together in the old *Rheinische Zeitung* days; it was a slogan from the botched revolution of 1848: 'The Salvation of the World Will Come from Germany.' I recite this to my valets and they ignore me.

I'm coming round to the view that I'm a German. True, I've never been in the country before, and I speak the language rather badly – but after all my parents were born here, my father's father was a rabbi right here in Berlin, and so was my great-grandfather before him. I've even discovered I have a taste for German food – the kind I used to be fed in my childhood. I only have to ask my valets politely and I'm served bratwurst with mustard, or red cabbage chopped and boiled with brown sugar and vinegar.

I feel sorry for the valets. My company must fatigue them. They pass the time by playing rummy and mumbling dirty jokes. They leave the wireless permanently on. Somebody with a harsh snappy voice is often

174

denouncing Jewish Bolsheviks and Bolshevik Jews. 'That's me!' I declare proudly. 'He's talking about me!' Then I start crying and the valets give me an injection and put me to bed.

A hundred soldiers in black and red uniforms were marching up and down the aisles of the vast new art deco Parsifal Kinema in the centre of Berlin tootling trumpets and banging drums yesterday evening. I didn't recognise the tune (I'm not very musical, you know) but it certainly was jolly and martial. I was one of the guests of honour on the special temporary podium at the back of the stalls. My valets were posted behind me; I could feel the barrels of their revolvers jutting into the small of my back. I was flanked by much-bemedalled officers and important-looking bored civilians in rigid hats. The audience – mostly black-shirted youths – filed in. I glanced up at the high domed concrete ceiling: quite an impressive feat of civil engineering, really. Ceremonial bunting was nailed along the arches, and it continued down both sides of the stage, twined around cement caryatids representing, I think, Teutonic gods. Wotan had a swastika stuck over his groin, figleaf fashion.

The Kinema darkened. The projector, just behind the podium, hummed. A cone of light passed not far above my head – bits of dust and hairs wandered in it – and shone on the screen. The audience applauded as the title flickered in giant scarlet letters:

HUMPHREY VEIL:
ÜBERMENSCH

The credits rolled.

The film was quite fun, really. It was the kind they call a 'talkie': the sound was perfectly synchronised with the picture. I wonder how they do it.

The storyline was about me! You see, soon after I'd arrived in Germany, a patient plump man had questioned me about my past, and – well, I've been interrogated so often – I'd told him everything I could remember. And I've got a sneaking feeling my valets have been reading my memoirs while I'm asleep – the pages are often mussed in the mornings . . . Of course, the director fictionalised my life a little . . .

'Humphrey Veil' is a tall slim blond fellow (played by a young actor named Heinz Deutsch). He is tempted in his youth by the multi-racial fleshpots of London and New York, but (with lots of close ups of lip-biting and brow-furrowing) he resists all that and becomes a German patriot. He is determined to overthrow Bolshevism singlehanded! He sabotages railways in the Crimea and sets fire to windmills. He infiltrates the highest circles and listens in to the deliberations of the Politbureau by means of a concealed phonograph. Finally, at the end of the film, he assassinates Lenin! Then the hero rests one foot on the recumbent corpse, brandishes his Mauser, and yells, 'Deutschland über Alles.' The German national anthem booms out. The closing credits roll.

Also, there's a romantic interest. 'Humphrey' is in love with a busty Rhine-maiden type called 'Sophia'. From time to time she trills merry songs in a piercing soprano. About three-quarters of the way through, she is parted from him by cruel fate and the Red Army. She wanders through a meadow gathering flowers, lilting a sweet ditty, 'Immer ist Humphrey Veil mein Veilchen' ('Humphrey Veil is my violet always').

It was really thrilling – except for the soppy bits. I was on the edge of my seat.

Afterwards, while the anthem was playing, everybody in the Kinema stood up and applauded. The house lights blazed on full then dimmed again. The actors who'd played 'Humphrey' and 'Sophia' – narrow young things with practised smiles – mounted the shallow stage in front of the screen and bowed and flirted with the audience for a while. Then they departed.

The band belted out a rousing march tune. The audience bravoed and clapped rhythmically. They howled in unison. It took me a while to understand: they were shouting my surname.

My valets gestured at me with their revolvers. I descended from the podium and ambled down the aisle. My valets were stalking behind me. Black-shirted youths and middle-aged matrons groped towards me as I passed by. They breathed my name and fondled the hem of my jacket.

I climbed on the stage and posed, feeling rather sweaty and self-conscious, down by the footlights. A single trumpeter played a Wagnerian fanfare. The house lights blinked out. A spotlight illuminated me alone. Blonde maidens hurled bouquets of smelly crimson roses with shocking accuracy at my feet. The music stopped. A huge banner unfolded on the screen behind me. Out of the corner of my eye I saw it was a giant swastika; my head was at its dead centre. I felt silly. I chewed my lip and gazed noncommittally at my shoes while everybody in the audience was extending their right arms in stiff erections and chanting, 'Heil Humphrey! Heil Humphrey! . . . '

176

4

'You look simply *awful*, Humph!'

'Well ... yes ... I suppose I ... you haven't changed one bit, Sophia!'

I was leaning on the garden gate of a dacha in the Crimea, sniffing the aroma of roses and my wife. A wonky driftwood sign was scorched with the house name: Mon Repos, plus, in smaller letters, its transliteration into Russian. A wooden arch rose over the gate for no obvious reason; a rose bush climbed over that. My guards had permitted me to visit Sophia on the morning of the day I was to leave the Soviet Union. Her face bloomed among the tight buds and thorns.

'You're lovely ... ' I said.

'Yes, isn't it? It's an early flowering variety.'

'I dreamed about you, every night, in Siberia. You and our baby. It's what kept me sane. I was never sure you were all right ... The letters stopped coming, and I was afraid ... '

'Well ... I'm perfectly healthy. It was very foolish of you to worry about me, Humph.'

'Of course.'

'You do look rather ... raddled, Humph. You're so skinny, and most of your hair's fallen out ... Have they been treating you well, in that ... labour camp of yours?'

My guards twiddled with the buttons on their uniforms and coughed discreetly.

I nodded.

'Now, do come in, Humph.'

I jutted my head forward to kiss her, but she bent to undo the latch. My chin brushed against her chignon, almost.

I followed her up the winding crazy-paved garden path. The guards traipsed after me. One of them knelt beside a clump of lavender and squeezed a sprig to bring out the aroma.

'All the years I was in Siberia, I kept thinking about you – '

177

'You've already made that remark, Humph.'

'Yes . . . I'm sorry.'

We sat on the veranda. Sophia gestured that I should lower myself into a rocking chair. She disposed herself on a high wooden stool, side-saddle. My guards leaned against the rusticated limestone columns supporting the veranda roof, and yawned.

I stretched my hand up towards her. She didn't grasp it. My arm stayed extended in a kind of salute.

'Sophia . . . '

'Yes, Humph?'

'It's . . . amazing . . . '

'The Crimea is such a fine climate, and so scenic. I tell all my friends from Moscow, when they come to visit, and many do, they should live here themselves. It was our little Crimean trip – do you remember it, Humph, just the two of us and poor dear Gritz? – that opened my eyes to the picturesqueness of this *paysage*. The locals are quite friendly – they speak a curiously gruff accent, but I understand them perfectly. And the sea is merely half an hour by automobile, if that.'

I withdrew my arm. The rocking chair tilted back. A green insect flitted past my nose, quietly. Sophia repeated, 'If that.'

I noticed a painting pinned to the inside of the window frame. It was a sheet of grey paper daubed with browns and yellows: an abstract landscape, presumably.

'Oh . . . so . . . keeping up the art, eh?'

'That little thing, Humph? It's a finger-painting, child's play . . . I teach art at the local school. Did I tell you that? The youngsters are simply delightful . . . '

She said in a loud voice, 'One does what one can to help the Union of Soviet Socialist Republics.' The guards nodded. She swatted an insect.

'And your own art?' I asked. 'Your waxworks?'

'Ah . . . tcha! We all did something in our youth which we regret. Isn't that so, Humph?'

A silence. A warm breeze. I rocked to and fro.

I said in a rush, 'I think you're so splendid, Sophia, honestly I do. Just surviving. Through all this. Keeping up your courage and your . . . beauty. Not giving in. You're a heroine!'

She pointed a finger down her cleavage. 'Heroine? Me?'

I rocked forward; my knees almost touched the ground. I said, 'I love you, Sophia!'

'Ah, Humph,' she said, 'I'd like you to meet my . . . him.'

She was pointing at a man in old ochre clothes who had just wandered out of the house. He was carrying a large pair of shears and nervously scratching his Adam's apple with the blades. He was a nondescript fellow . . . but I knew I'd met him somewhere before.

I recognised him.

He gave me a weak wave, and smiled.

'Humph,' said Sophia. 'Meet my . . . ' She blew her nose delicately on a petite hankie, then stuffed it back up her sleeve. 'Meet my husband.'

'But, Sophia . . . You're married to me!'

'Oh, you and I had a divorce. Didn't they tell you in your . . . in Siberia? No? . . . It was nothing grand or elaborate. A quiet little ceremony . . . Well, Humph, aren't you going to say hello?'

I said nothing.

Sophia's husband toddled down the garden path. He began snipping away at the rose bush.

'My husband's ever so good around the house, and the garden. He's a novelist, of course. Not that he's published much . . . at all. He can write the beginnings very well, but he always has trouble with the endings . . . '

Wrinkled yellowish flowers tumbled from the rose bush. The secateurs clicked.

'And I think the climate here's so much more healthy than in the big city. Spiritually refreshing. For a creative artist, I mean, like my husband. We honestly did find Moscow rather . . . ' She searched for the right word. Her hand rotated from breast to chin to breast. Her hankie fell out of her sleeve. I scooped it up.

A whole dry thorny branch cracked off the rose bush and fell on the path. The man pushed it to one side with his foot and went on cutting.

' . . . hurlyburly,' said Sophia.

I stared at her swinging stockinged ankle.

'About our . . . about the . . . ' Sophia patted her cheeks as if applying rouge. 'About what you were asking. Our . . . the . . . it was a miscarriage. That is to say . . . oh, what would I have done with a baby, Humph? You can't imagine me as a mother, surely? I'm not cut out for that sort of thing.'

One guard coughed. One guard tapped his wristwatch.

Her husband took a long metal apparatus from behind the Mon Repos sign, and pointed it at the rose bush. He pushed a pump and a fine glittery spray settled on the flowers and leaves.

179

A guard tapped my elbow. Another guard beckoned me to rise.

'Sophia,' I said, 'I have to go now. I don't know where they're taking me, but I have to go. Will you . . . abandon your garden and your dacha and your husband and your rose bush and your automobile and your veranda and the children at the local school and your crazy-paved winding path and follow me anywhere I go in the whole wide world?'

The guards pulled me sharply upright and led me away. The chair rocked backwards and forwards.

Sophia was weeping.

Vadim swore, '*Greenfly!*'

5
POSTSCRIPT

My younger self is leaning over my shoulder and reading these words as I write them. Strictly speaking, he's not I – he's that bony fair boy, Heinz Deutsch, who acted me in the film.

Heinz has told me he's going to star in a stage play about the exploits of the great Aryan superspy 'Humphrey Veil', and he's come to pick up a few character details and physical traits. We're permitted to spend one hour in each other's presence. He screws up his eyes and inspects me from different angles as if he loved me. I gaze longingly back.

We speak in English. He spent some years in Hollywood and, give or take an idiosyncratic accent and Germanic intonation, is fluent in my mother tongue.

I don't believe this nonsense about a 'stage play'; obviously he's some kind of spy. I tell him so, using the idiom, 'Pull the other one!'

I think he understands because he shakes his head and tut-tuts.

I inform him (please note the following words, Heinz) I KNOW NOTHING ABOUT HUMPHREY VEIL . . . and he clicks his tongue in a way which communicates both disbelief and amazement at my modesty.

I refer him to the scrapbook containing my press cuttings. (It's over there – on the desk, beside the stack of illegible diaries. That's right.) Everything in it is so incredible it might just be true. There are several grainy photographs of 'Humphrey Veil' among those cuttings; oddly, the pictures look more like Heinz than me.

Now Heinz is narrating some peculiar oriental parable – but I'm not listening. I'm too busy. I want to write the postscript to my autobiography *right now* and I can't spare the time.

Let me set down my credo.

1) I believe in Marxism-Leninism.

Oh, and before I forget – I want to apologise for the errors of fact in my memoirs. No doubt I misnamed streets and misdated historical events.

Well, what have I got to rely on but my memory and diaries? I've always done my best.

But there's one kind of 'error' for which I won't apologise. It may seem, at first reading, that my dating is incorrect. Much that I've described in the Moscow of Lenin's time didn't appear there till later – or so 'history records'. For instance, historically the League of Militant Godless was inaugurated by Stalin. Historically it was Stalin who invented Grandfather Frost. Above all, historically, the Moscow metro wasn't begun or even planned till after Stalin had come into power.

So there must be some mistake. Something is a tissue of lies: this autobiography – or your history book. And who dictated the contents of your history book? Either I am a composer of fiction – for whatever reasons of ambition, craziness, artistic urge and self-delusion – or Stalin is.

Reader: which seems to you the more likely?

Heinz is tapping me on the shoulder. He's saying, listen, we haven't much time . . . Heinz, I *am* listening.

Now he's telling me about a beautiful princess called Scheherezade whose husband, the King, plotted to execute her as soon as she'd finished narrating her tales. So (he concludes) she never did finish them.

Just so, according to Heinz, I'm being kept alive for the sake of my autobiography. Each night, my valets photograph what I've written that day, and dispatch it to the *Abwehr*. Heinz himself has been shown a copy. At first, my account of the Moscow metro and dissident artistic movements interested the spymasters; that kind of information could have strategic use. But then I started scribbling away about prisons and love – and they know all they want to know about that kind of thing already.

What can I do? Unlike Scheherezade I've already reached my post-script. I've nothing much more to set down.

Heinz informs me, using the expression 'to cut a long story short' several times, plus plenty of stammered pauses, that Germany has already decided to dispose of Humphrey Veil and replace him by . . . (he gulps hard) Heinz himself. He's under orders to stand in for me at rallies and movie premières.

His eyes are damp. I never know what to say at times like these.

Ten minutes have passed. The sun is setting. My desk is lit by a single candle.

There's been a power cut which (so Heinz whispers) was deliberately caused by himself (he removed the fuse in the mains supply) to help me, because he too is a devout Marxist-Leninist.

I ask him if he intends to save my life somehow.

He breathes out softly and the flame flickers.

Outside, in the city beyond the barred window, electric bulbs and the moon glow. A reflection of my room hovers out there, in the night. A moth flutters through that other room – and somehow, through a slim gap in a pane, penetrates this one. It settles on the vase of roses on my desk. Its wings are striped with shadow like the pages of a riffled book. Then it takes off: it voyages round and round the candle . . .

They say that Stalin has completed the Moscow metro system. They say the trains run fast and frequently, linking the whole city by means of concealed underground connections. They say that Stalin has had the stations decorated in fine majestic style, with chandeliers and statues of exemplary metro workers.

I should like to have travelled in the perfected Moscow metro once in my lifetime.

Heinz says he can't save my life but he can save something more important. When the Nazis are overthrown and a Communist government comes to power, he promises he'll have my autobiography published. I must give it to him, this evening and he'll smuggle it away.

I consider his proposition. What upsets me, I tell him, is that I'll never have the chance to revise my autobiography and make it perfect . . . but of course nobody ever can.

Anyway, how will he snatch the manuscript from under the noses of my valets? Surely they'd soon discover its absence, and Heinz would be the obvious suspect.

He says he plans to knock over the candle and pretend the manuscript is burnt away.

Obviously, this stratagem is absurd. His face is serious and well-meaning. He looks so much like my self of a decade ago, I hate to disillusion him.

He disillusions me. If only we create a huge distraction, something so dramatic that this place is filled with noisy policemen and rushing ambulancemen and . . . He breaks off his account because one of my valets is glancing at us with excessive interest.

I think I follow. He and I must fight each other (I illustrate this ruse in quick dumb show) so as to draw attention away from him.

He opens his coat slightly, and closes it. A gust of warm air is forced out; I smell his nervous sweat. I glimpse his revolver.

He explains the plot. I will hit him. He, in 'self-defence', will shoot me. In the resultant fuss, he'll sneak out with the manuscript. Just before leaving, he'll knock over the candle and set fire to something or another (I volunteer a handkerchief; I lay it beside this manuscript) so if anybody wonders afterwards what has happened to my papers, there'll be an explanation.

But suppose I recover from the gunshot wound, then I'd be tortured and forced to reveal everything. So (I whisper to him) he *must* shoot to kill.

I wish we could comfort each other somehow.

One of my valets is approaching. Perhaps he understands a little English, or the language of facial expressions. He says something to Heinz in German, too quick for me to follow.

Now we must wait another few minutes, until the valets have settled down again. Meanwhile we shouldn't talk (Heinz insists) but communicate – if we have to – only by writing on this sheet of paper.

What will I write?

Sophiasophiasophia.

The candle's more than half melted already. Guttering away. The wax is dribbling into strange swollen forms like the domes of Russian churches . . . and these shapes themselves dissolve into others . . . which turn into . . .

This candle flame, toppled, will set fire to my handkerchief. Which will set fire to the chair. Which will set fire to the desk. Which will set fire to the carpet and the curtain. Which will kindle the building which will ignite the district. And the whole of Berlin will go up in smoke. The Reichstag will crackle like a fireworks display. The cages at the zoo will burn and the animals will go free and burn too. All Germany will become a conflagration, and all Europe, and America, and the old bourgeois world will vanish in the flames . . . it will melt like wax . . . and re-form itself in a new mould.

I'm afraid.

Well, when I mock-attack Heinz, I'd better shout something at him, some Marxist slogans . . . Best to write them down now. That way I won't fluff my lines on the night.

Workers of the World unite! You have nothing to lose but your chains!

History repeats itself, the first time as tragedy and the second time as farce!

Previous philosophers have interpreted the world. My object is to change it!

oh God, I'm frightened oh Marx oh Heinz oh Sophia I can't go through with it *read this, Heinz*:

    I CAN'T GO THROUGH WITH IT, HEINZ

        WHY NOT?

    I CAN'T BEAR TO HIT YOU – YOU LOOK LIKE MY YOUNGER SELF

        NEVERTHELESS?

    WHAT?

        SURELY?

    I HATE THAT ME WHO WENT TO MOSCOW WHEN WE COULD HAVE STAYED ON IN LONDON OR COMFY NEW YORK. I WANT TO HIT ME SO HARD I

        WHEN YOU'RE READY TO ATTACK ME, HUMPHREY, WRITE 'YES'?

    AND WHEN YOU'RE READY TO SHOOT, HEINZ, YOU WRITE 'YES'?

        YES

    YES

        YES

    YES

A NOTE ON THE AUTHOR

Jonathan Treitel was born in London in 1959. He has worked as a physicist and lived in San Francisco and Tokyo. He is a published poet and short-story writer.